P9-CRX-176

Claire

and the
Bakery Thief

For Star & Al — J.P.

Text and illustrations © 2008 Janice Poon

All rights reserved. No part of this publication may be
reproduced, stored in a retrieval system or transmitted, in any
form or by any means, without the prior written permission
of Kids Can Press Ltd. or, in case of photocopying or other
reprographic copying, a license from The Canadian Copyright
Licensing Agency (Access Copyright). For an Access
Copyright license, visit www.accesscopyright.ca
or call toll free to 1-800-893-5777.

This is a work of fiction and any resemblance of characters to
persons living or dead is purely accidental.

Kids Can Press acknowledges the financial support of the
Government of Ontario, through the Ontario Media
Development Corporation's Ontario Book Initiative; the
Ontario Arts Council; the Canada Council for the Arts; and
the Government of Canada, through the BPIDP, for our
publishing activity.

Published in Canada by
Kids Can Press Ltd.
29 Birch Avenue
Toronto, ON M4V 1E2

Published in the U.S. by
Kids Can Press Ltd.
2250 Military Road
Tonawanda, NY 14150

www.kidscanpress.com

Edited by Karen Li
Designed by Marie Bartholomew and Kathleen Gray
Printed and bound in Singapore

The hardcover edition of this book is smyth sewn casebound.
The paperback edition of this book is limp sewn with drawn-on cover.

CM 08 0 9 8 7 6 5 4 3 2 1
CM PA 08 0 9 8 7 6 5 4 3 2 1

Library and Archives Canada Cataloguing in Publication

Poon, Janice
    Claire and the bakery thief / Janice Poon.

ISBN 978-1-55453-286-5 (bound)
ISBN 978-1-55453-245-2 (pbk.)

I. Title.

PS8631 O638C53 2008   jC813'.6   C2007-903298-2

Kids Can Press is a *l*©**r**∪**s**™ Entertainment company

Claire
and the
Bakery Thief

Written and illustrated by
JANICE POON

Kids Can Press

Dear Diary:

My whole life is changing. Things got kinda weird after Dad lost his job. But then he goes and buys an old bakery in the country! And now we have to move there. He says it will be good for us to get back to the earth. I think I'd rather go to Mars.

Claire

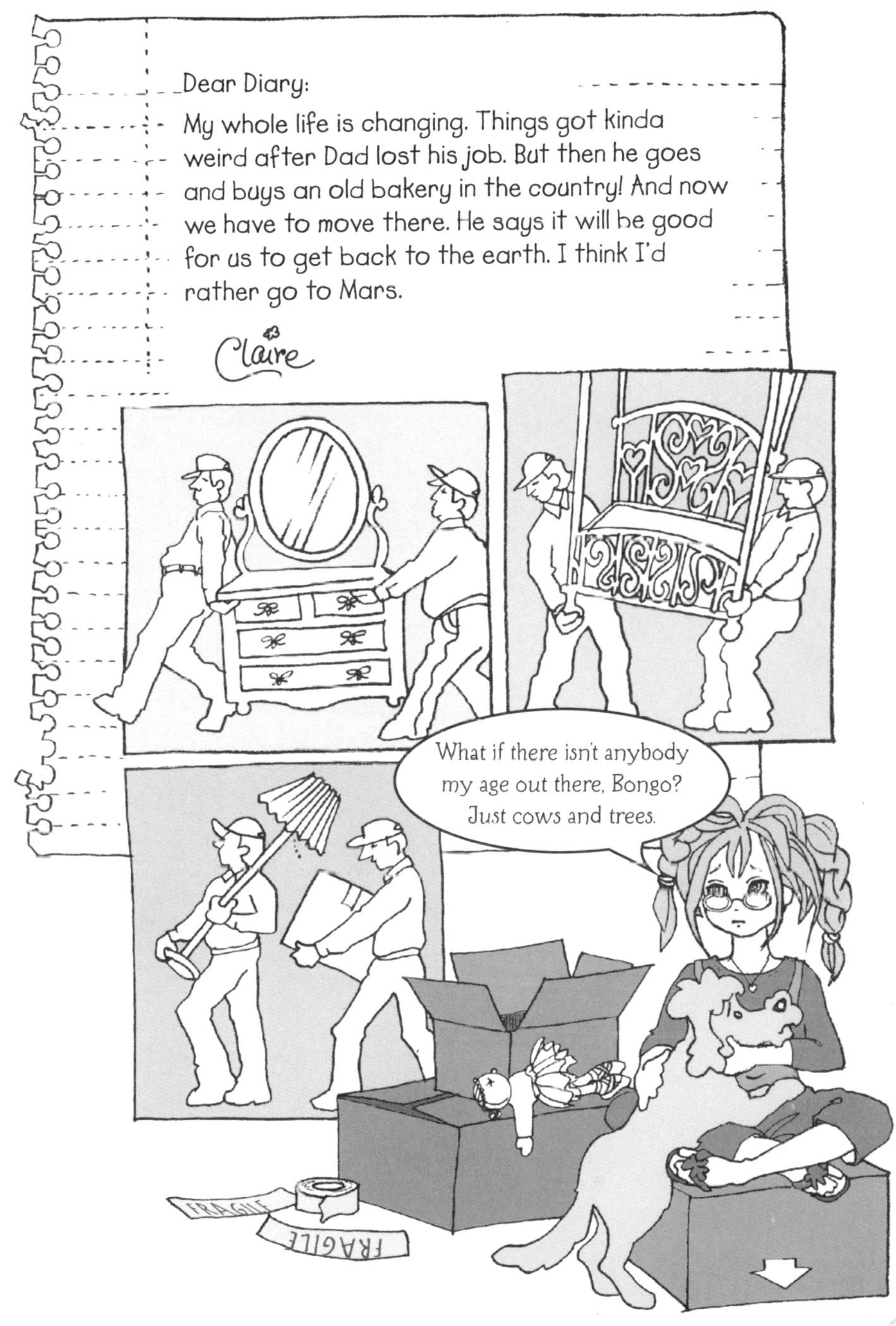
What if there isn't anybody my age out there, Bongo? Just cows and trees.
FRAGILE
FRAGILE

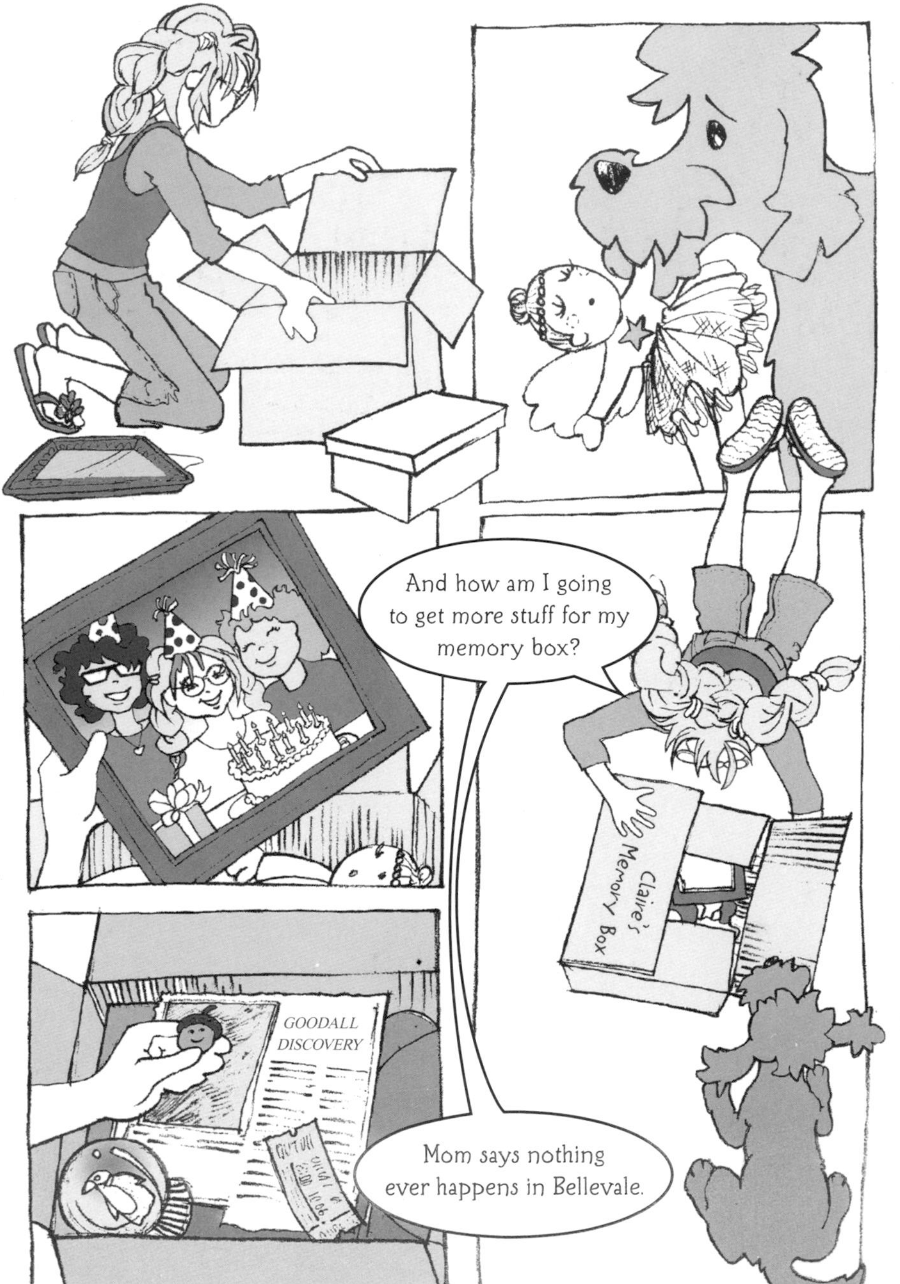
And how am I going to get more stuff for my memory box?
Claire's Memory Box
GOODALL DISCOVERY
Mom says nothing ever happens in Bellevale.

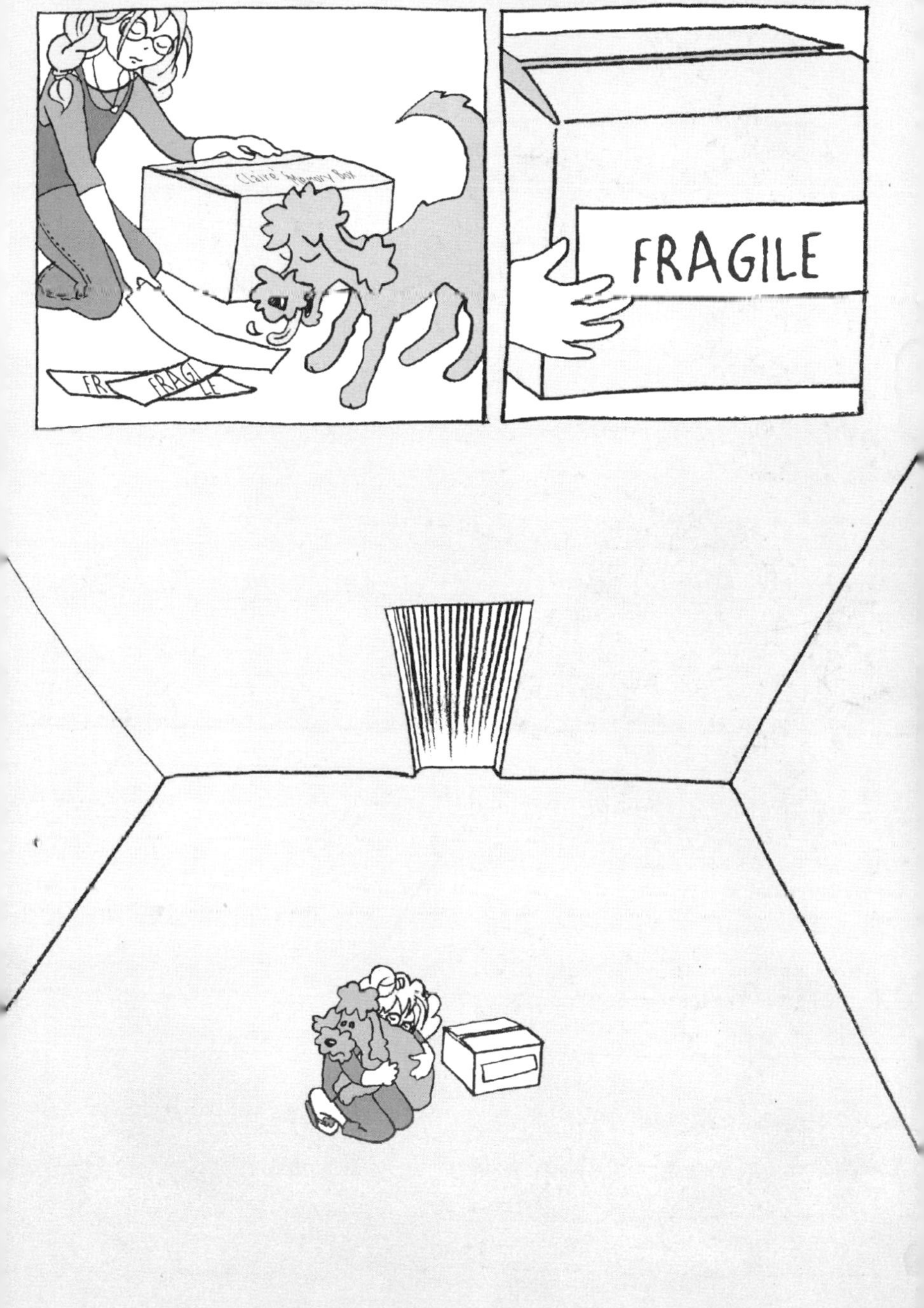
Claire's Memory Box
FR
FRAG
LE
FRAGILE

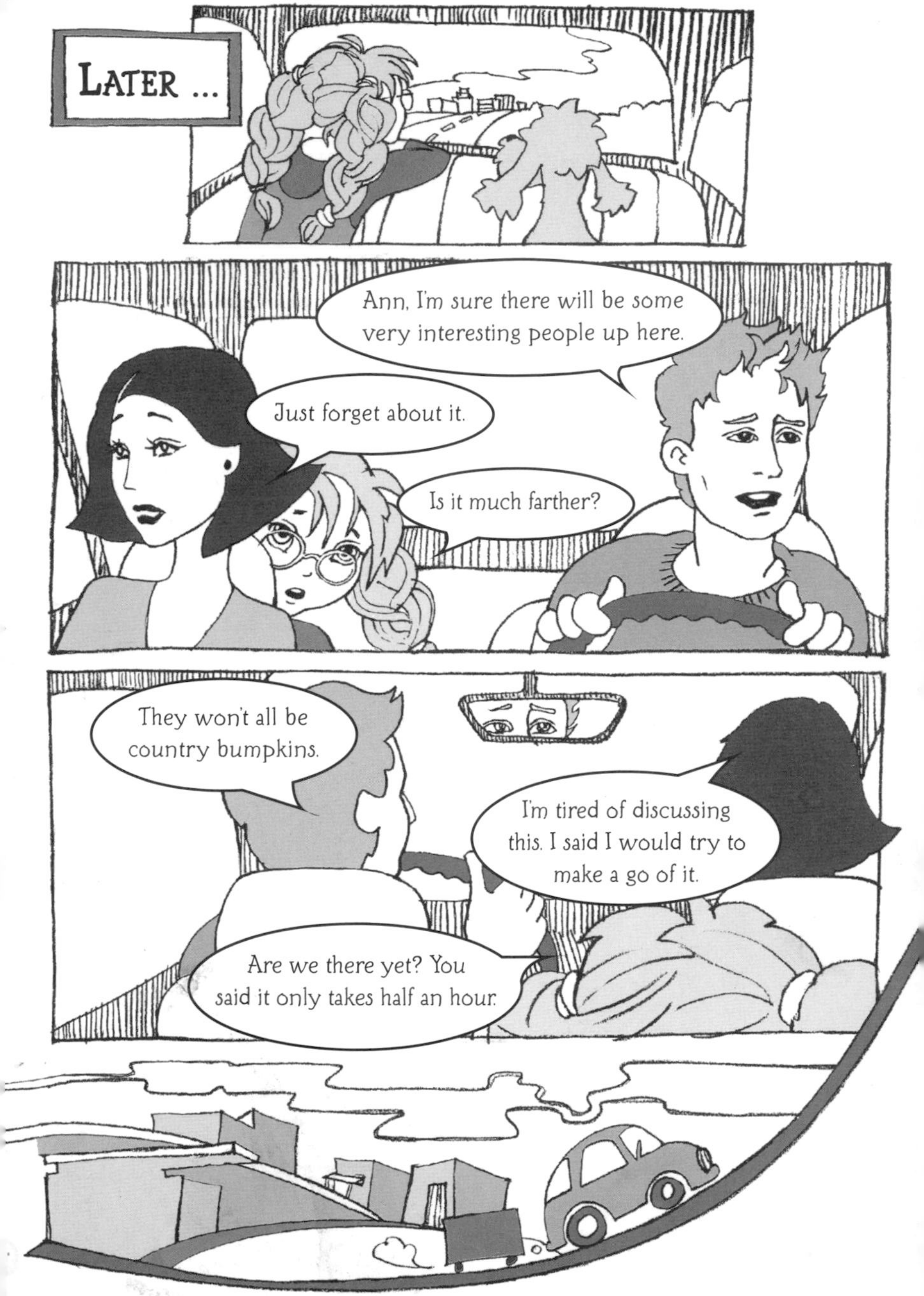
LATER ...
Ann, I'm sure there will be some very interesting people up here.
Just forget about it.
Is it much farther?
They won't all be country bumpkins.
I'm tired of discussing this. I said I would try to make a go of it.
Are we there yet? You said it only takes half an hour.

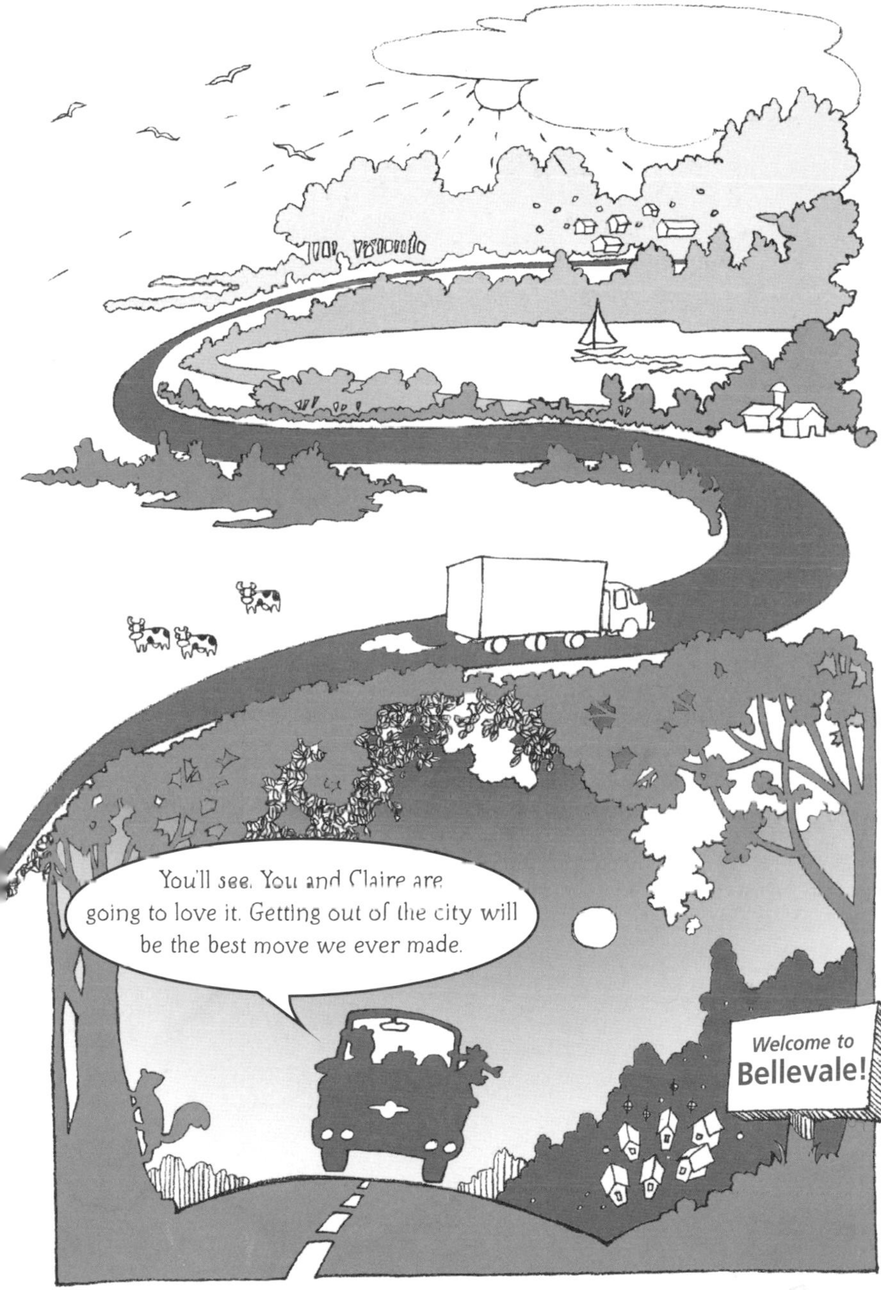
You'll see. You and Claire are going to love it. Getting out of the city will be the best move we ever made.
Welcome to Bellevale!

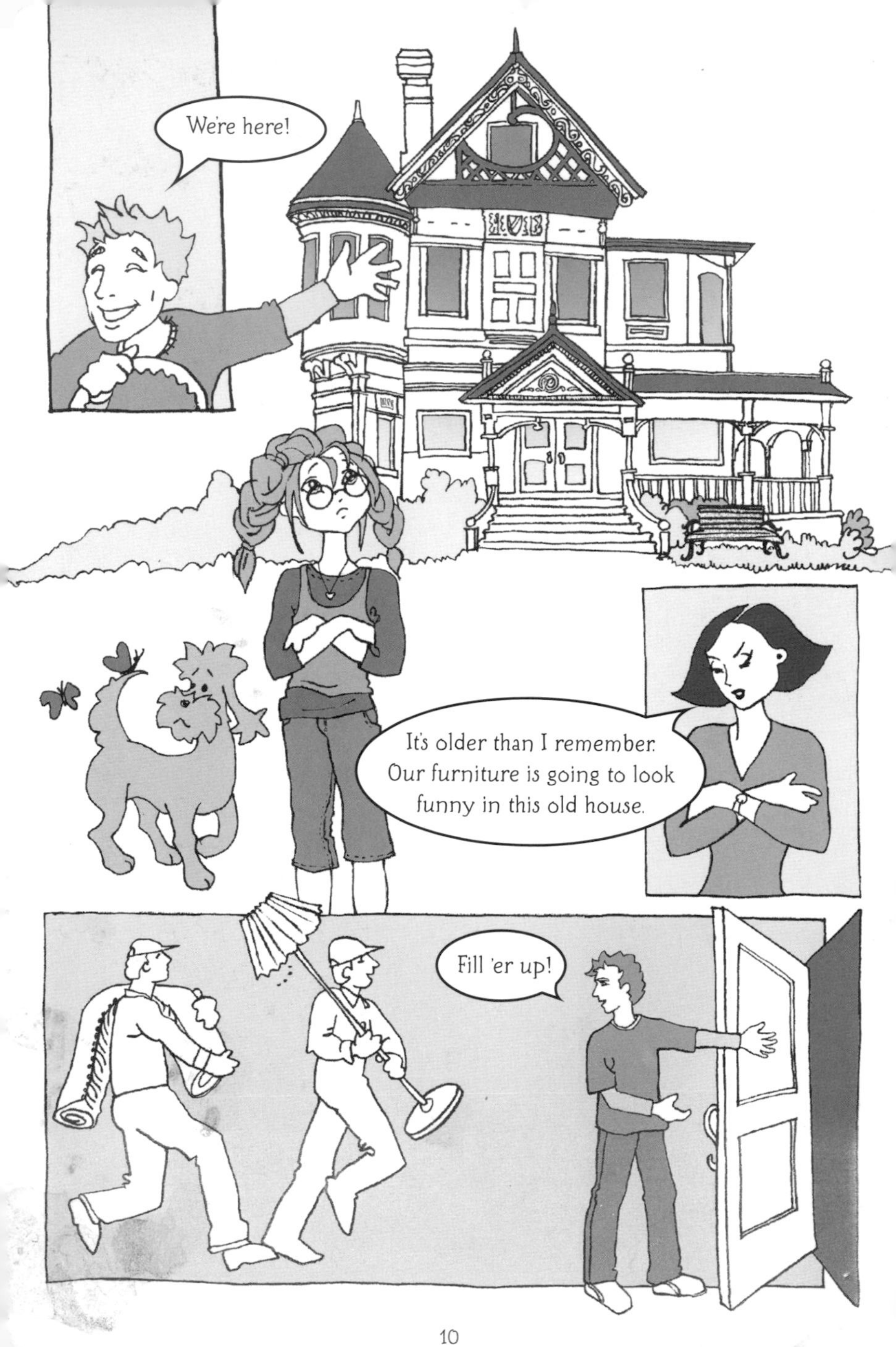
We're here!
It's older than I remember. Our furniture is going to look funny in this old house.
Fill 'er up!

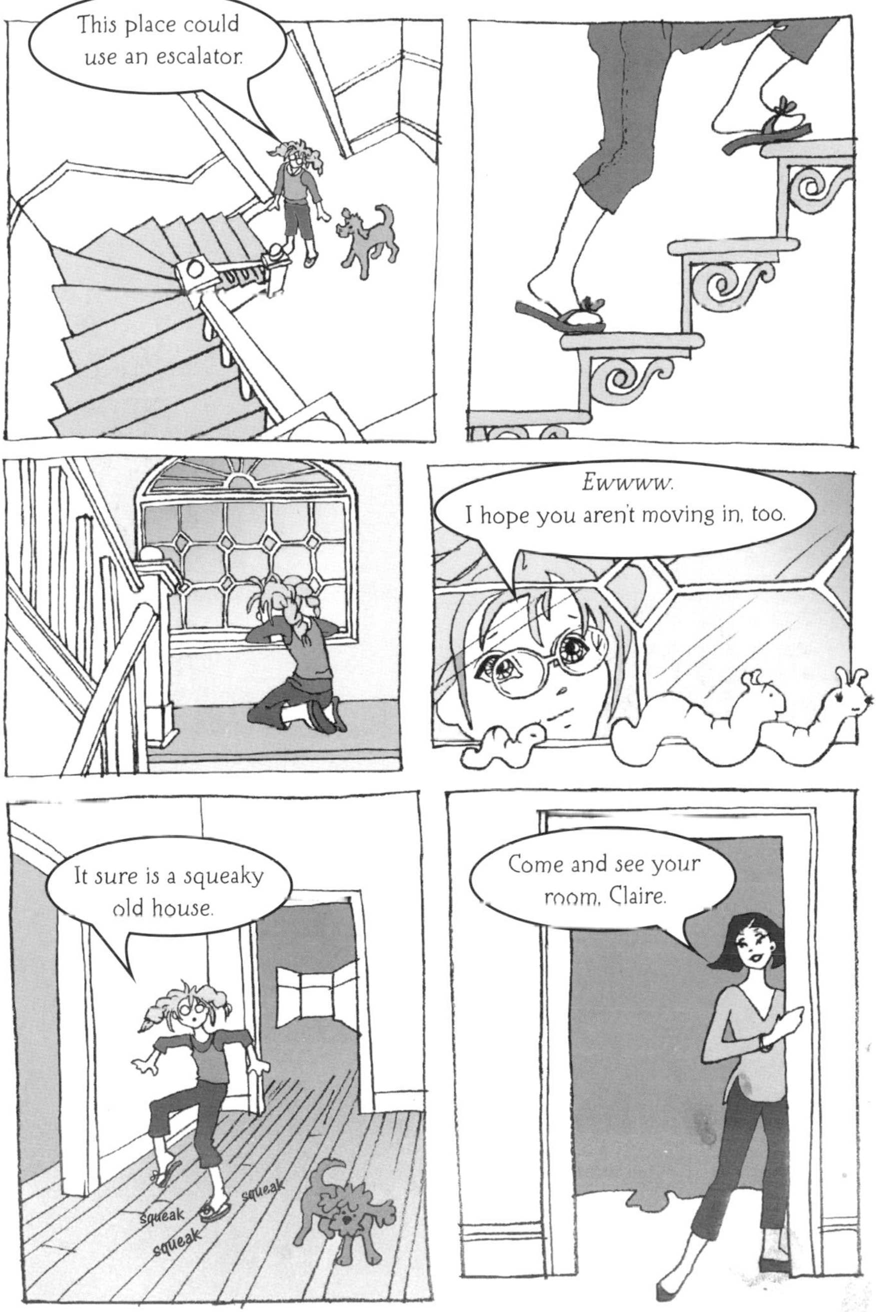
This place could use an escalator.
Ewwww.
I hope you aren't moving in, too.
It sure is a squeaky old house.
squeak
squeak
squeak
Come and see your room, Claire.

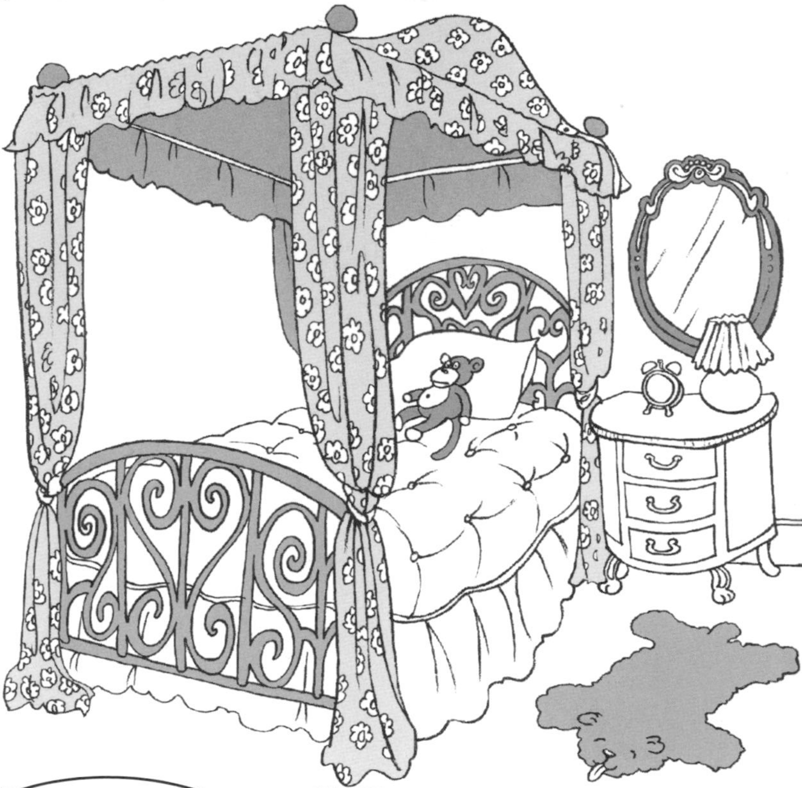

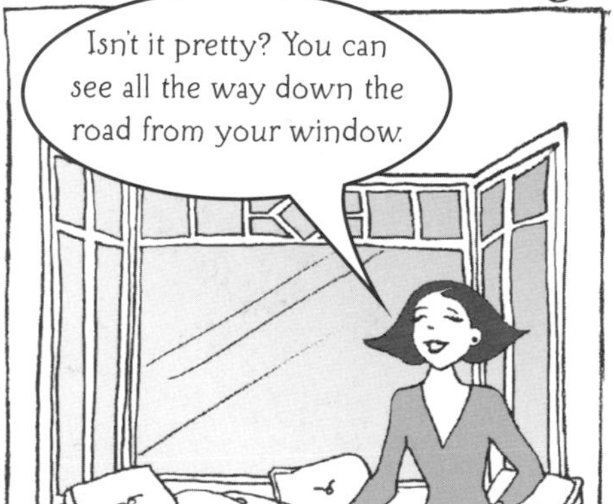
Isn't it pretty? You can see all the way down the road from your window.

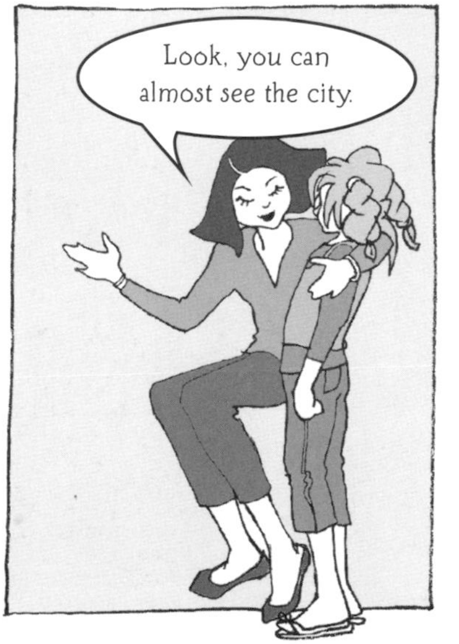
Look, you can almost see the city.

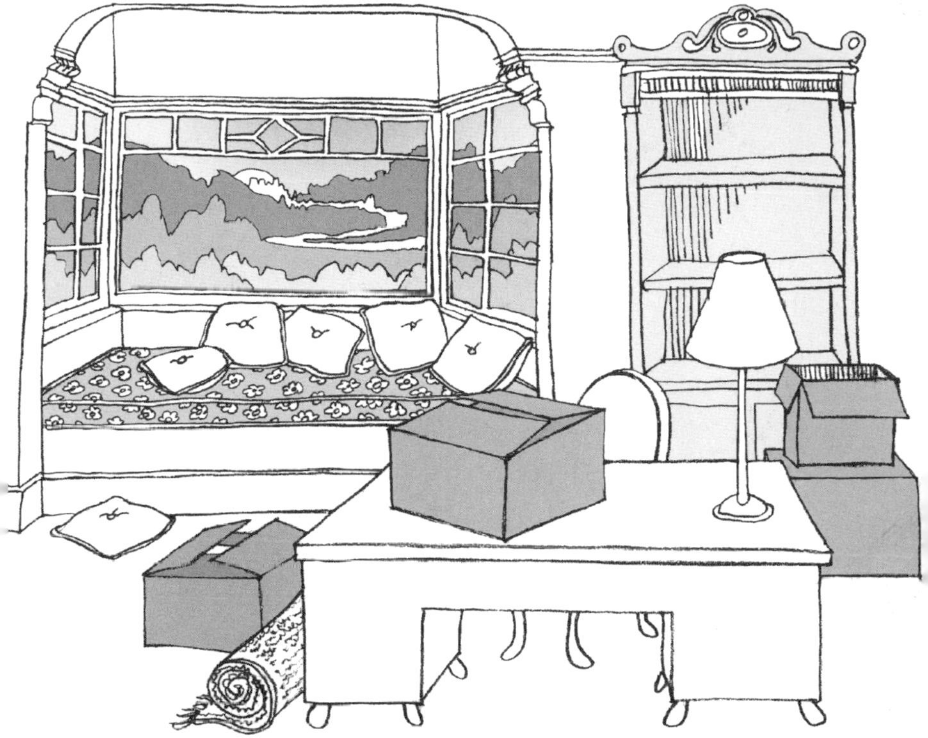

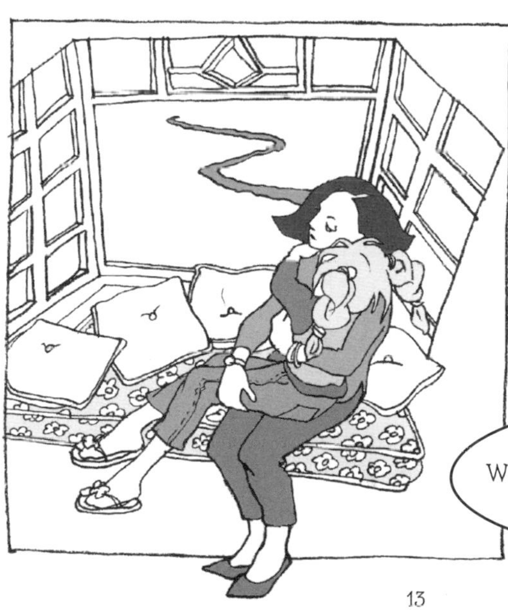

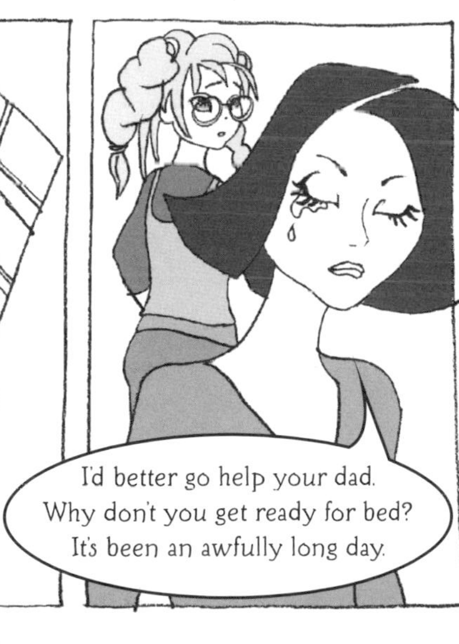
I'd better go help your dad.
Why don't you get ready for bed?
It's been an awfully long day.

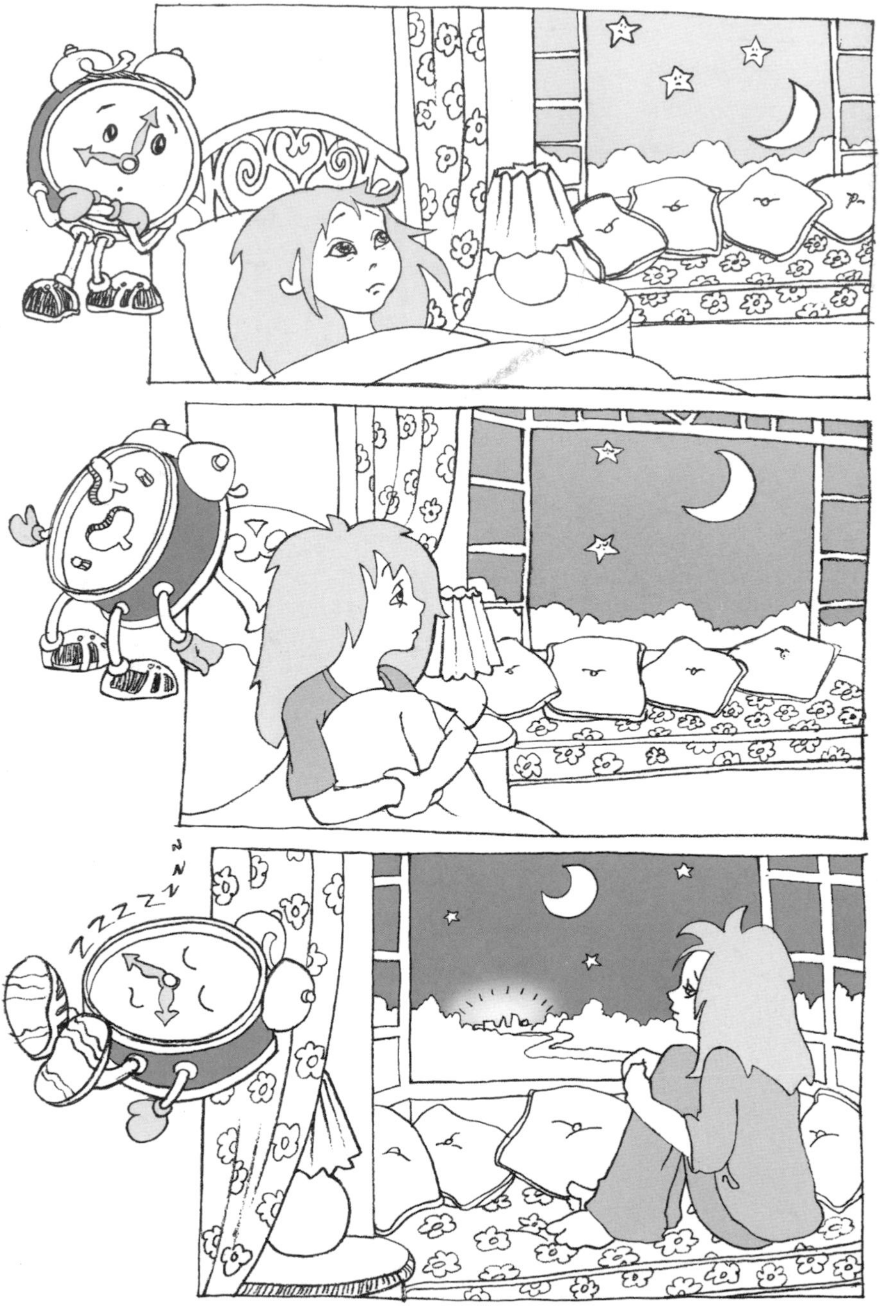

Dear Diary:

I guess it's not so bad here. Everyone is really friendly, and I met the girl who lives next door. Her name is Emma. She's OK, I guess.

The woods are full of amazing things. Here's a leaf I found yesterday when I was out on my bike.

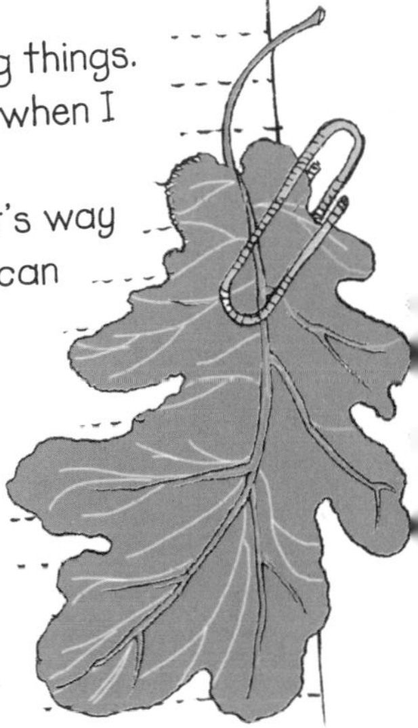

My bedroom is pretty cool. It's way bigger than my old room. And I can walk right into my closet. It's a mini room with slopey walls, kind of like a hobbit-house. That's where I hide out most of the time. I'm in the way everywhere else. Mom and Dad are really busy fixing up the bakery. Why do they want a bakery when all they do is argue about it? They should open a bickery instead.

Claire

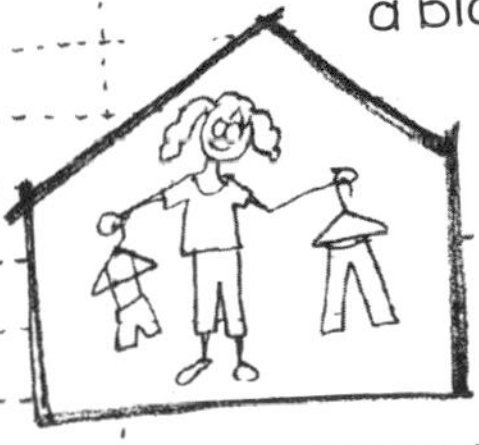

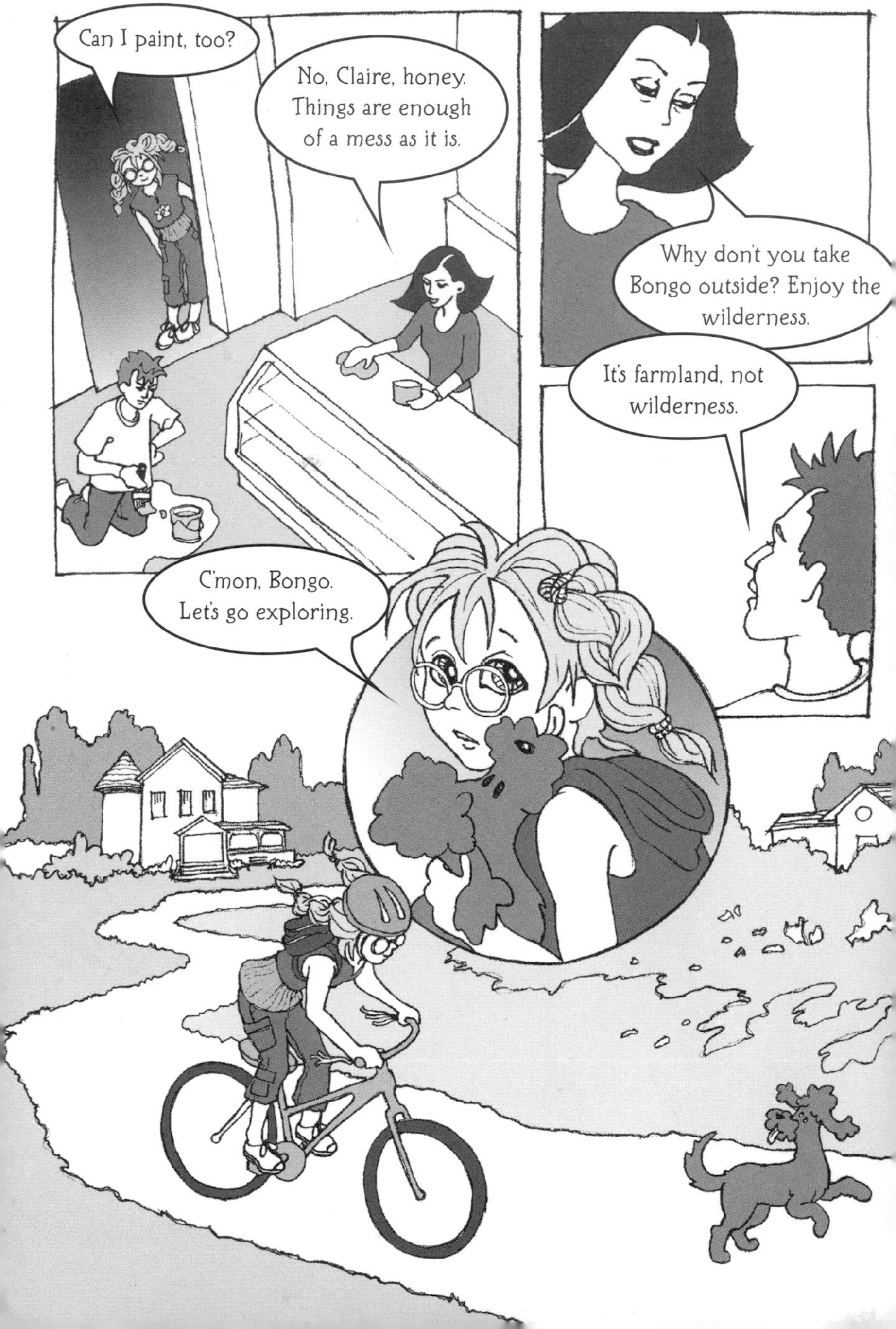
Can I paint, too?
No, Claire, honey. Things are enough of a mess as it is.
Why don't you take Bongo outside? Enjoy the wilderness.
It's farmland, not wilderness.
C'mon, Bongo. Let's go exploring.

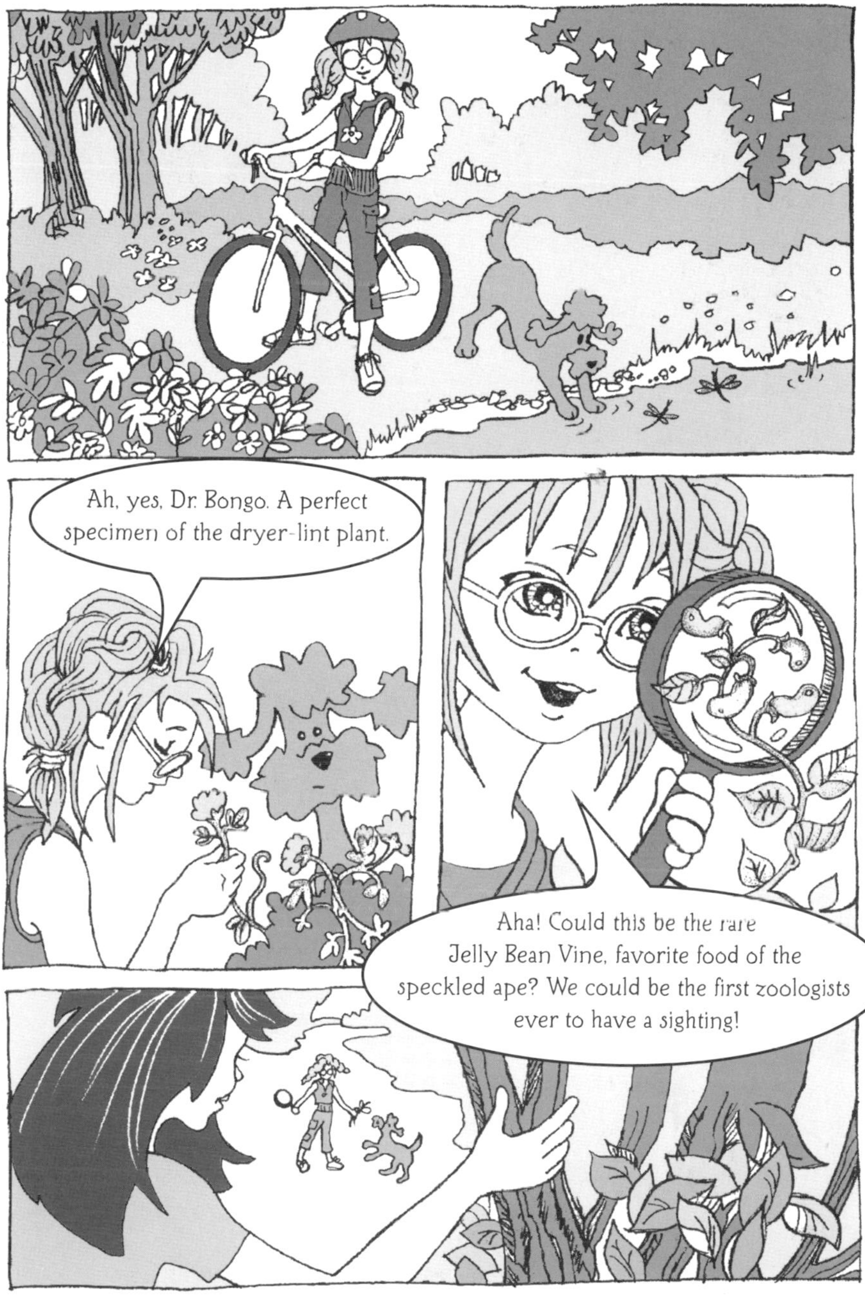
Ah, yes, Dr. Bongo. A perfect specimen of the dryer-lint plant.
Aha! Could this be the rare Jelly Bean Vine, favorite food of the speckled ape? We could be the first zoologists ever to have a sighting!

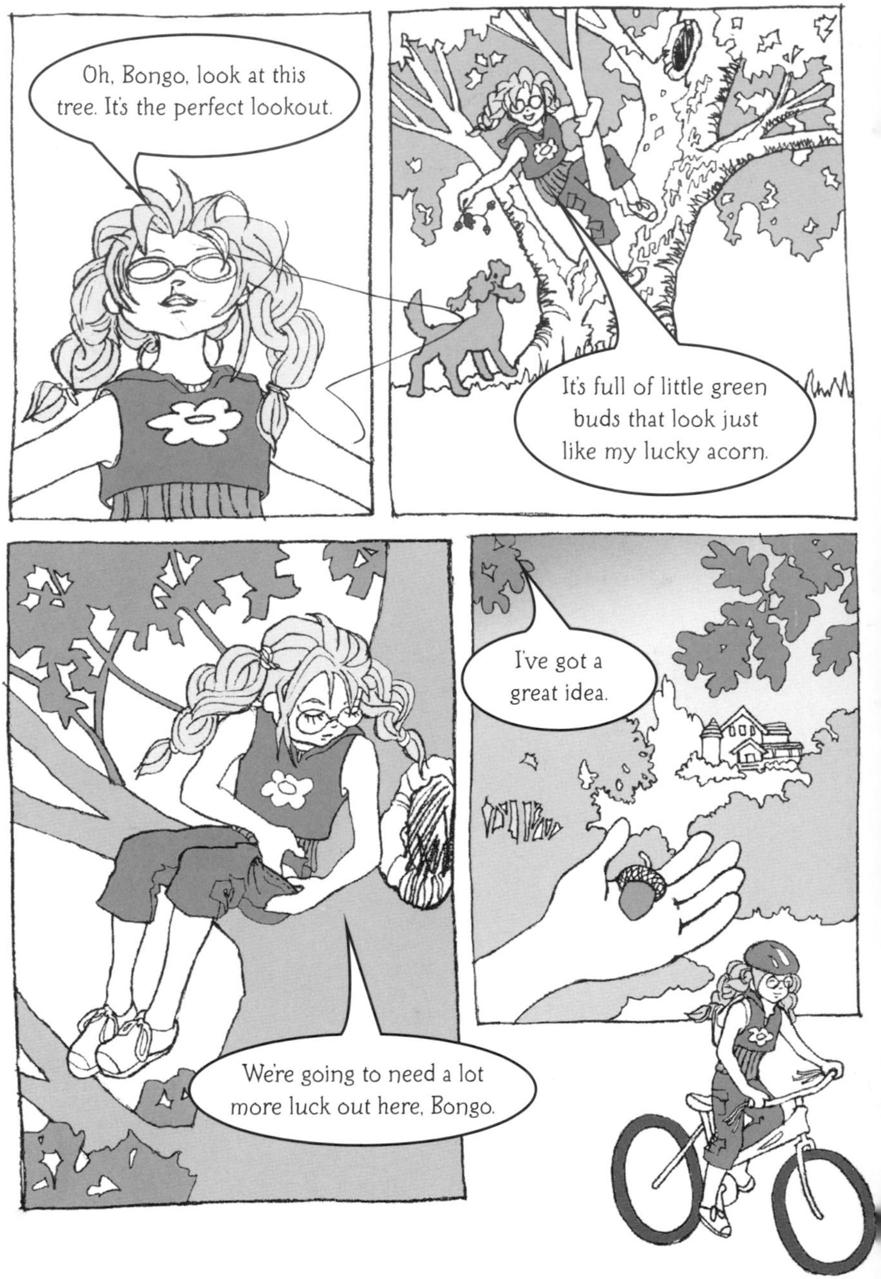
Oh, Bongo, look at this tree. It's the perfect lookout.
It's full of little green buds that look just like my lucky acorn.
We're going to need a lot more luck out here, Bongo.
I've got a great idea.

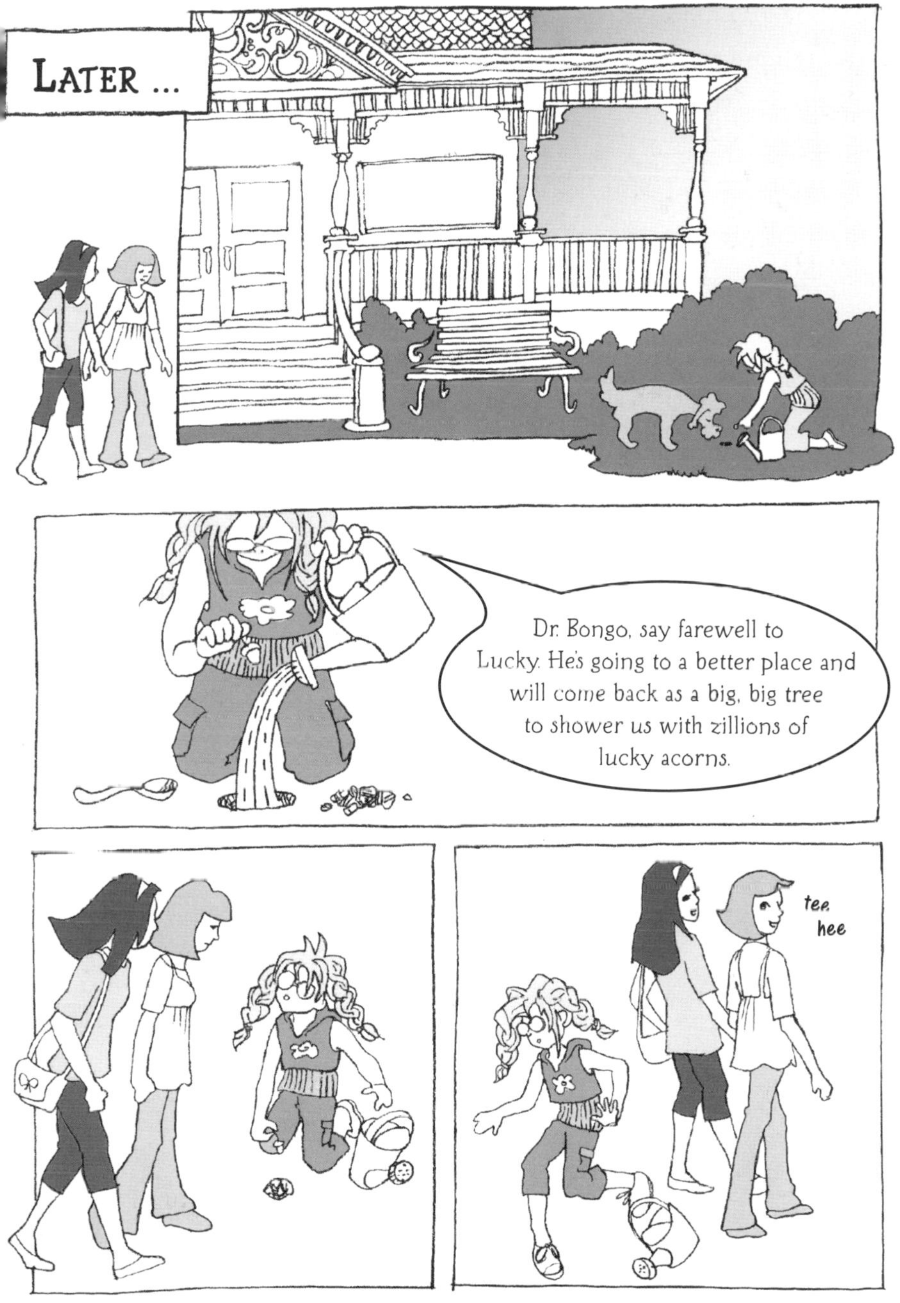

LATER ...
Dr. Bongo, say farewell to Lucky. He's going to a better place and will come back as a big, big tree to shower us with zillions of lucky acorns.
tee hee

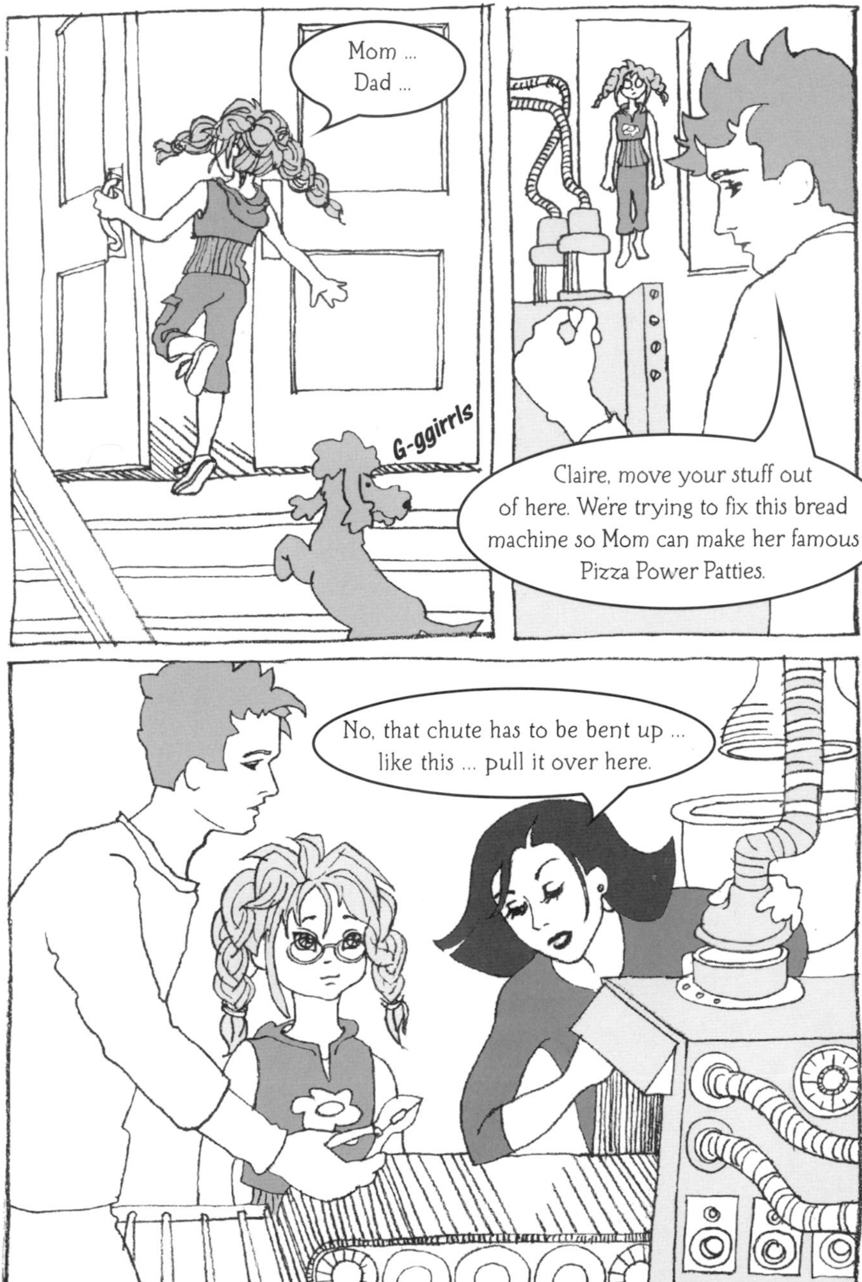
Mom ...
Dad ...
G-ggirrls
Claire, move your stuff out of here. We're trying to fix this bread machine so Mom can make her famous Pizza Power Patties.
No, that chute has to be bent up ... like this ... pull it over here.

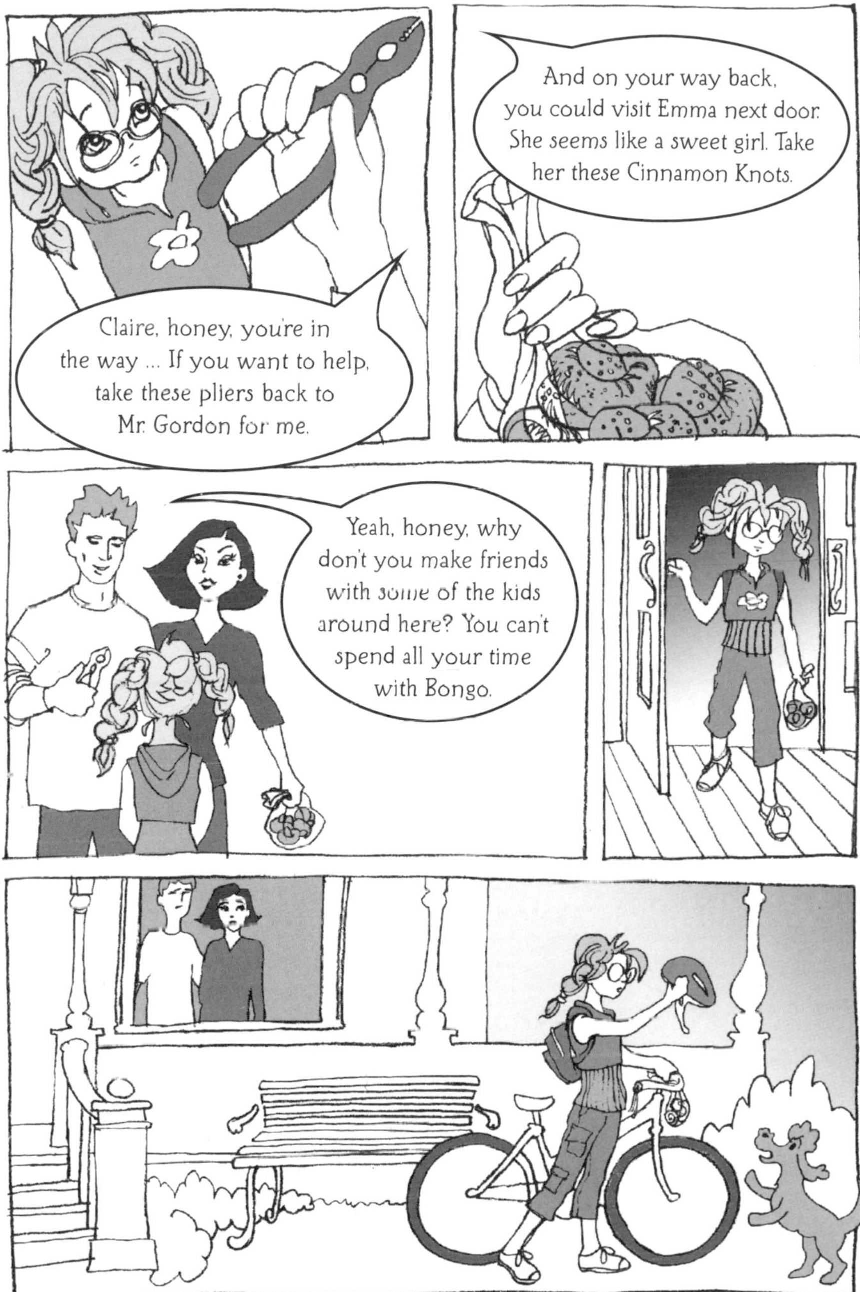

Claire, honey, you're in the way ... If you want to help, take these pliers back to Mr. Gordon for me.
And on your way back, you could visit Emma next door. She seems like a sweet girl. Take her these Cinnamon Knots.
Yeah, honey, why don't you make friends with some of the kids around here? You can't spend all your time with Bongo.

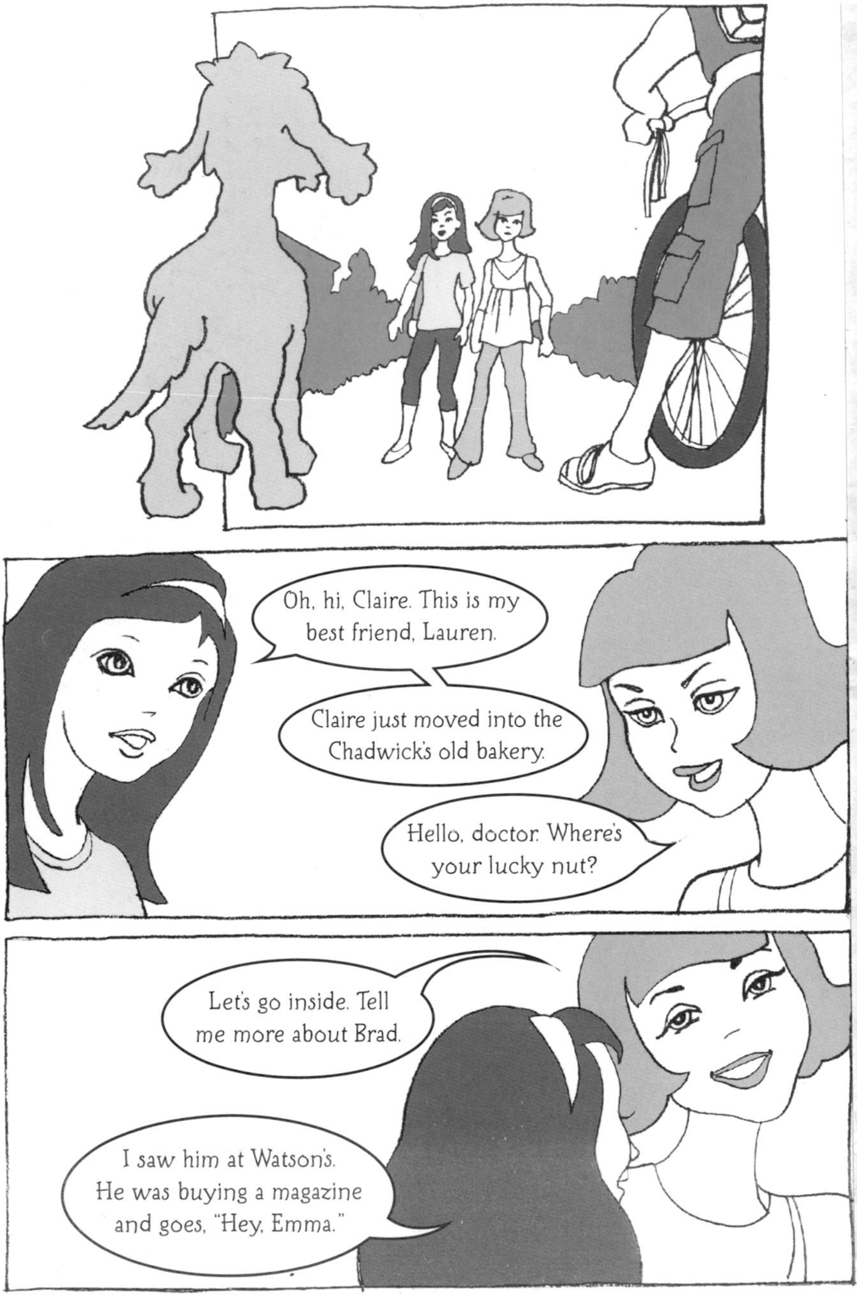
Oh, hi, Claire. This is my best friend, Lauren.
Claire just moved into the Chadwick's old bakery.
Hello, doctor. Where's your lucky nut?
Let's go inside. Tell me more about Brad.
I saw him at Watson's. He was buying a magazine and goes, "Hey, Emma."

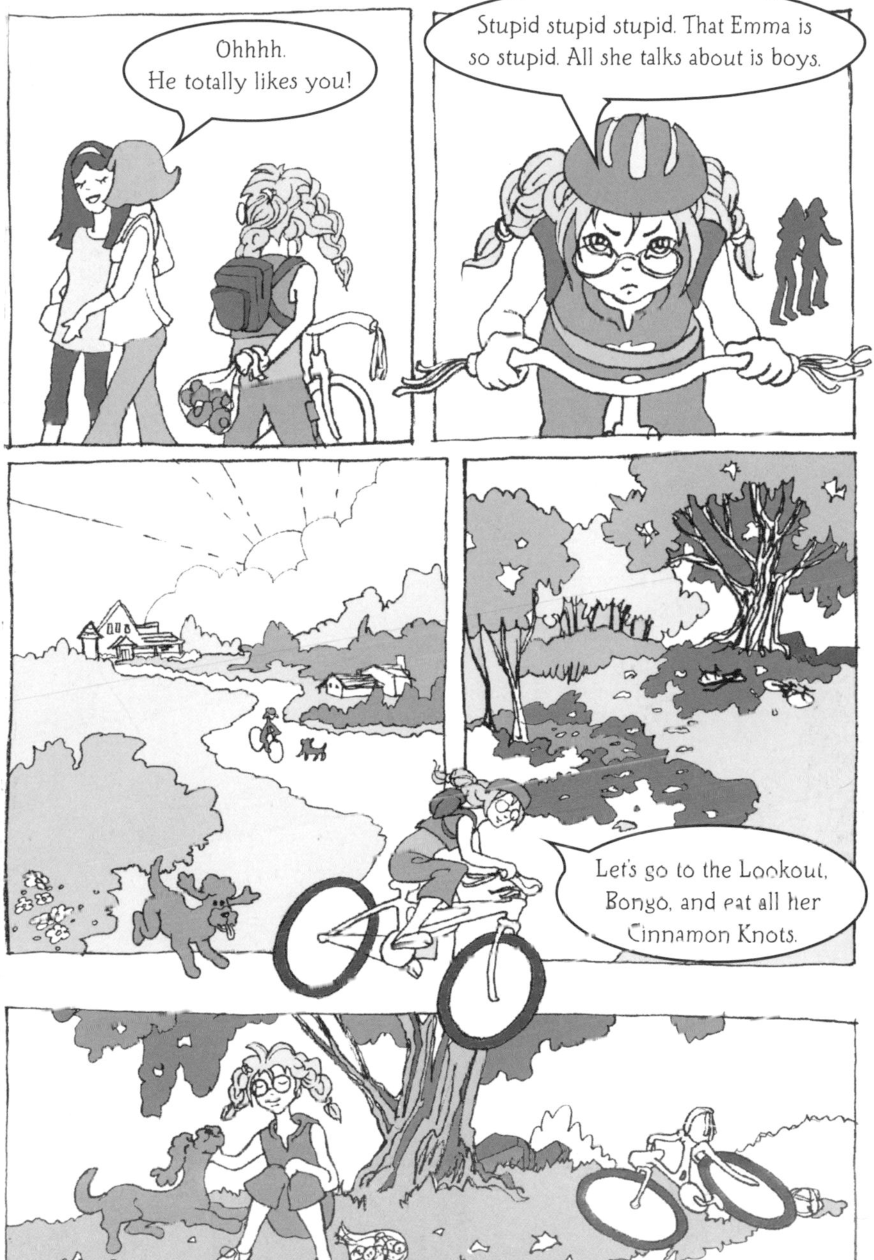
Ohhhh.
He totally likes you!
Stupid stupid stupid. That Emma is so stupid. All she talks about is boys.
Let's go to the Lookout, Bongo, and eat all her Cinnamon Knots.

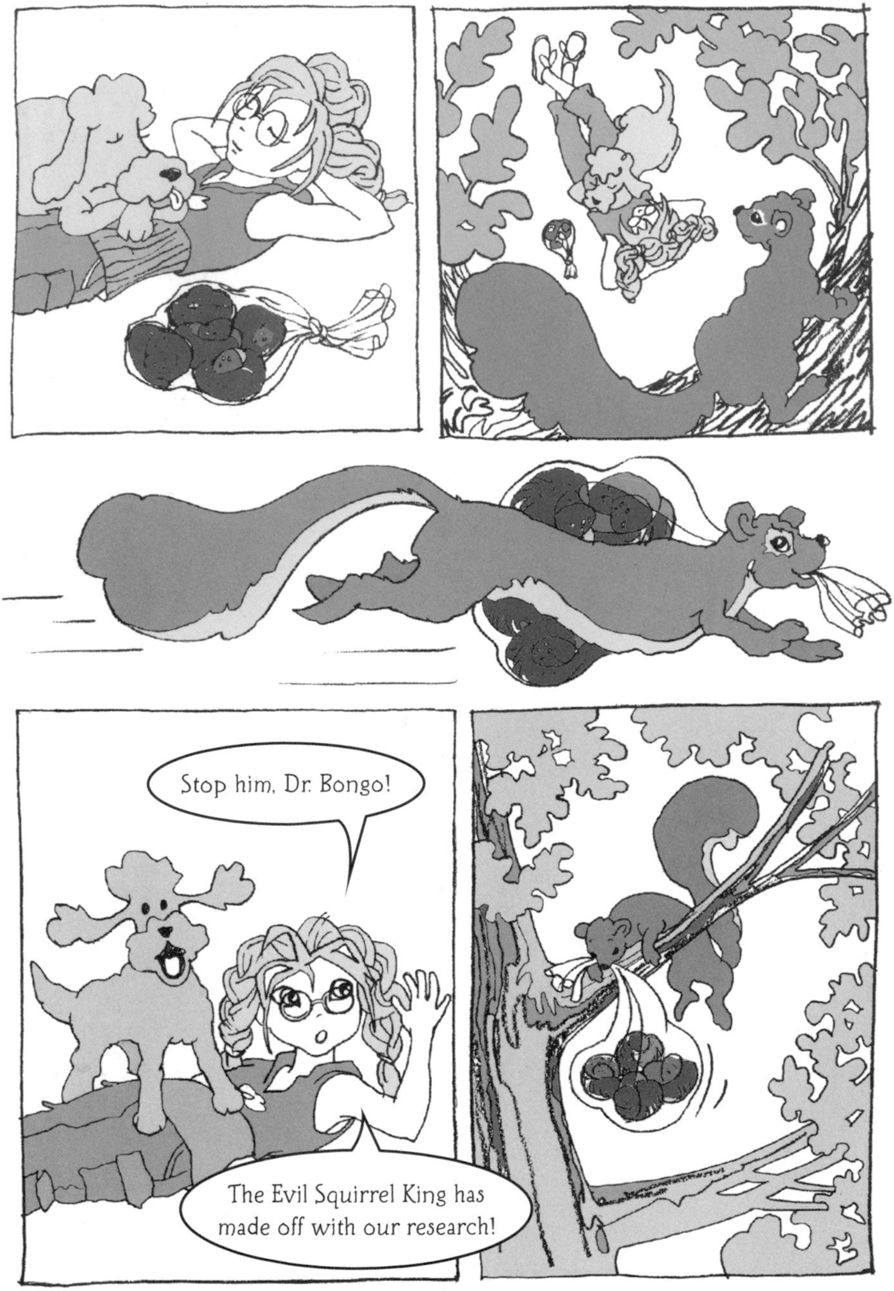
Stop him, Dr. Bongo!
The Evil Squirrel King has made off with our research!

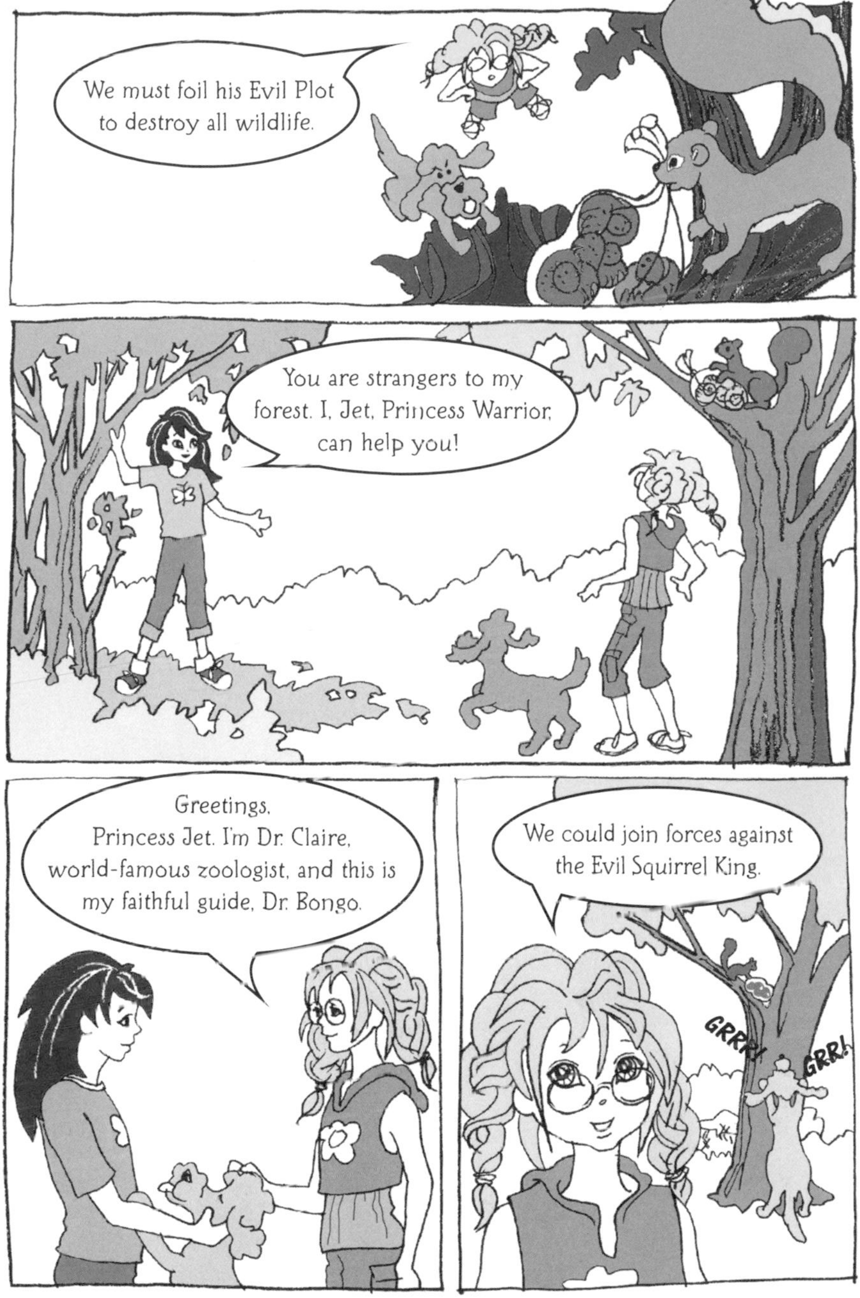
We must foil his Evil Plot to destroy all wildlife.
You are strangers to my forest. I, Jet, Princess Warrior, can help you!
Greetings, Princess Jet. I'm Dr. Claire, world-famous zoologist, and this is my faithful guide, Dr. Bongo.
We could join forces against the Evil Squirrel King.
GRRR!
GRR!

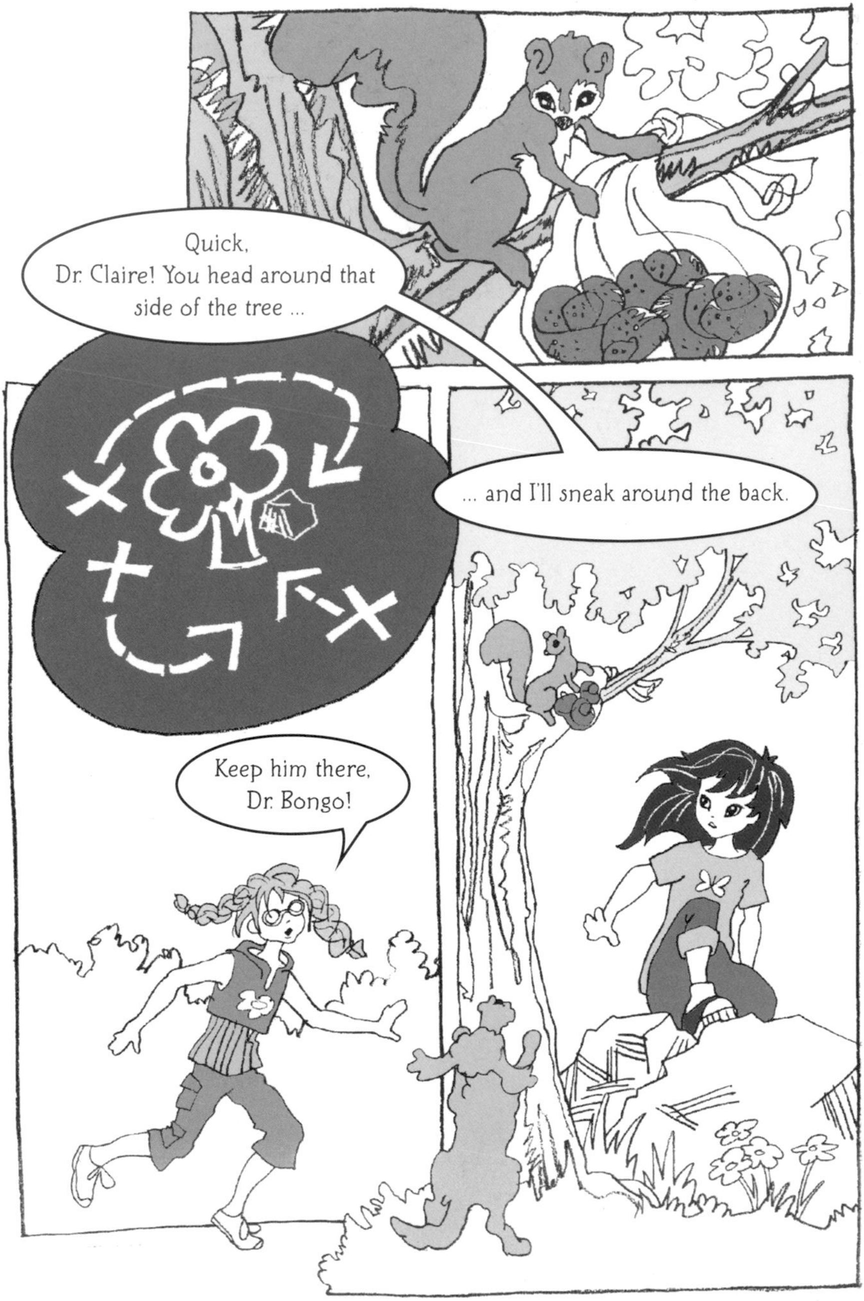
Quick,
Dr. Claire! You head around that
side of the tree ...
... and I'll sneak around the back.
Keep him there,
Dr. Bongo!

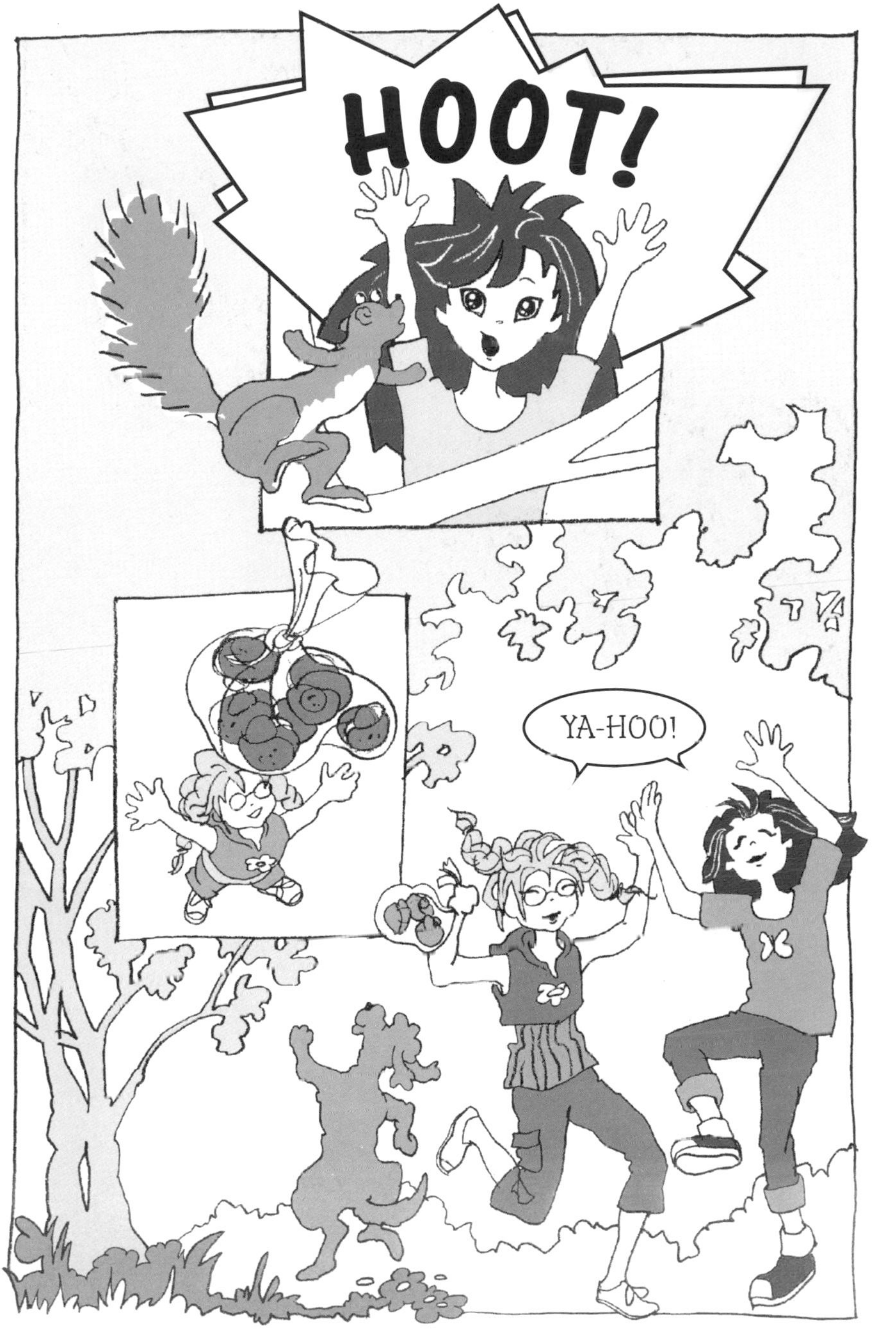
HOOT!
YA-HOO!

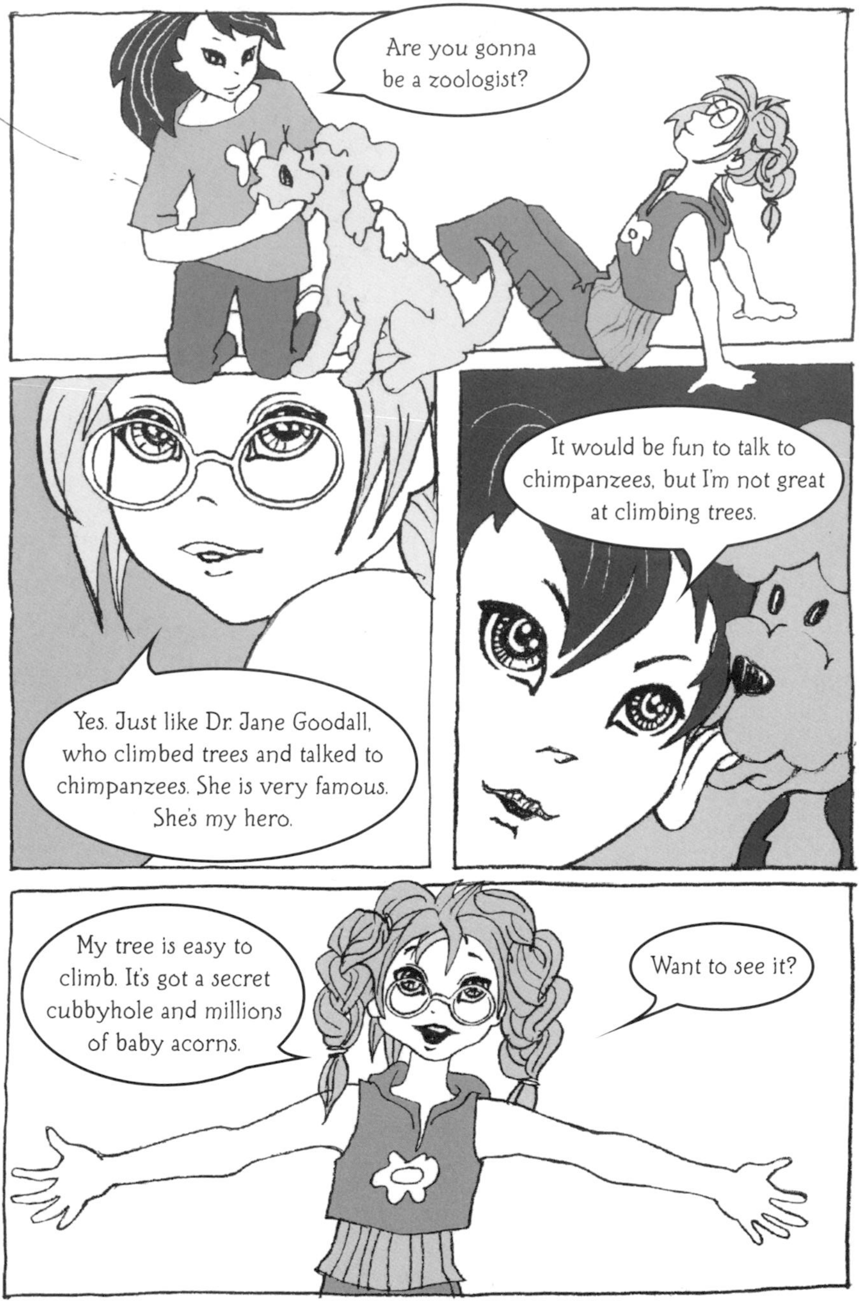
Are you gonna be a zoologist?
Yes. Just like Dr. Jane Goodall, who climbed trees and talked to chimpanzees. She is very famous. She's my hero.
It would be fun to talk to chimpanzees, but I'm not great at climbing trees.
My tree is easy to climb. It's got a secret cubbyhole and millions of baby acorns.
Want to see it?

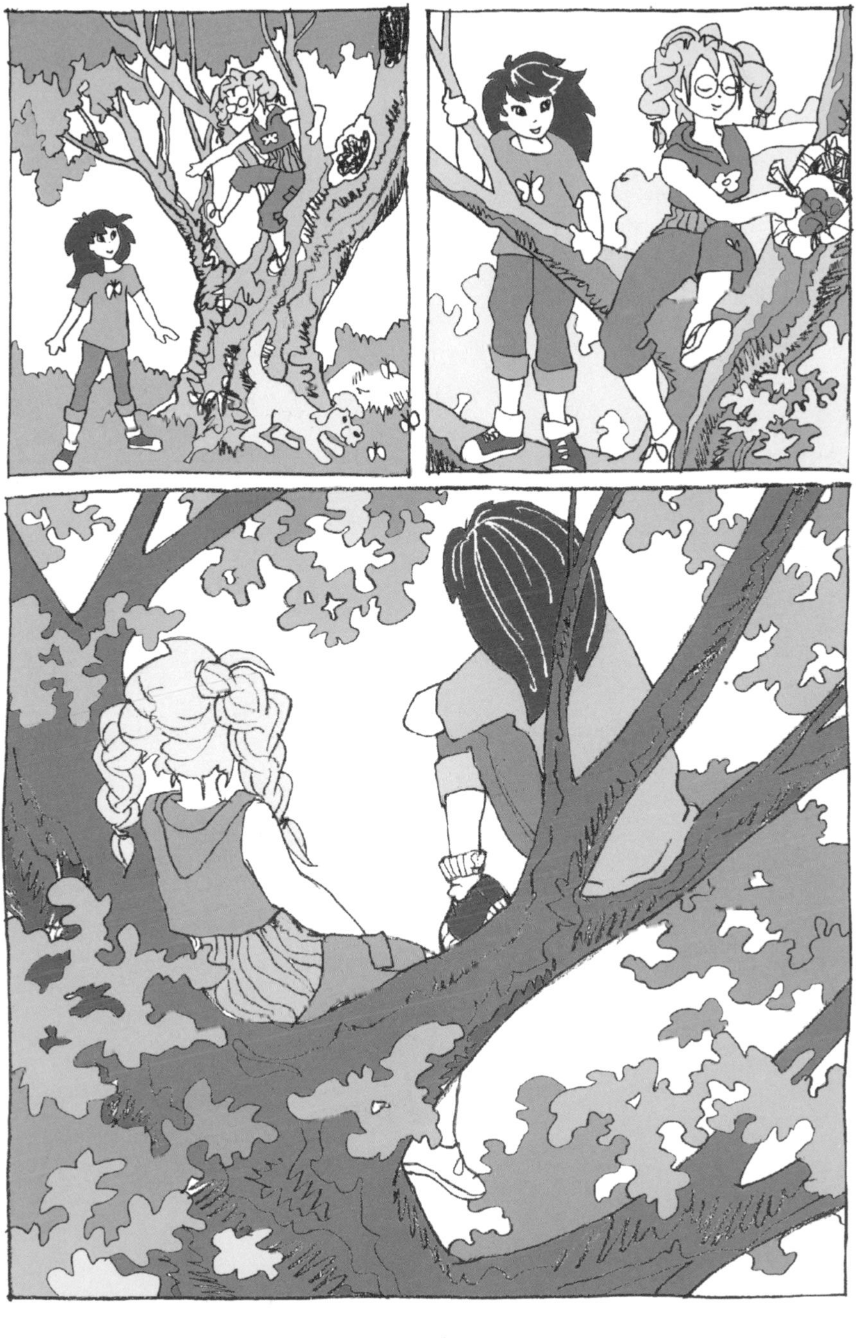

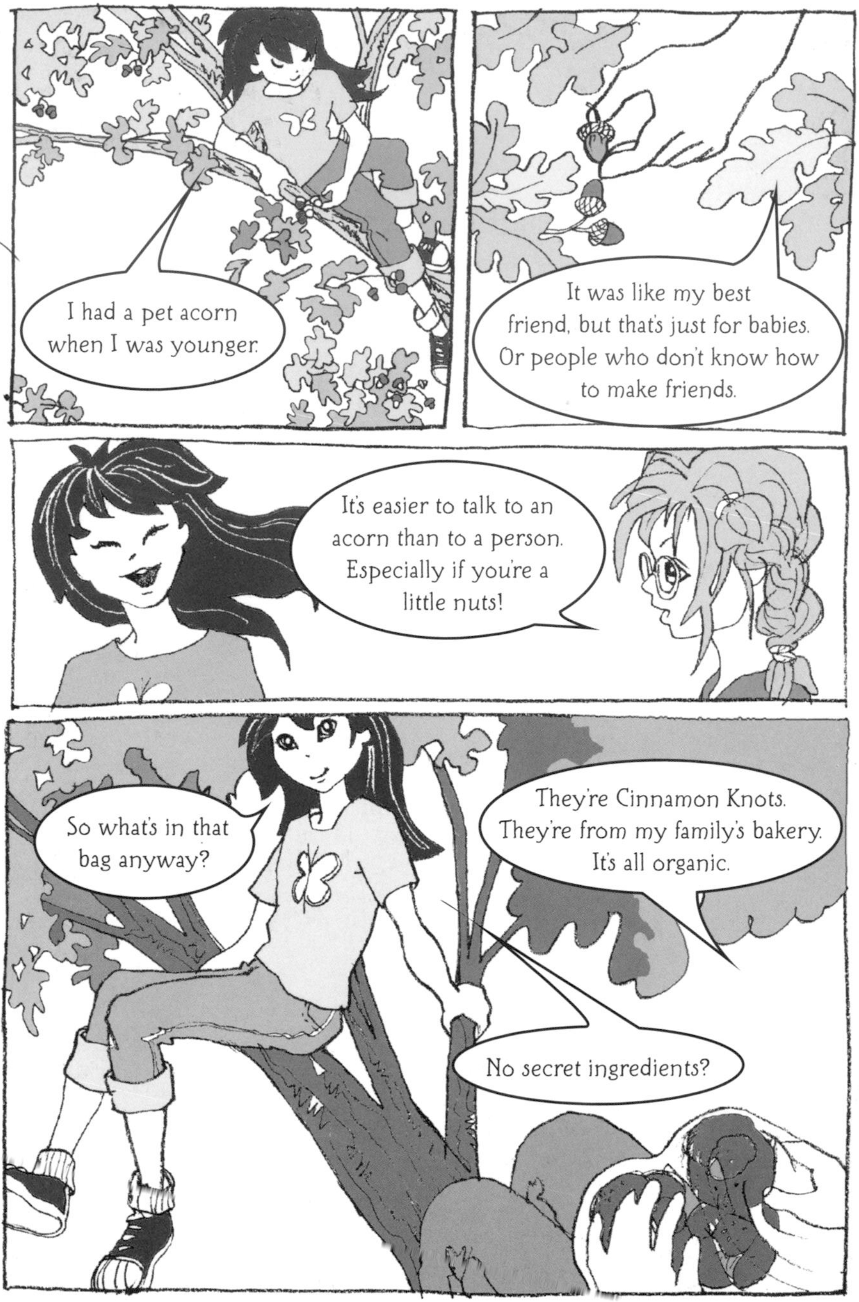
I had a pet acorn when I was younger.
It was like my best friend, but that's just for babies. Or people who don't know how to make friends.
It's easier to talk to an acorn than to a person. Especially if you're a little nuts!
So what's in that bag anyway?
They're Cinnamon Knots. They're from my family's bakery. It's all organic.
No secret ingredients?

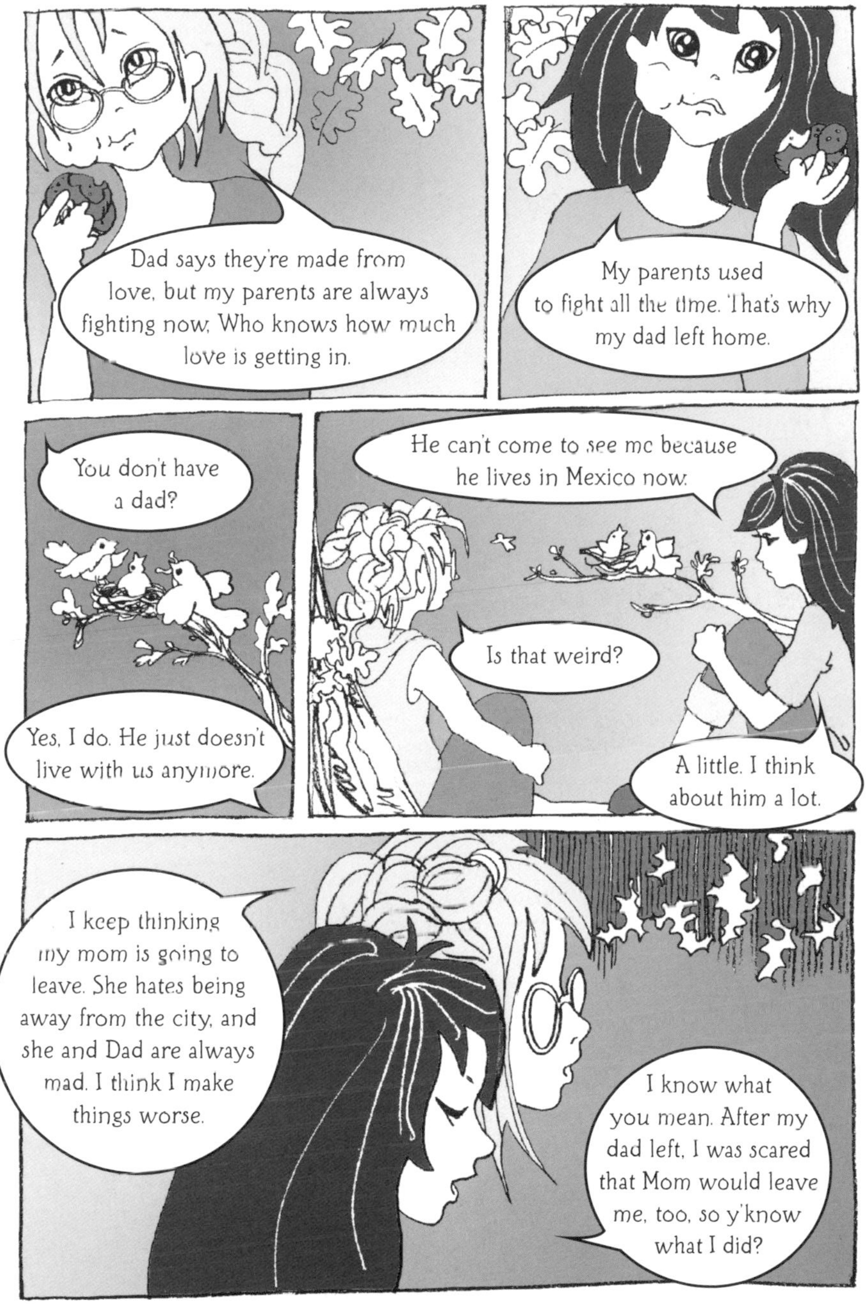
Dad says they're made from love, but my parents are always fighting now. Who knows how much love is getting in.
My parents used to fight all the time. That's why my dad left home.
You don't have a dad?
Yes, I do. He just doesn't live with us anymore.
He can't come to see me because he lives in Mexico now.
Is that weird?
A little. I think about him a lot.
I keep thinking my mom is going to leave. She hates being away from the city, and she and Dad are always mad. I think I make things worse.
I know what you mean. After my dad left, I was scared that Mom would leave me, too, so y'know what I did?

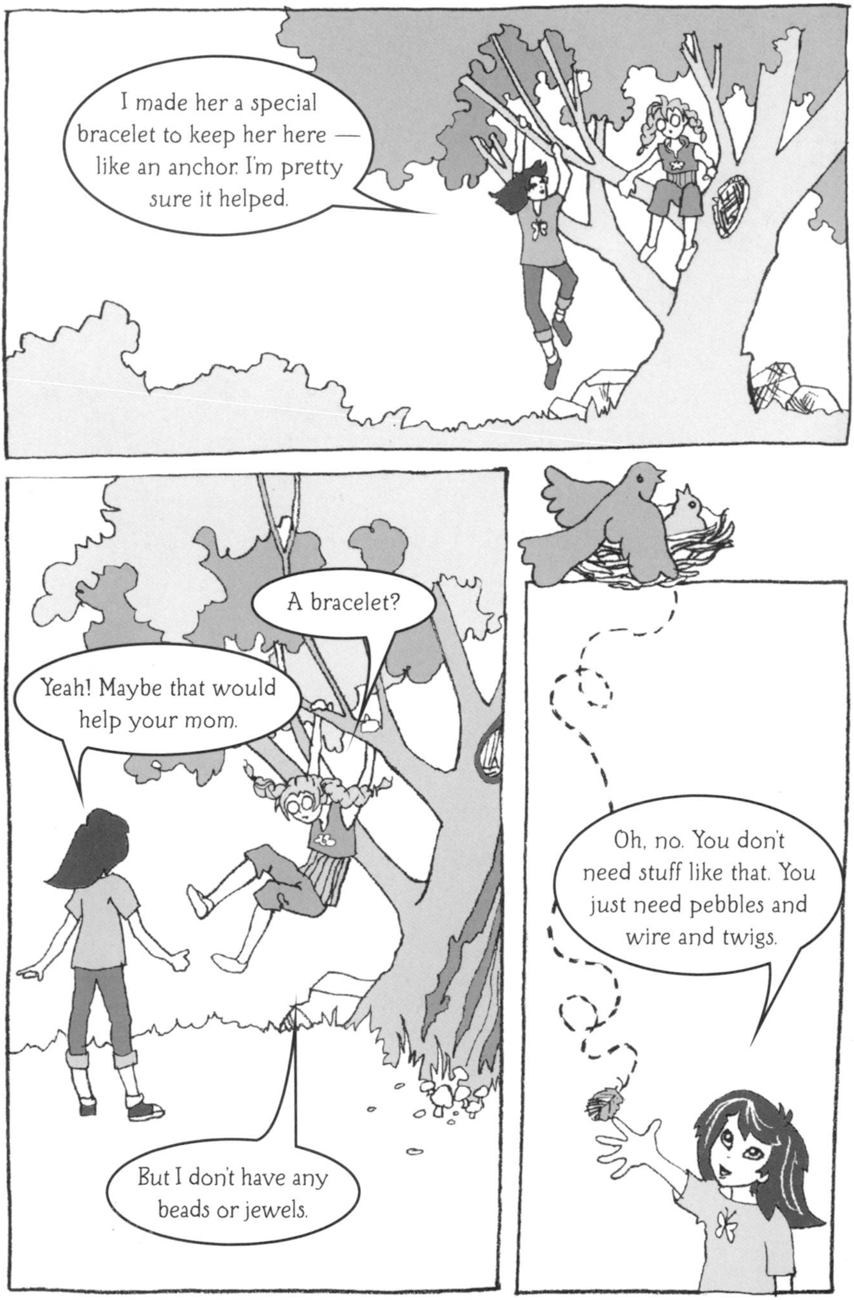
I made her a special bracelet to keep her here — like an anchor. I'm pretty sure it helped.
A bracelet?
Yeah! Maybe that would help your mom.
But I don't have any beads or jewels.
Oh, no. You don't need stuff like that. You just need pebbles and wire and twigs.

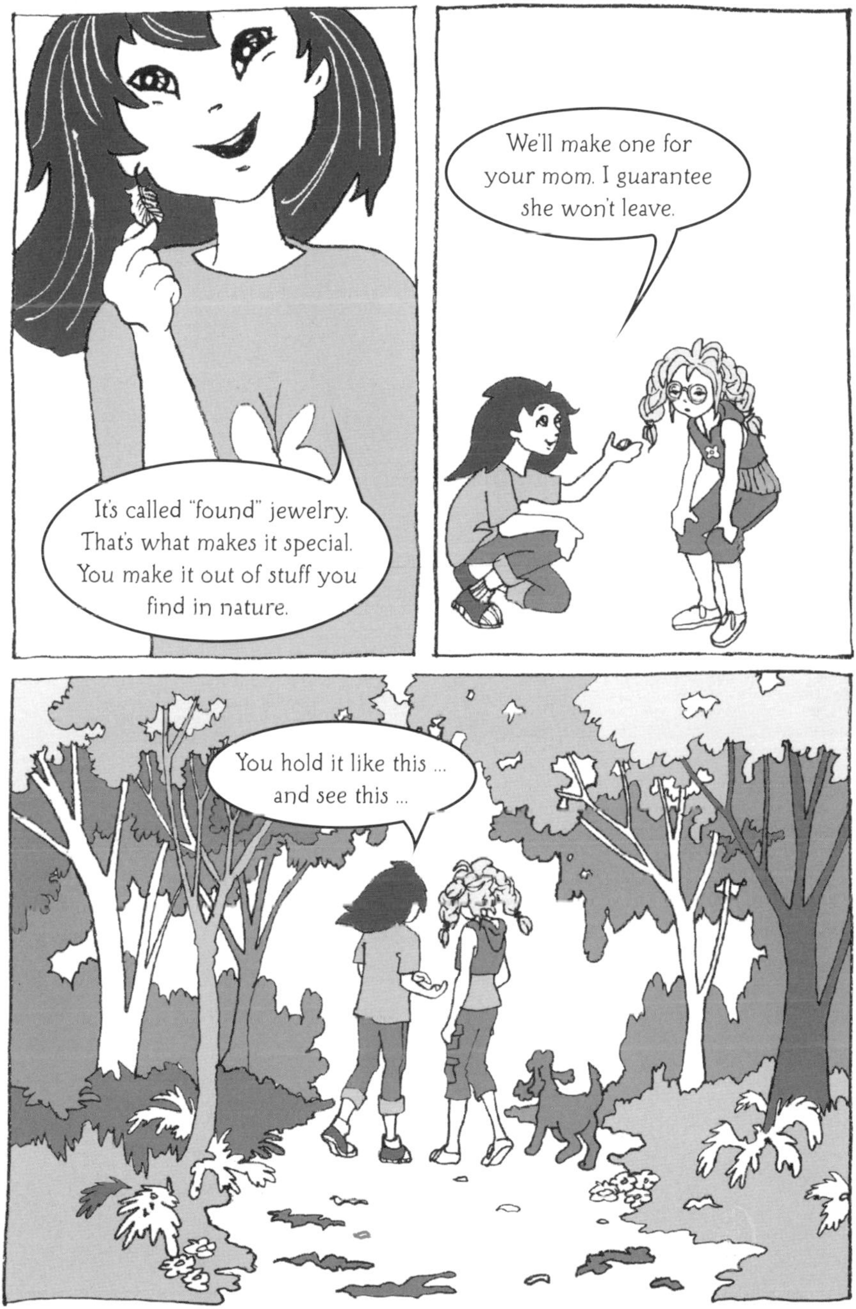
It's called "found" jewelry. That's what makes it special. You make it out of stuff you find in nature.
We'll make one for your mom. I guarantee she won't leave.
You hold it like this ... and see this ...

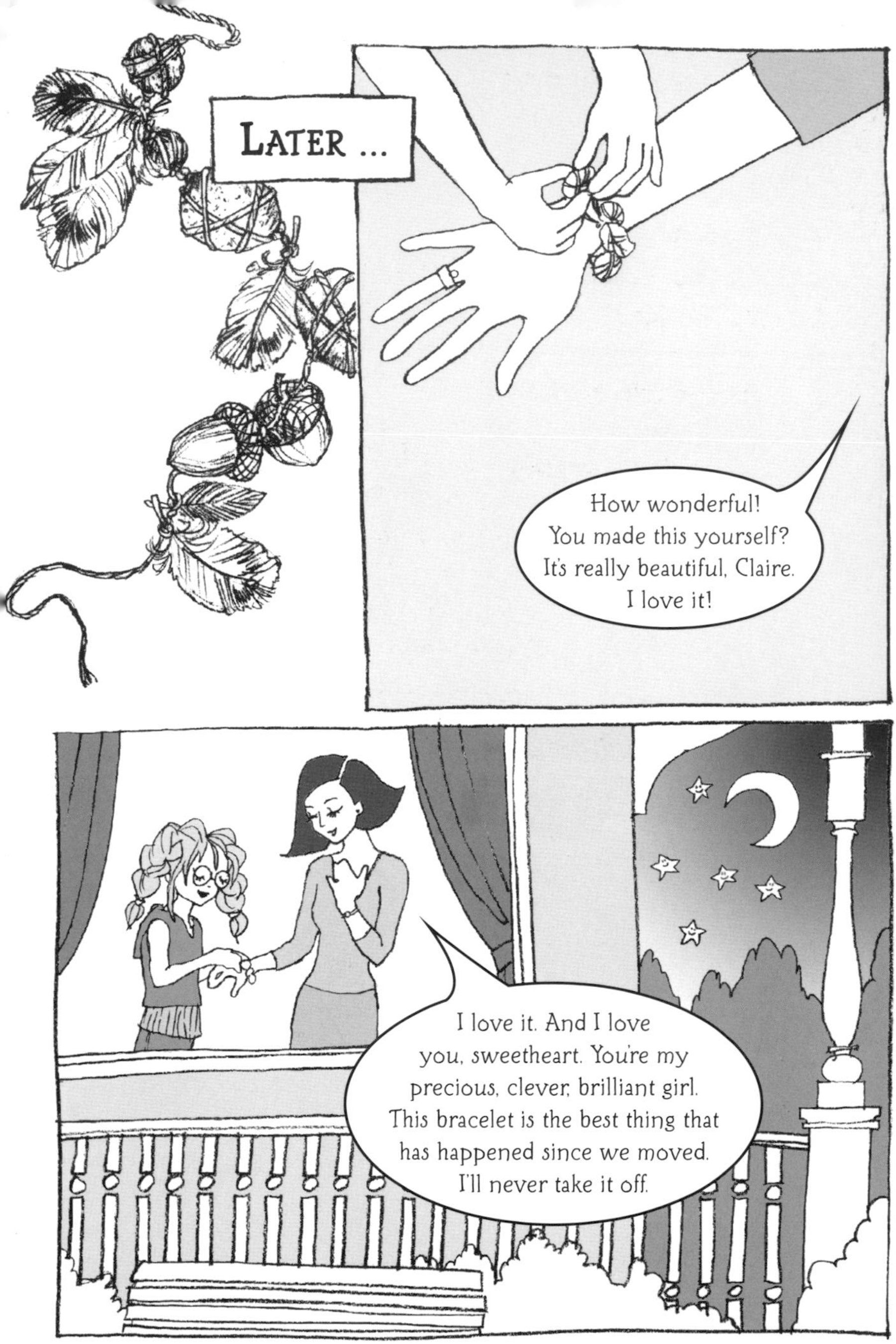
LATER ...
How wonderful! You made this yourself? It's really beautiful, Claire. I love it!
I love it. And I love you, sweetheart. You're my precious, clever, brilliant girl. This bracelet is the best thing that has happened since we moved. I'll never take it off.

Dear Diary:

The bakery is a big huge giant hit! We're calling it "The Grain of Truth" because it's organic, get it? More and more people come every day. It's practically famous now.

Dad is really happy. But he and Mom are still fighting. I hear them at night when they think I'm sleeping.

I sure hope Jet is right about the bracelet keeping Mom anchored. Maybe I should have made her a belt or a coat. Something bigger and heavier. No joke, Dear Diary. I'm really, really worried.

Claire

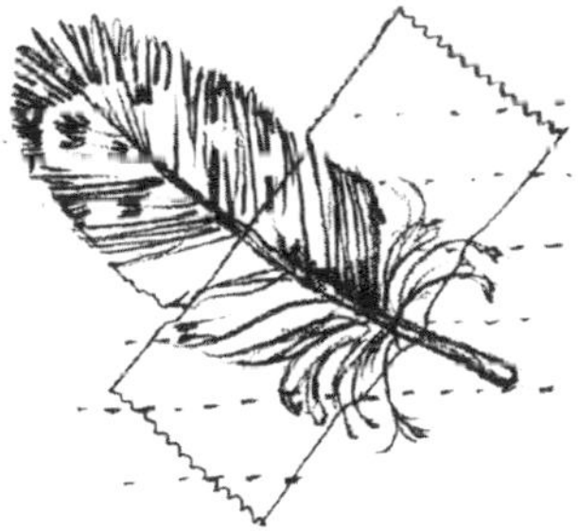

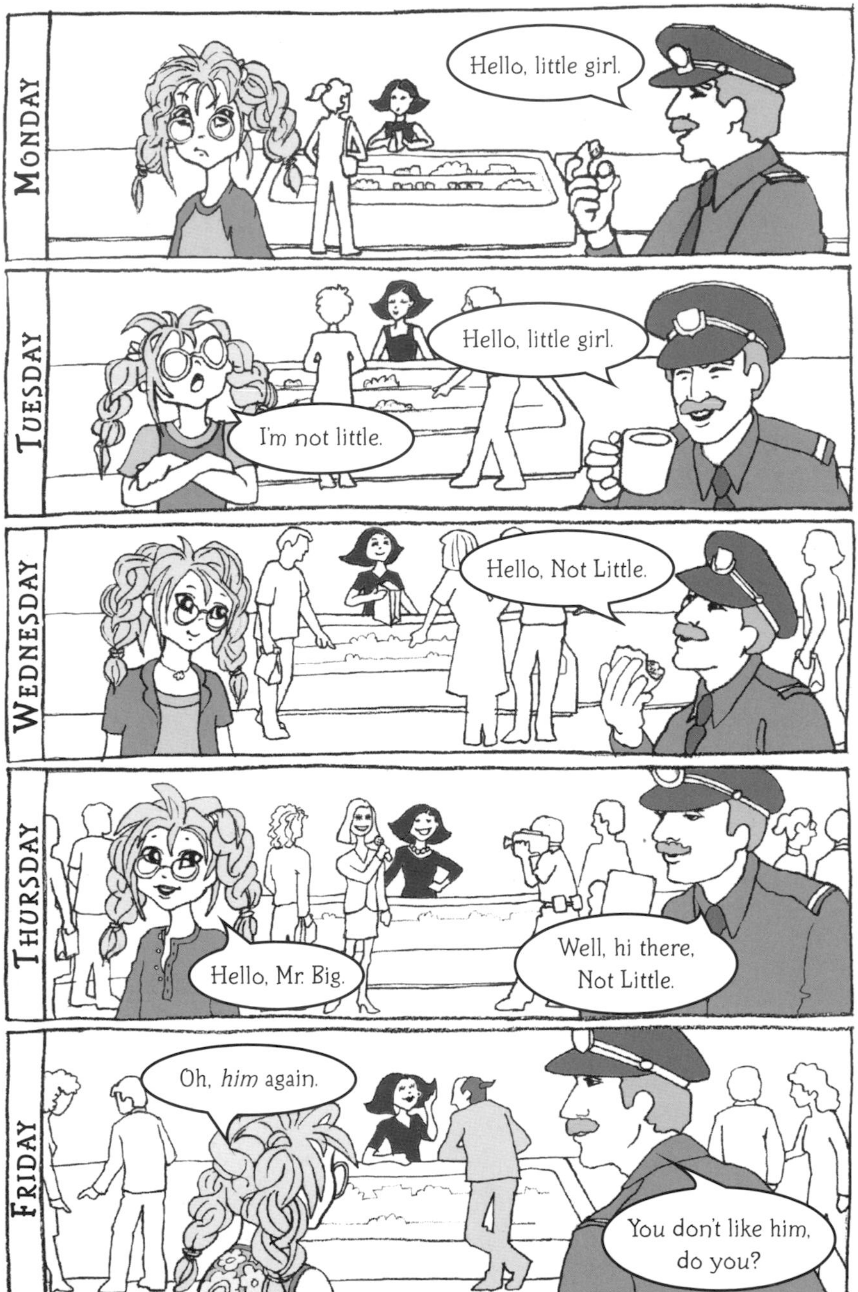
MONDAY
Hello, little girl.
TUESDAY
Hello, little girl.
I'm not little.
WEDNESDAY
Hello, Not Little.
THURSDAY
Hello, Mr. Big.
Well, hi there, Not Little.
FRIDAY
Oh, *him* again.
You don't like him, do you?

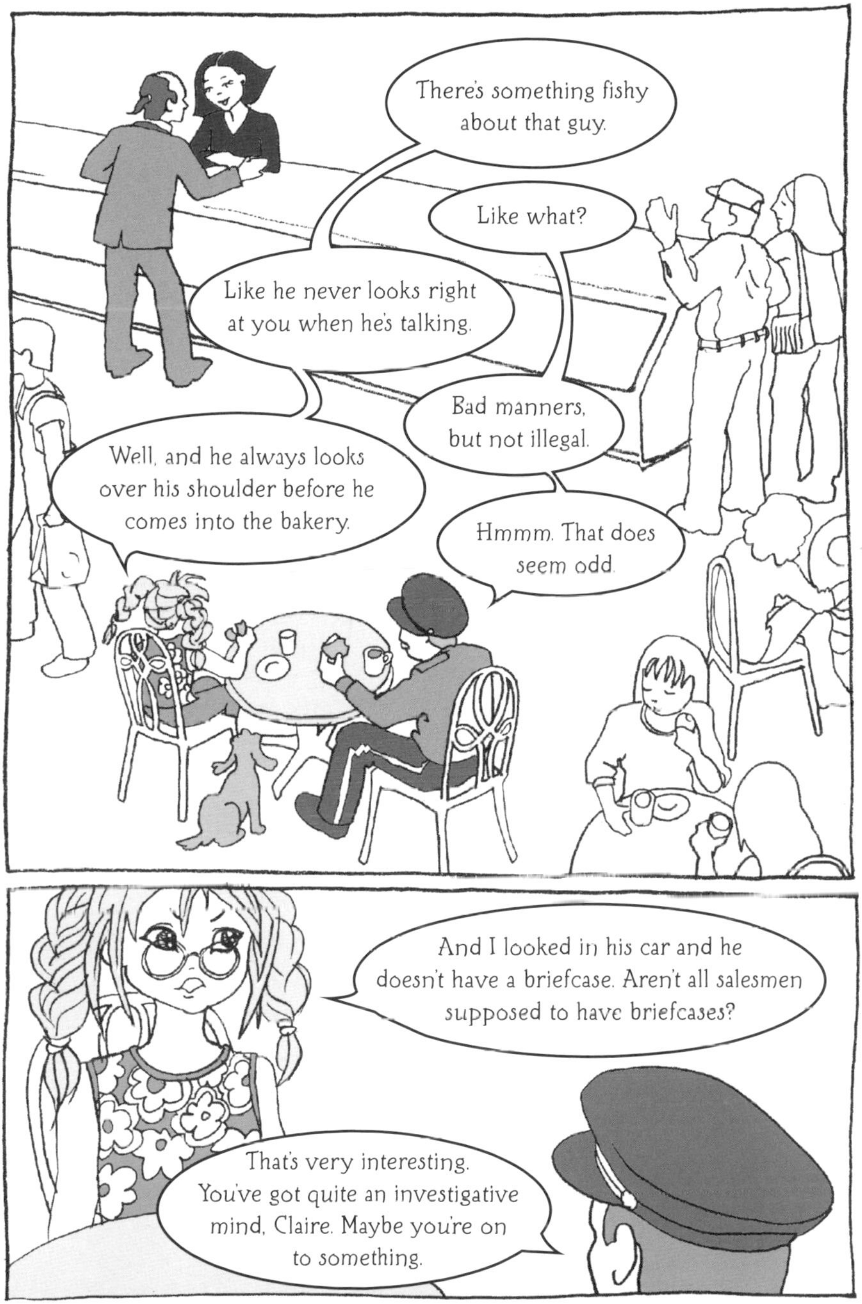
There's something fishy about that guy.
Like what?
Like he never looks right at you when he's talking.
Bad manners, but not illegal.
Well, and he always looks over his shoulder before he comes into the bakery.
Hmmm. That does seem odd.
And I looked in his car and he doesn't have a briefcase. Aren't all salesmen supposed to have briefcases?
That's very interesting. You've got quite an investigative mind, Claire. Maybe you're on to something.

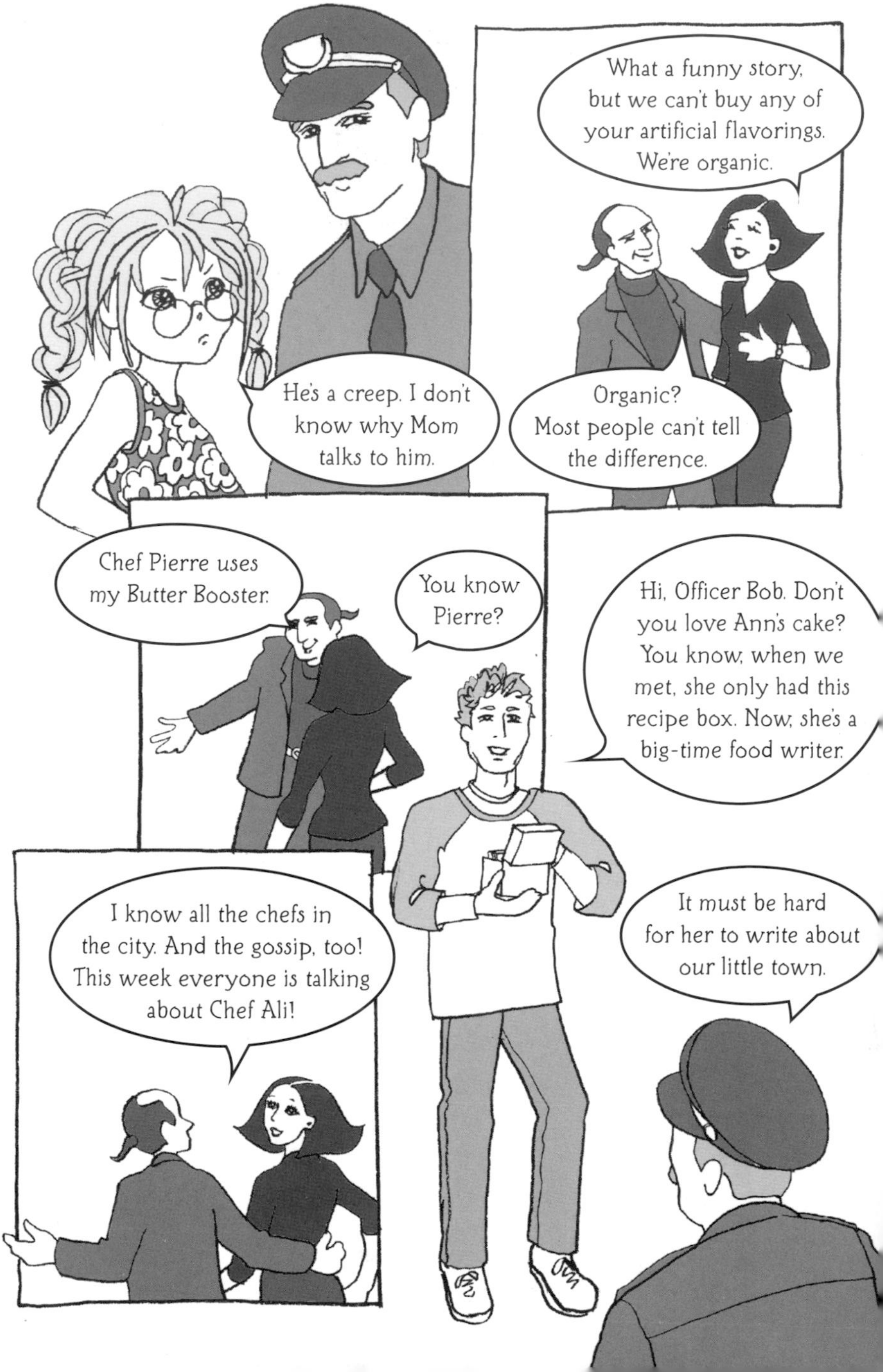
He's a creep. I don't know why Mom talks to him.
What a funny story, but we can't buy any of your artificial flavorings. We're organic.
Organic? Most people can't tell the difference.
Chef Pierre uses my Butter Booster.
You know Pierre?
Hi, Officer Bob. Don't you love Ann's cake? You know, when we met, she only had this recipe box. Now, she's a big-time food writer.
I know all the chefs in the city. And the gossip, too! This week everyone is talking about Chef Ali!
It must be hard for her to write about our little town.

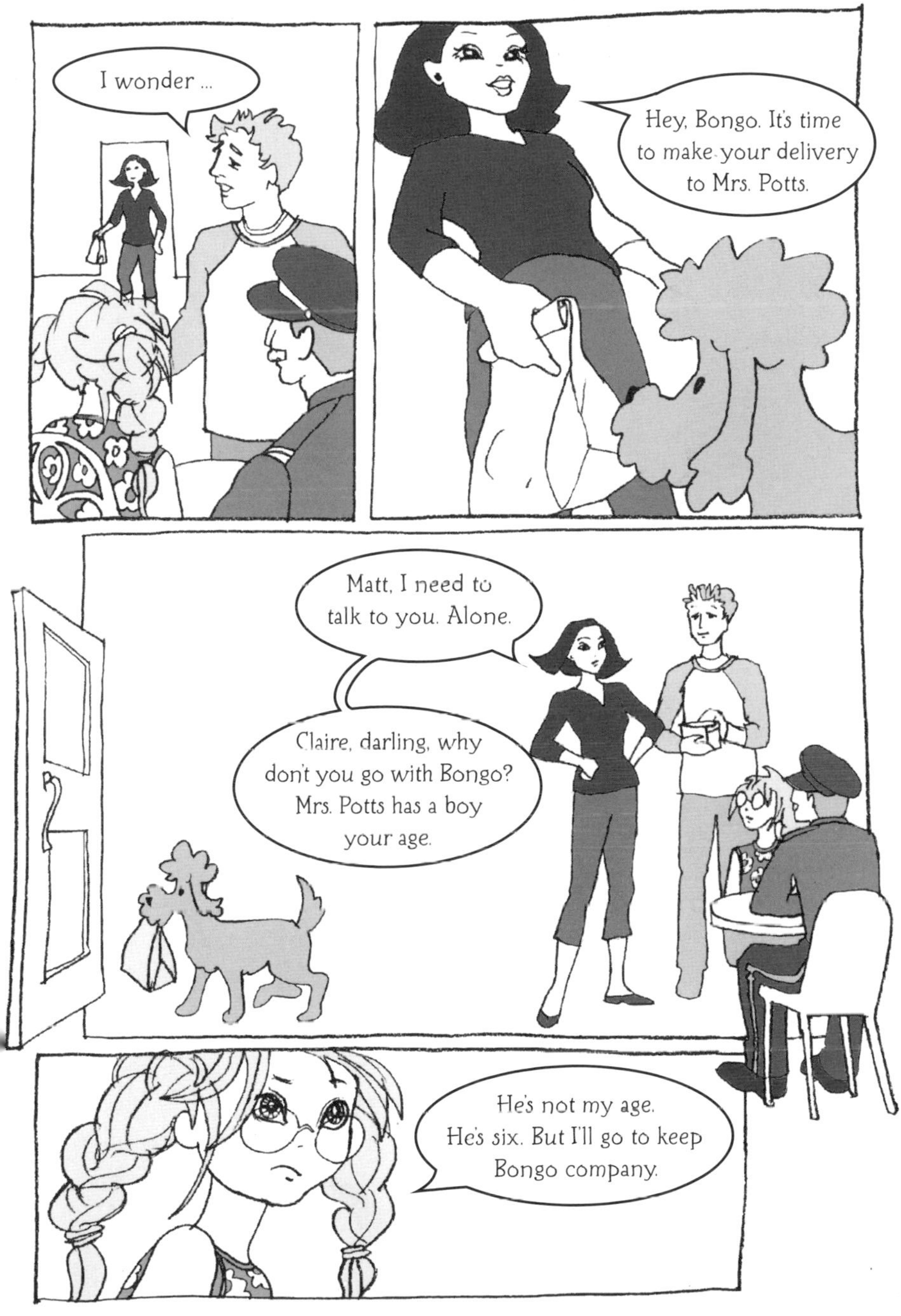
I wonder ...
Hey, Bongo. It's time to make your delivery to Mrs. Potts.
Matt, I need to talk to you. Alone.
Claire, darling, why don't you go with Bongo? Mrs. Potts has a boy your age.
He's not my age. He's six. But I'll go to keep Bongo company.

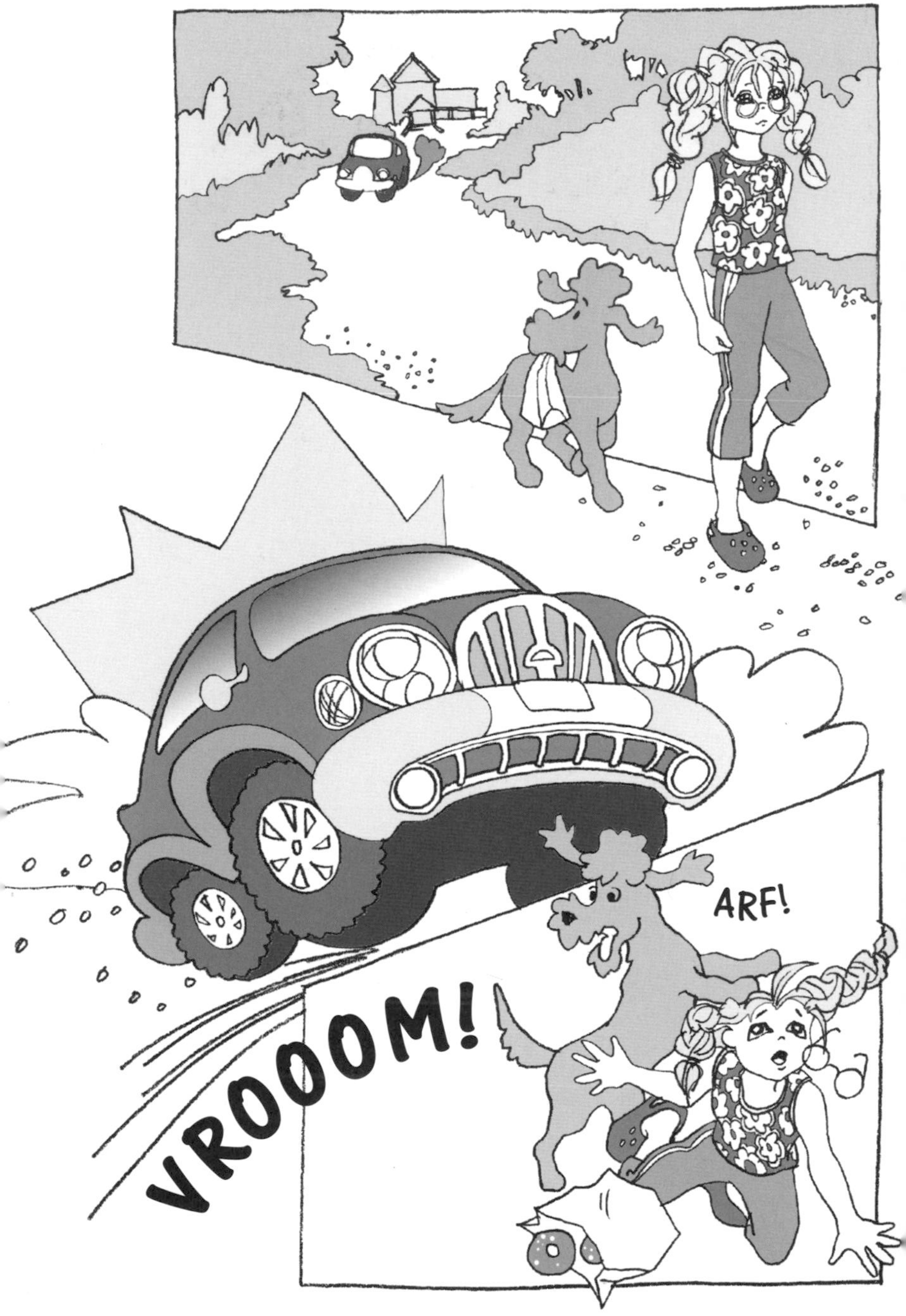
VROOOM!
ARF!

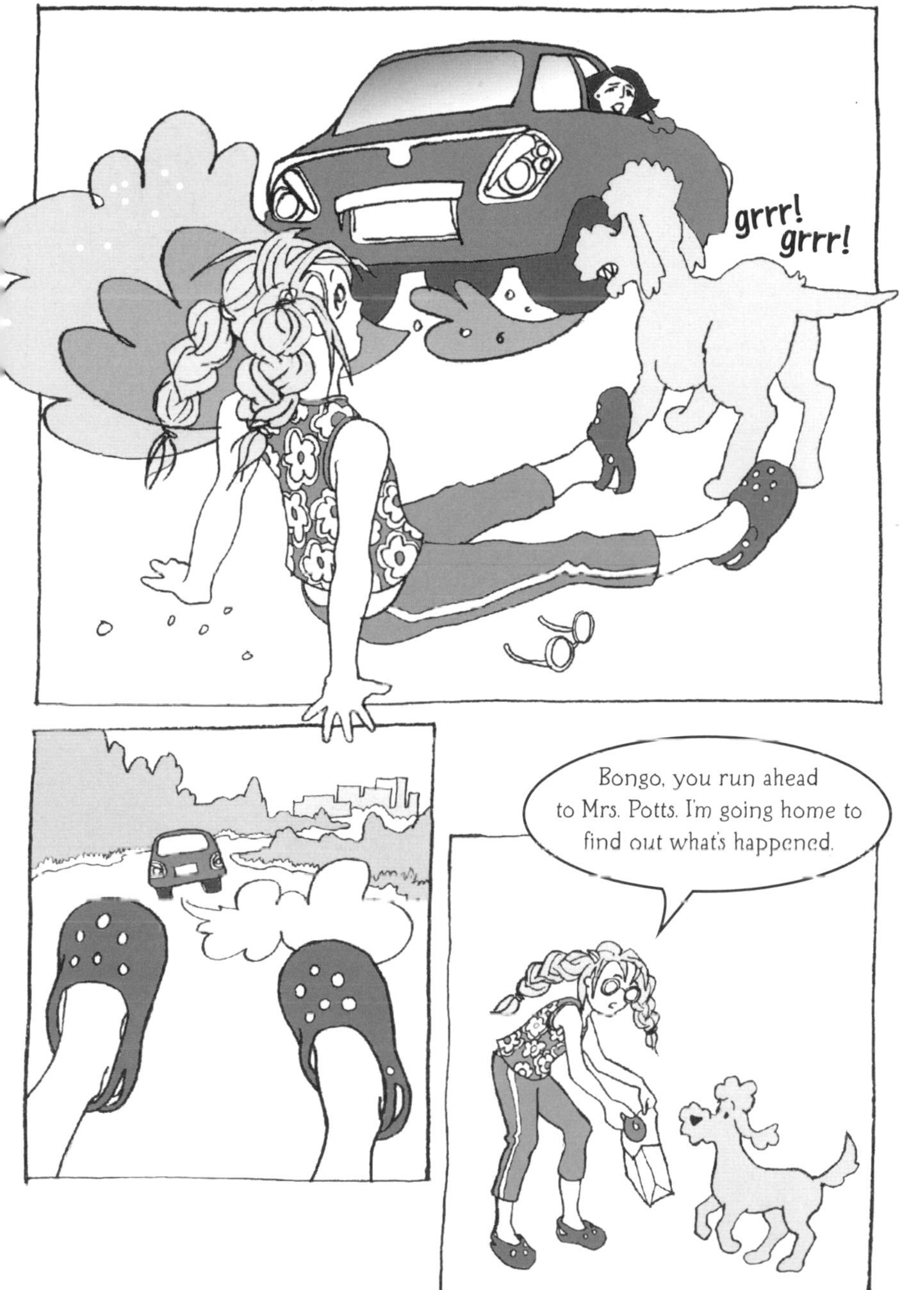
grrr!
grrr!
Bongo, you run ahead to Mrs. Potts. I'm going home to find out what's happened.

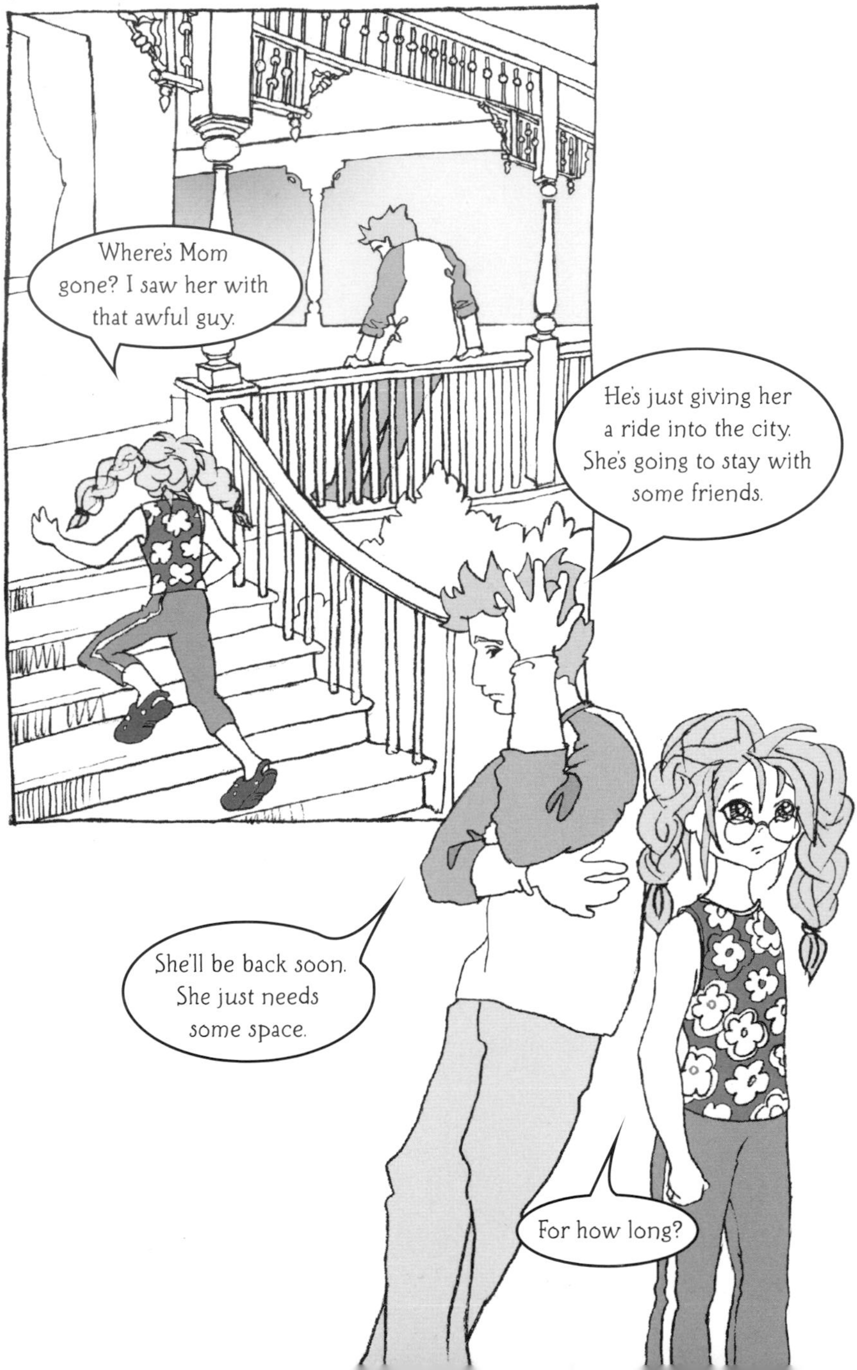
Where's Mom gone? I saw her with that awful guy.
He's just giving her a ride into the city. She's going to stay with some friends.
She'll be back soon. She just needs some space.
For how long?

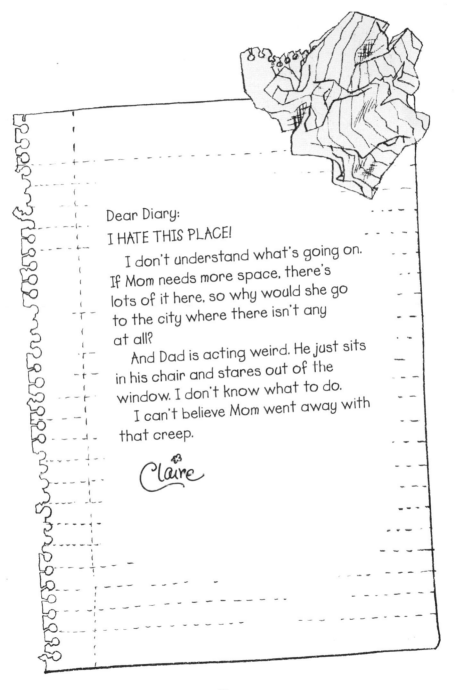

Dear Diary:

I HATE THIS PLACE!

I don't understand what's going on. If Mom needs more space, there's lots of it here, so why would she go to the city where there isn't any at all?

And Dad is acting weird. He just sits in his chair and stares out of the window. I don't know what to do.

I can't believe Mom went away with that creep.

Claire

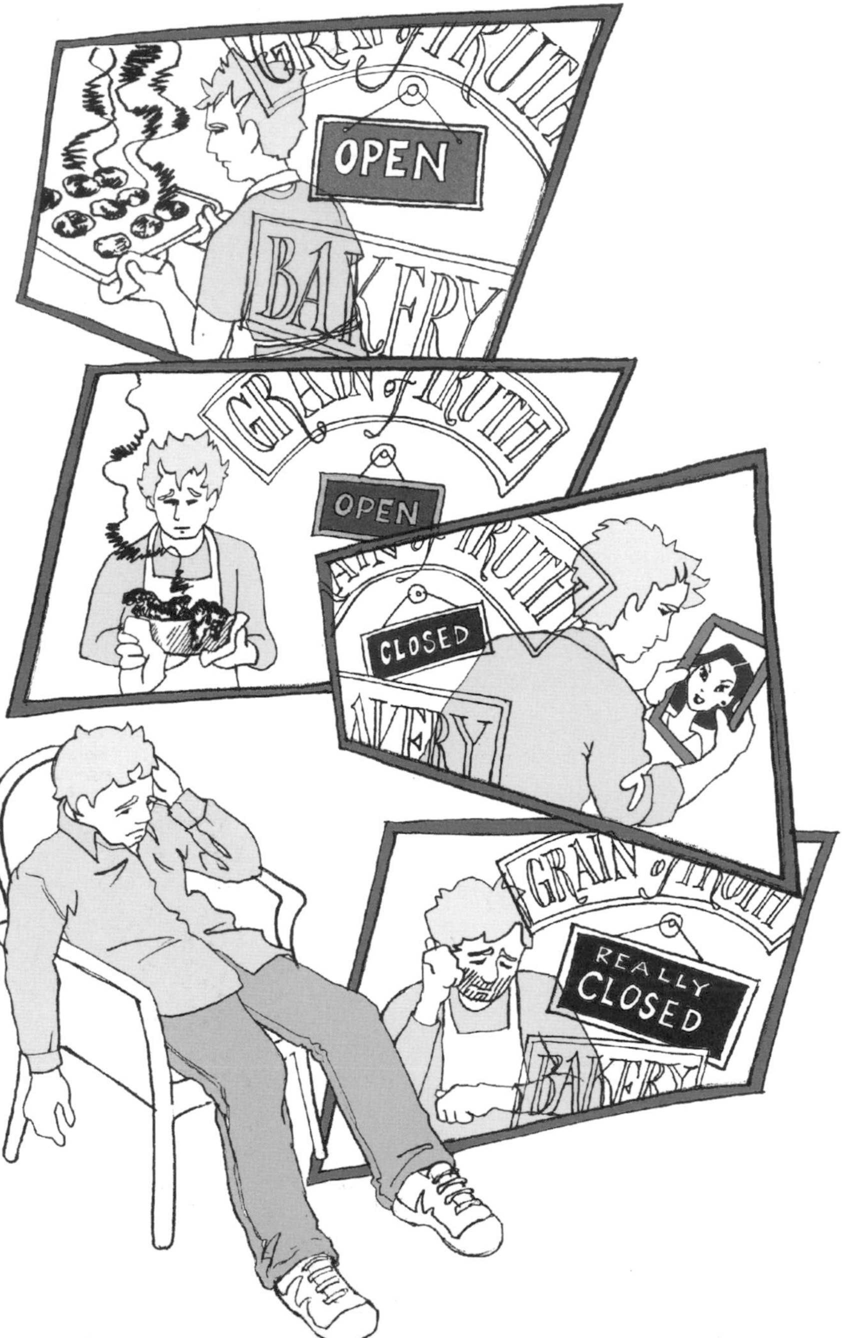
OPEN
BAKERY
GRAIN of TRUTH
OPEN
CLOSED
GRAIN
REALLY CLOSED
BAKERY

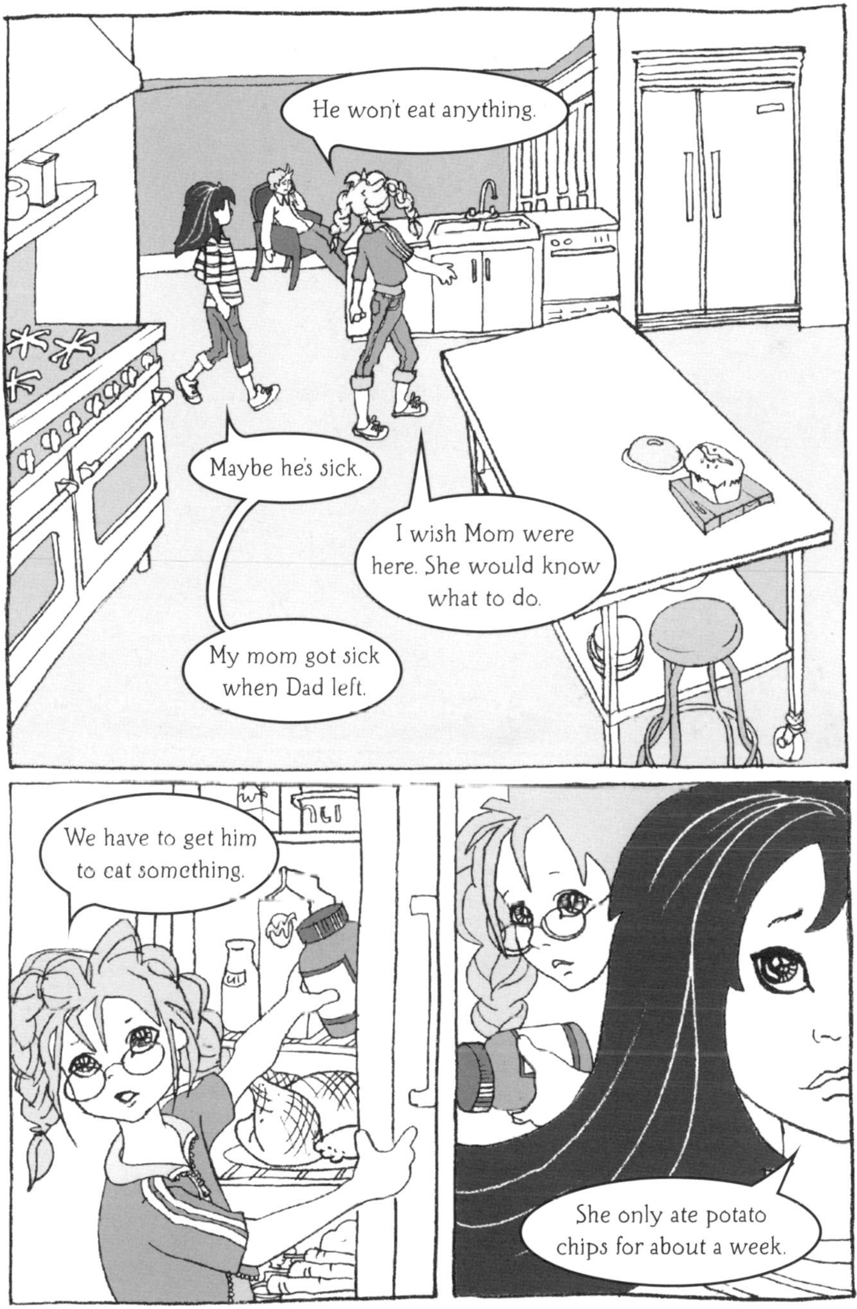
He won't eat anything.
Maybe he's sick.
I wish Mom were here. She would know what to do.
My mom got sick when Dad left.
We have to get him to eat something.
She only ate potato chips for about a week.

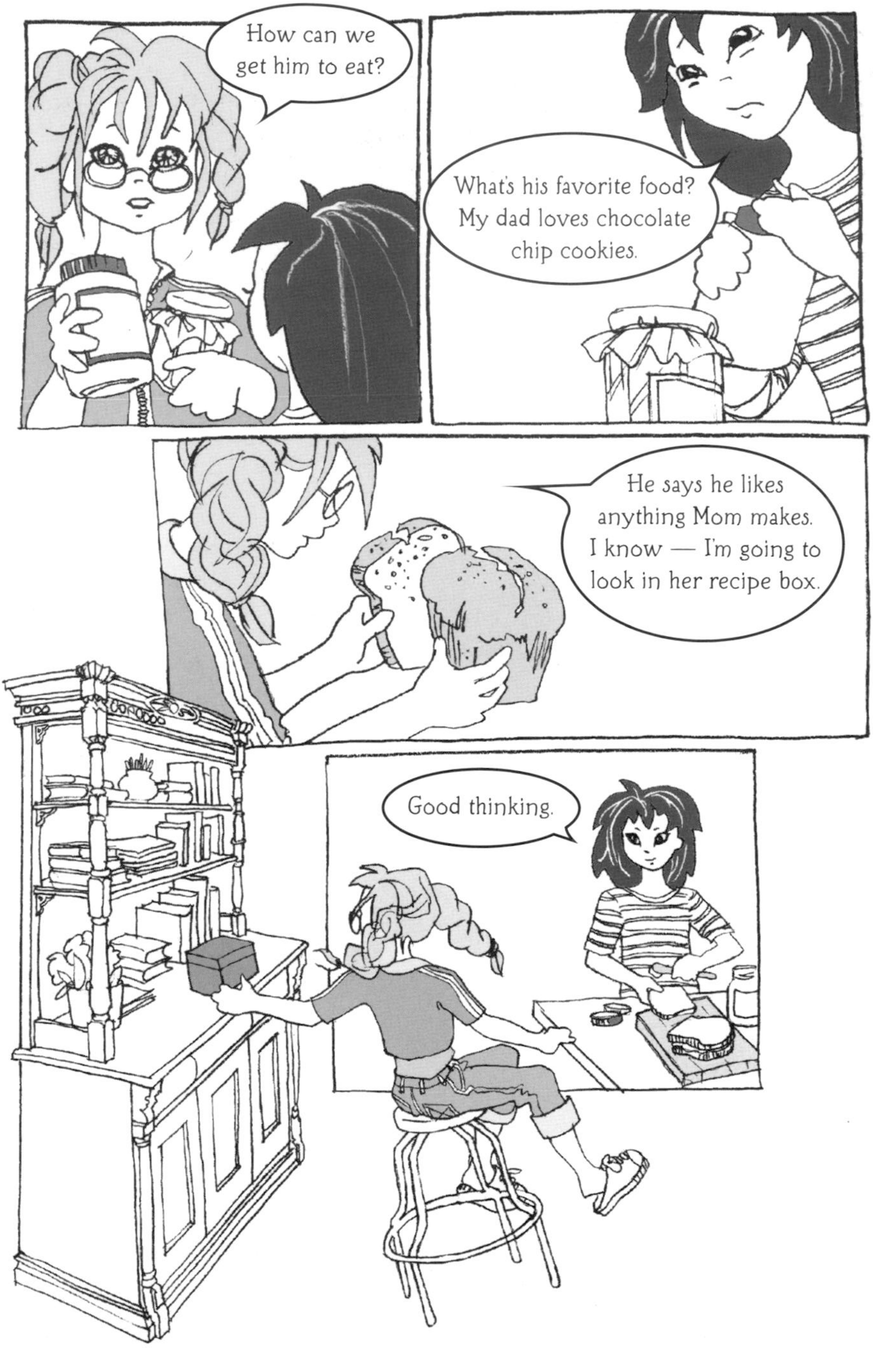
How can we get him to eat?
What's his favorite food? My dad loves chocolate chip cookies.
He says he likes anything Mom makes. I know — I'm going to look in her recipe box.
Good thinking.

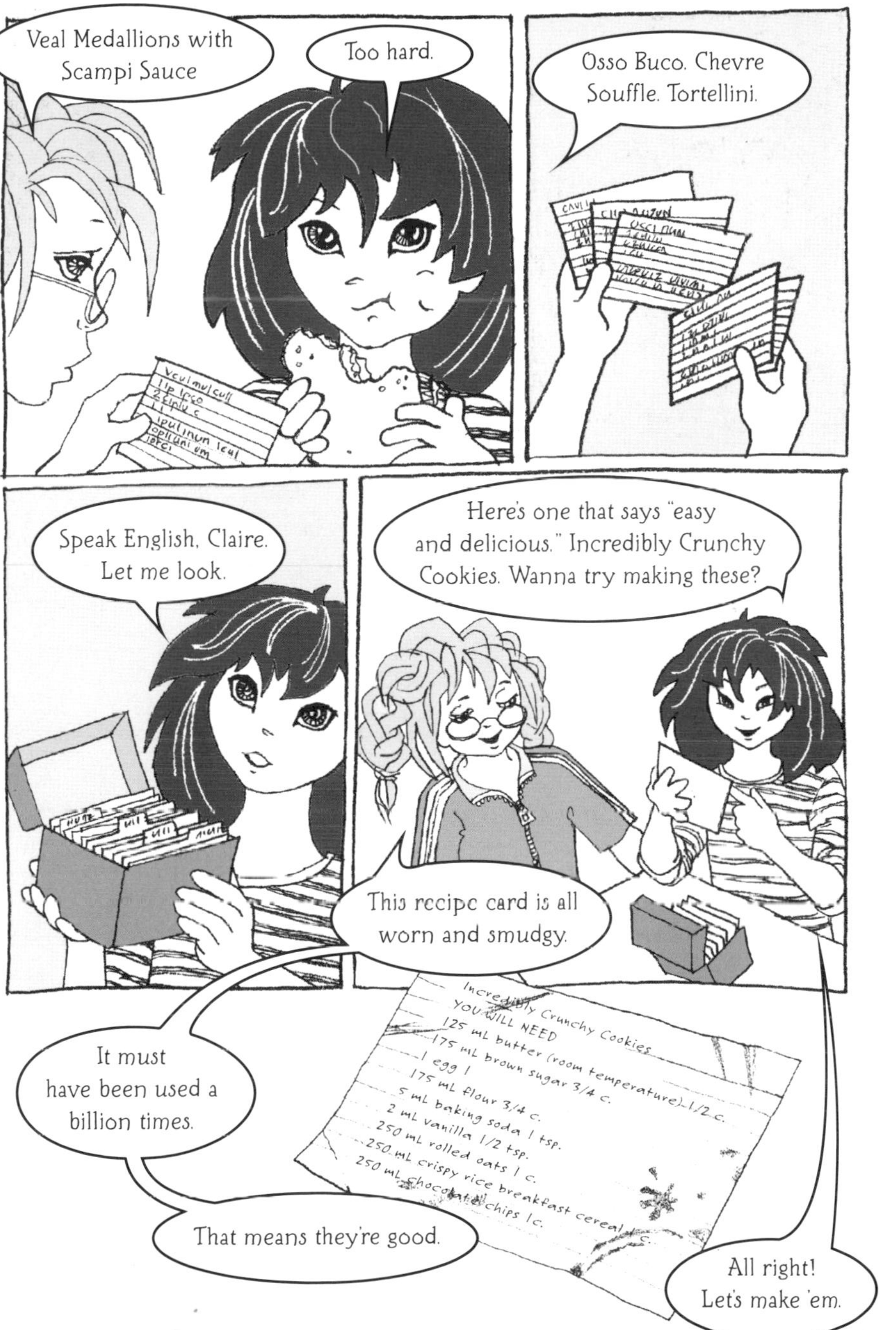
Veal Medallions with Scampi Sauce
Too hard.
Osso Buco. Chevre Souffle. Tortellini.
Speak English, Claire. Let me look.
Here's one that says "easy and delicious." Incredibly Crunchy Cookies. Wanna try making these?
This recipe card is all worn and smudgy.
It must have been used a billion times.
That means they're good.
Incredibly Crunchy Cookies
YOU WILL NEED
125 mL butter (room temperature) 1/2 c.
175 mL brown sugar 3/4 c.
1 egg 1
175 mL flour 3/4 c.
5 mL baking soda 1 tsp.
2 mL vanilla 1/2 tsp.
250 mL rolled oats 1 c.
250 mL crispy rice breakfast cereal 1 c.
250 mL chocolate chips 1c.
All right! Let's make 'em.

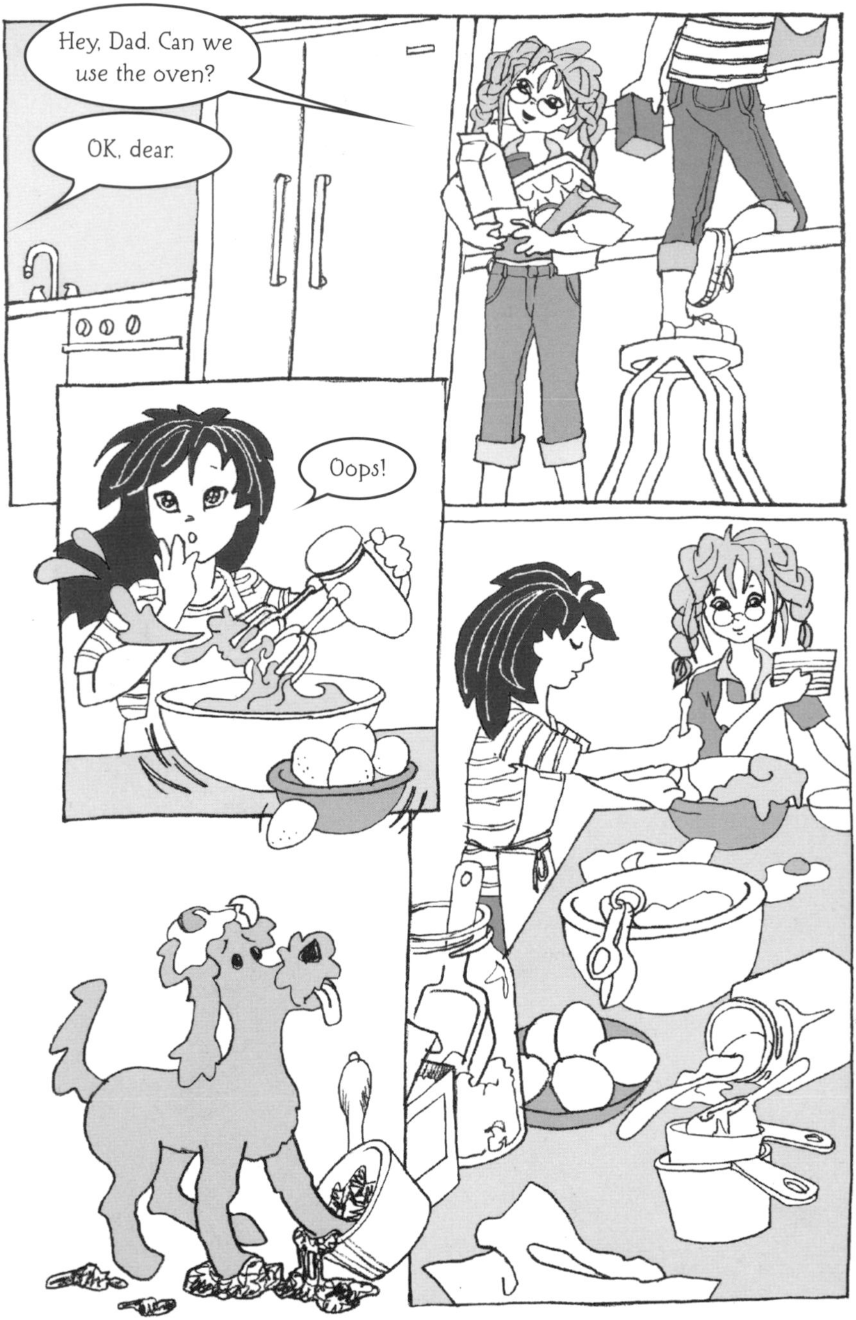
Hey, Dad. Can we use the oven?
OK, dear.
Oops!

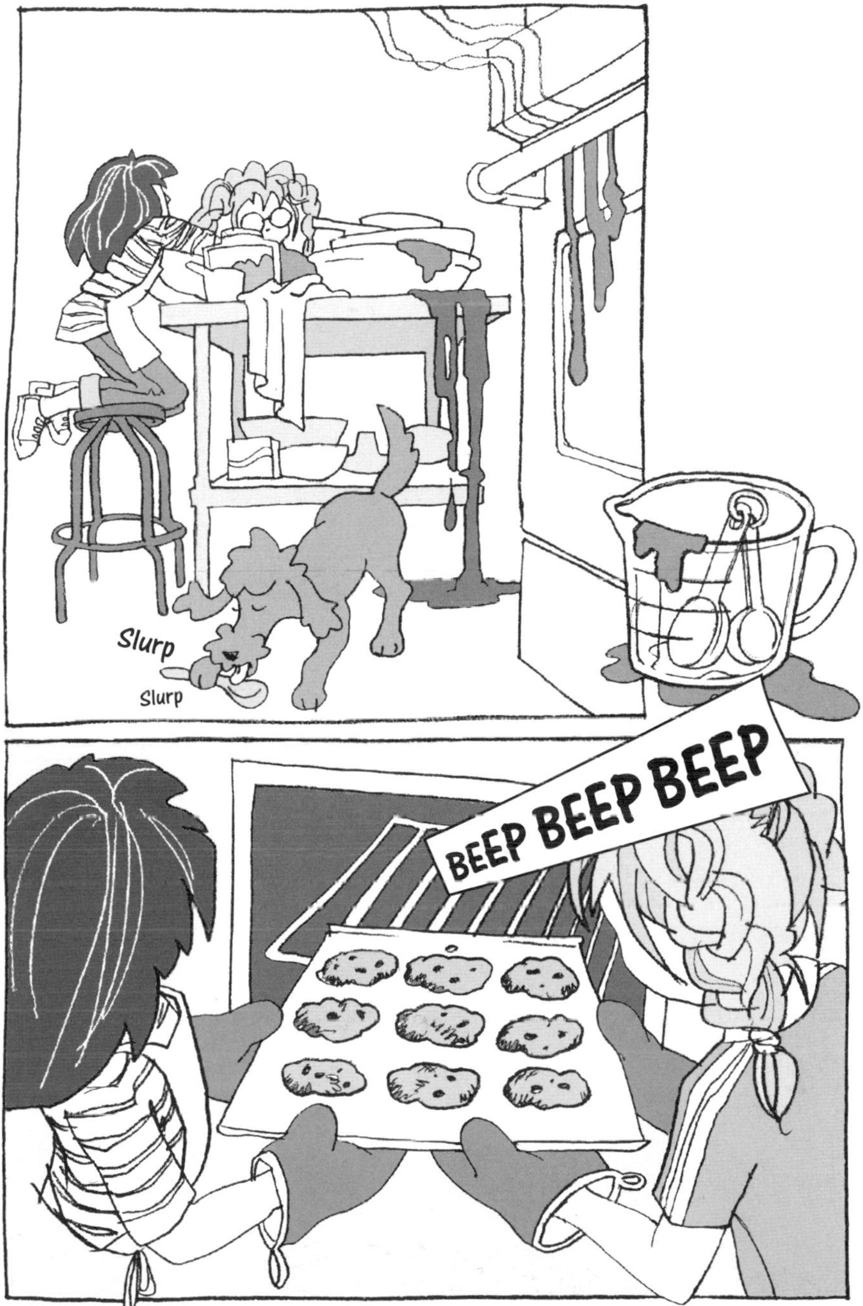
Slurp
Slurp
BEEP BEEP BEEP

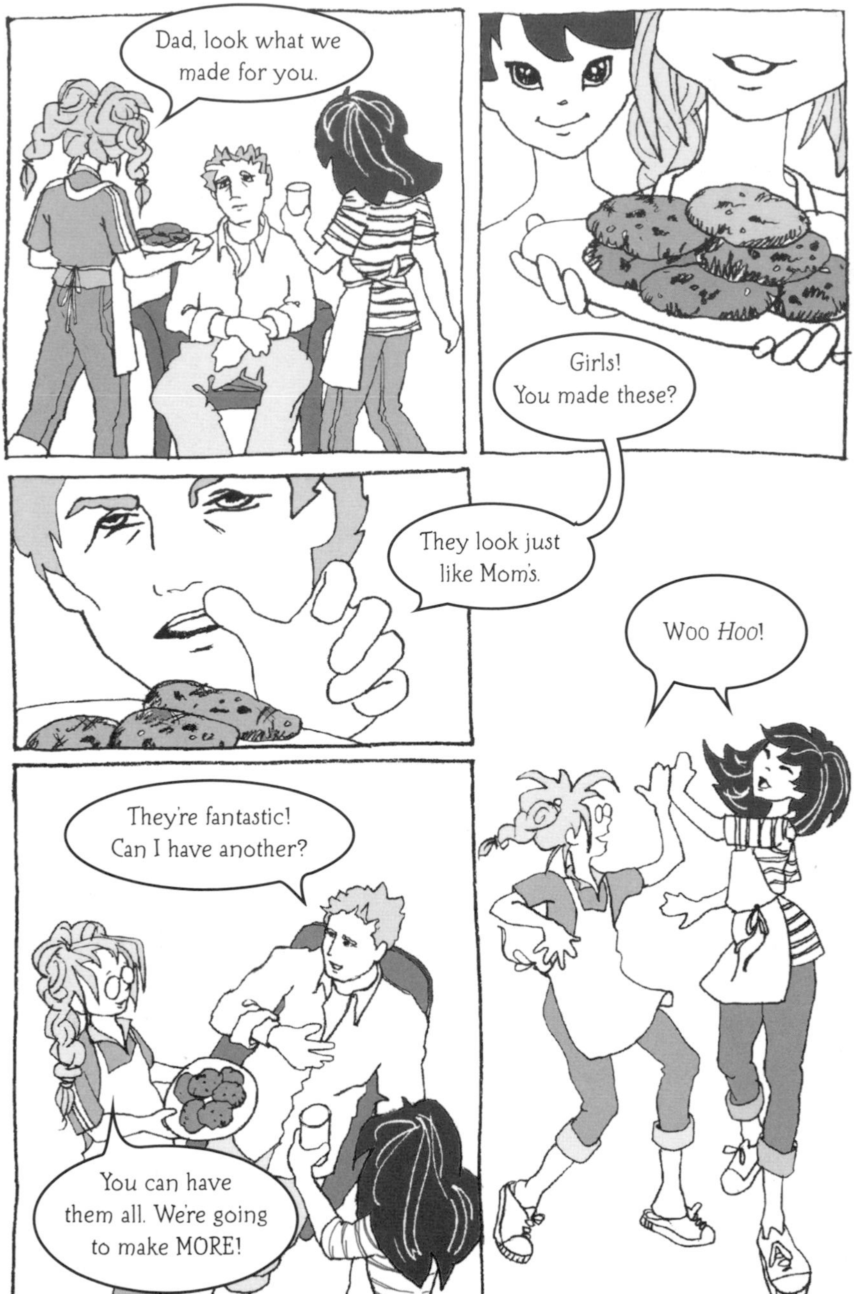
Dad, look what we made for you.
Girls! You made these?
They look just like Mom's.
They're fantastic! Can I have another?
You can have them all. We're going to make MORE!
Woo *Hoo*!

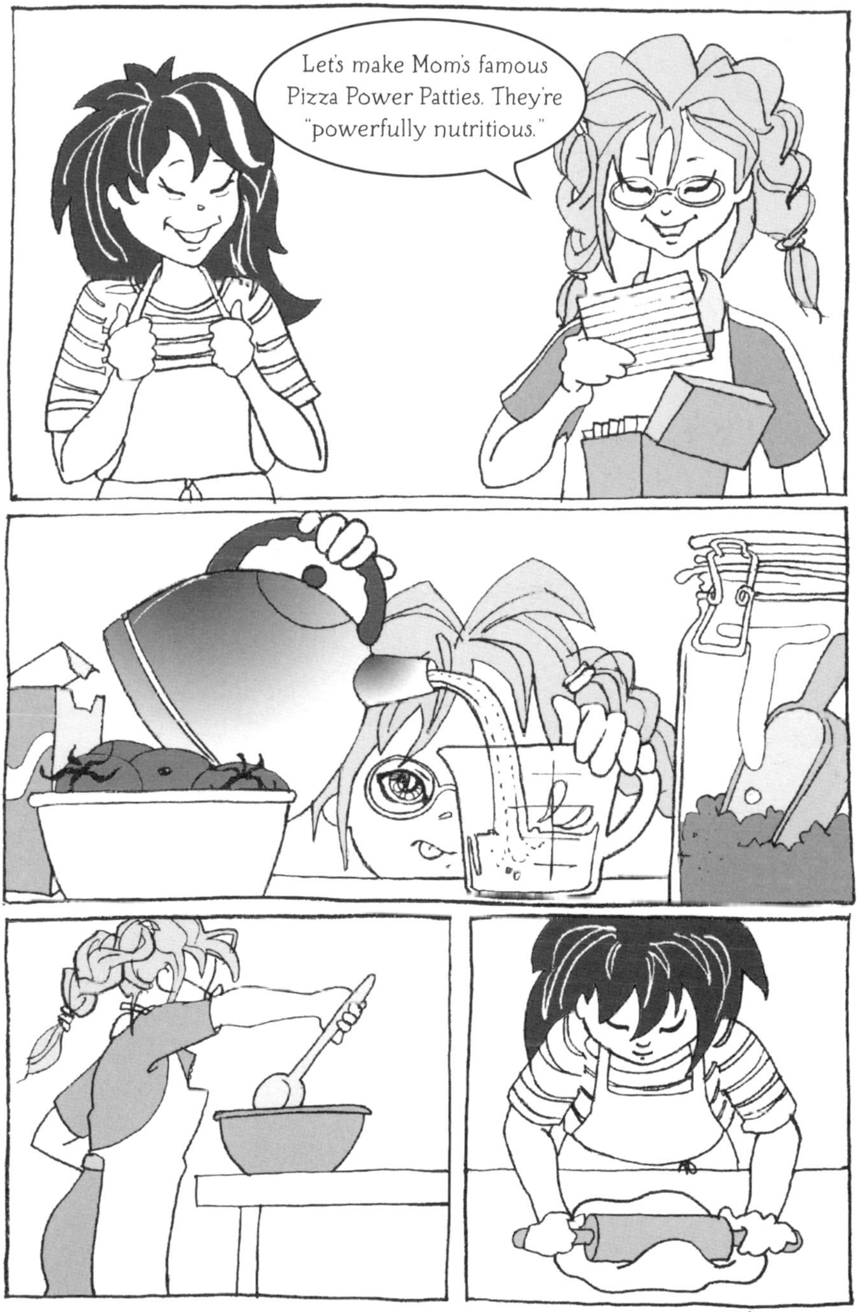
Let's make Mom's famous Pizza Power Patties. They're "powerfully nutritious."

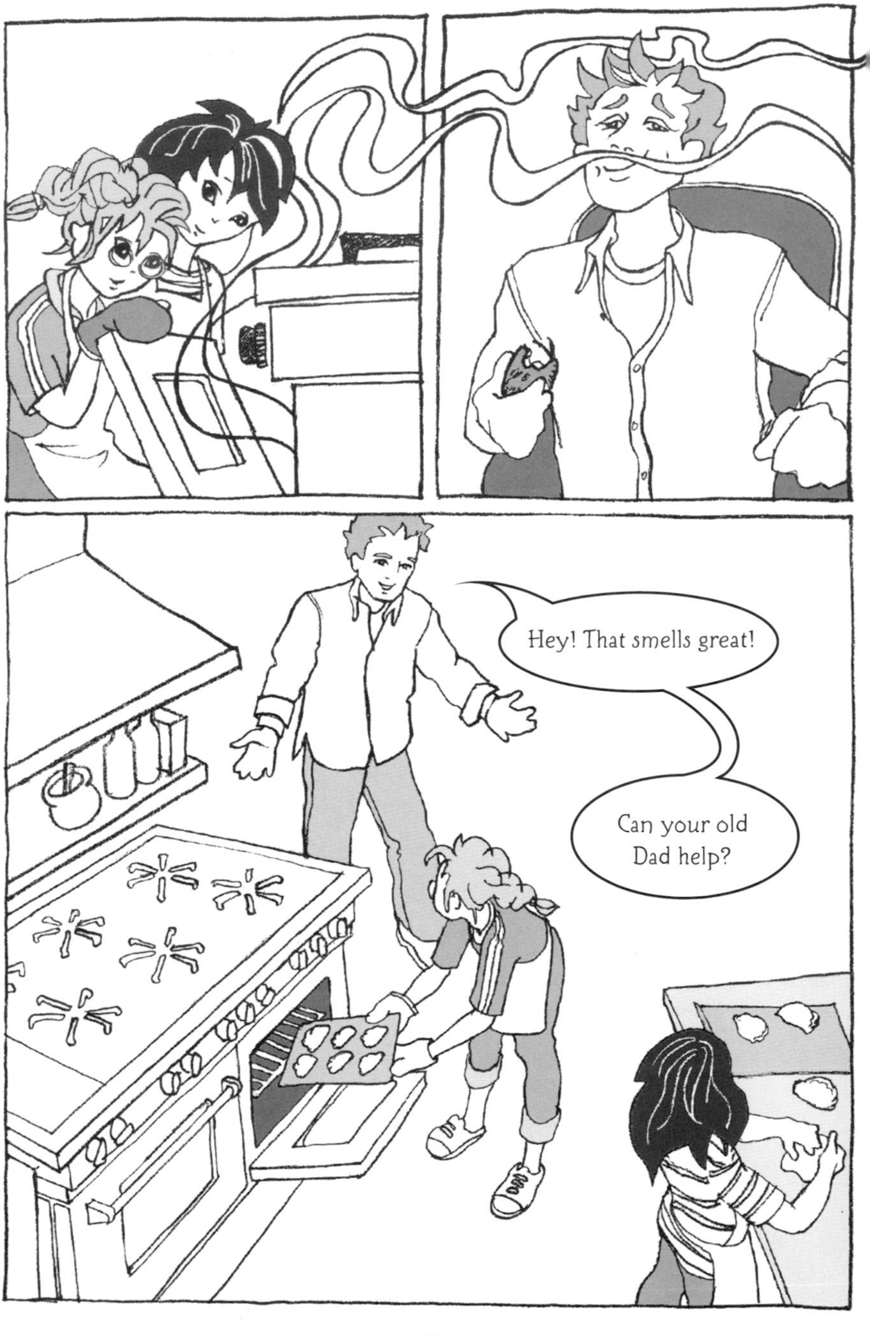
Hey! That smells great!
Can your old Dad help?

Dear Diary:

Dad is feeling better. The Pizza Power Patties were exactly what he needed. He's got the bakery open again. I thought I would feel better once Dad was happy, but it's weird. Everyone is kind of acting like nothing's wrong. Even Jet. Is she crazy? I feel like shouting.

Mom is gone. Nothing's right.

Claire

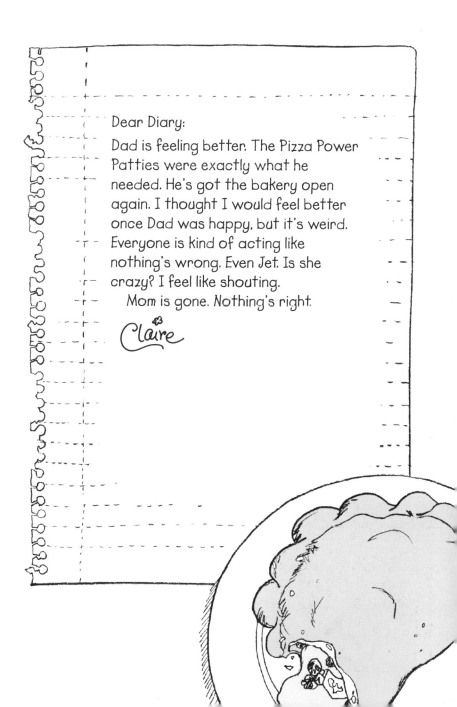

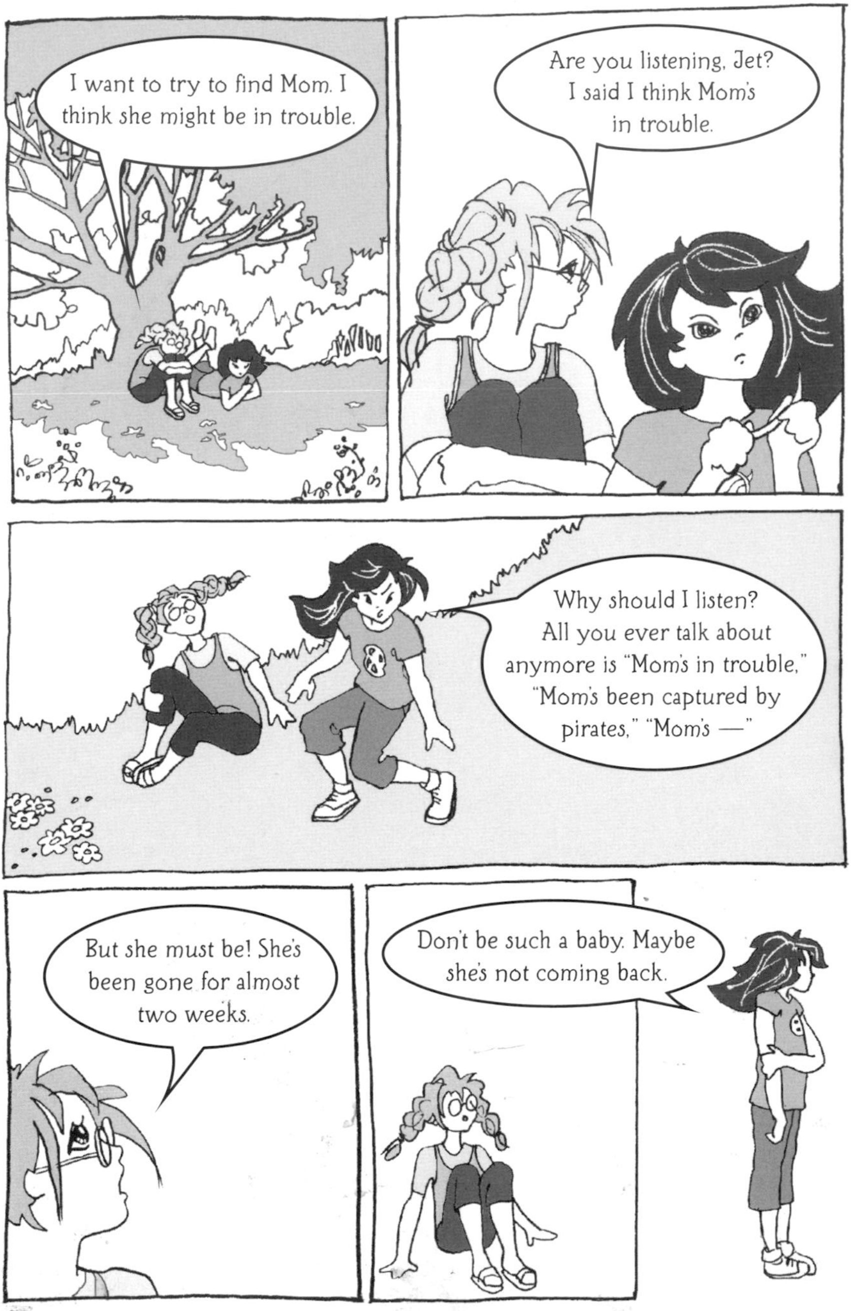
I want to try to find Mom. I think she might be in trouble.
Are you listening, Jet? I said I think Mom's in trouble.
Why should I listen? All you ever talk about anymore is "Mom's in trouble," "Mom's been captured by pirates," "Mom's —"
But she must be! She's been gone for almost two weeks.
Don't be such a baby. Maybe she's not coming back.

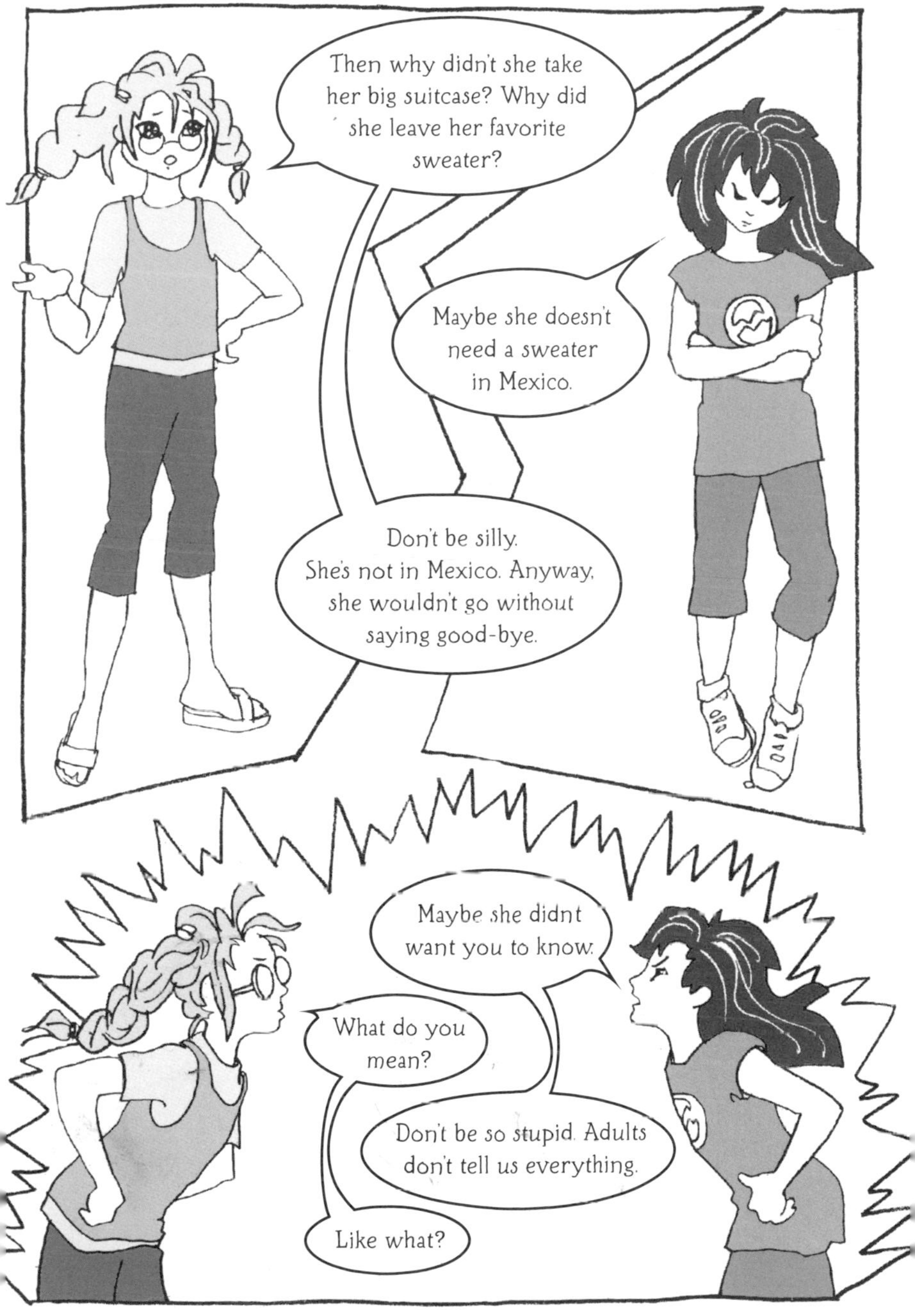
Then why didn't she take her big suitcase? Why did she leave her favorite sweater?
Maybe she doesn't need a sweater in Mexico.
Don't be silly. She's not in Mexico. Anyway, she wouldn't go without saying good-bye.
Maybe she didnt want you to know.
What do you mean?
Don't be so stupid. Adults don't tell us everything.
Like what?

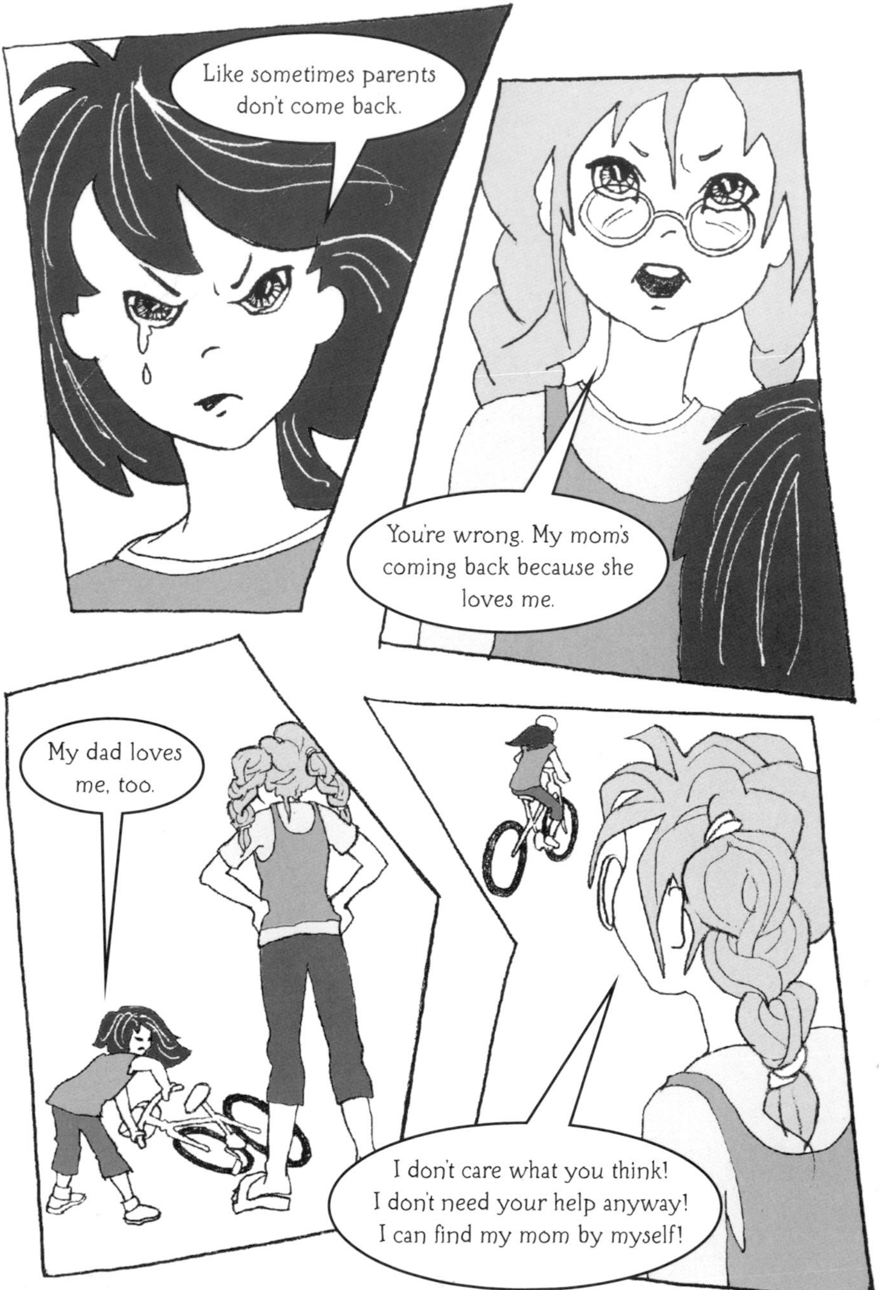
Like sometimes parents don't come back.
You're wrong. My mom's coming back because she loves me.
My dad loves me, too.
I don't care what you think! I don't need your help anyway! I can find my mom by myself!

Dear Diary:

I asked Bongo to help me be brave. He's my only friend. Dad never mentions Mom anymore. And Jet is mad at me. I saw her when I was in Watson's buying the map and compass, but she didn't even look at me. She's the baby, not me.

So, guess what, dear Diary ... I'm going to find Mom myself. I have a plan with maps and everything hidden at the Lookout. (If Dad found out I was going to the city alone, he'd freak out.)

I'll have to sneak away before Bongo wakes up. He'll want to come, but Dad needs him here.

Nervous, but excited,

Claire

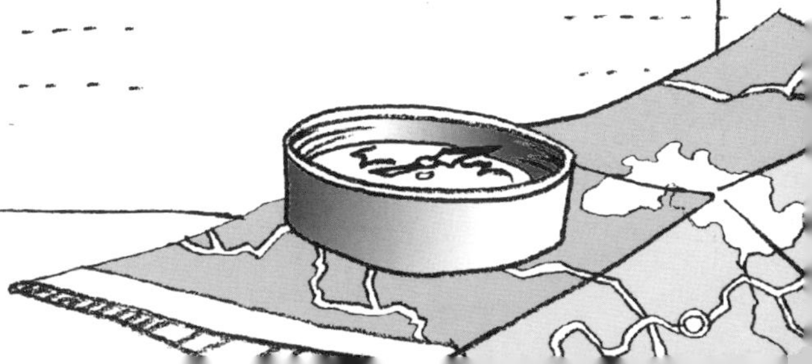

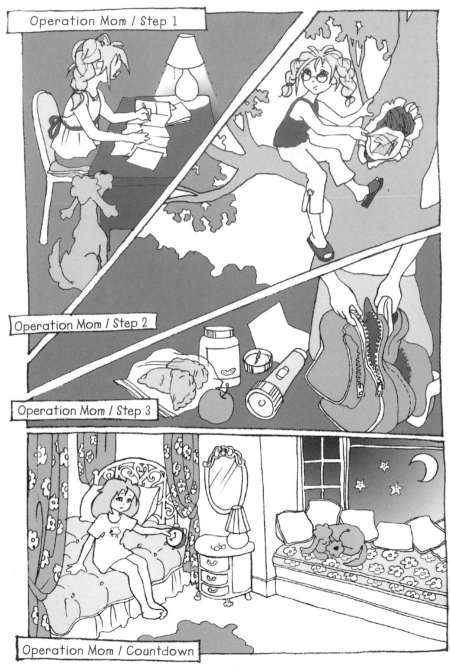

Operation Mom / Step 1

Operation Mom / Step 2

Operation Mom / Step 3

Operation Mom / Countdown

58

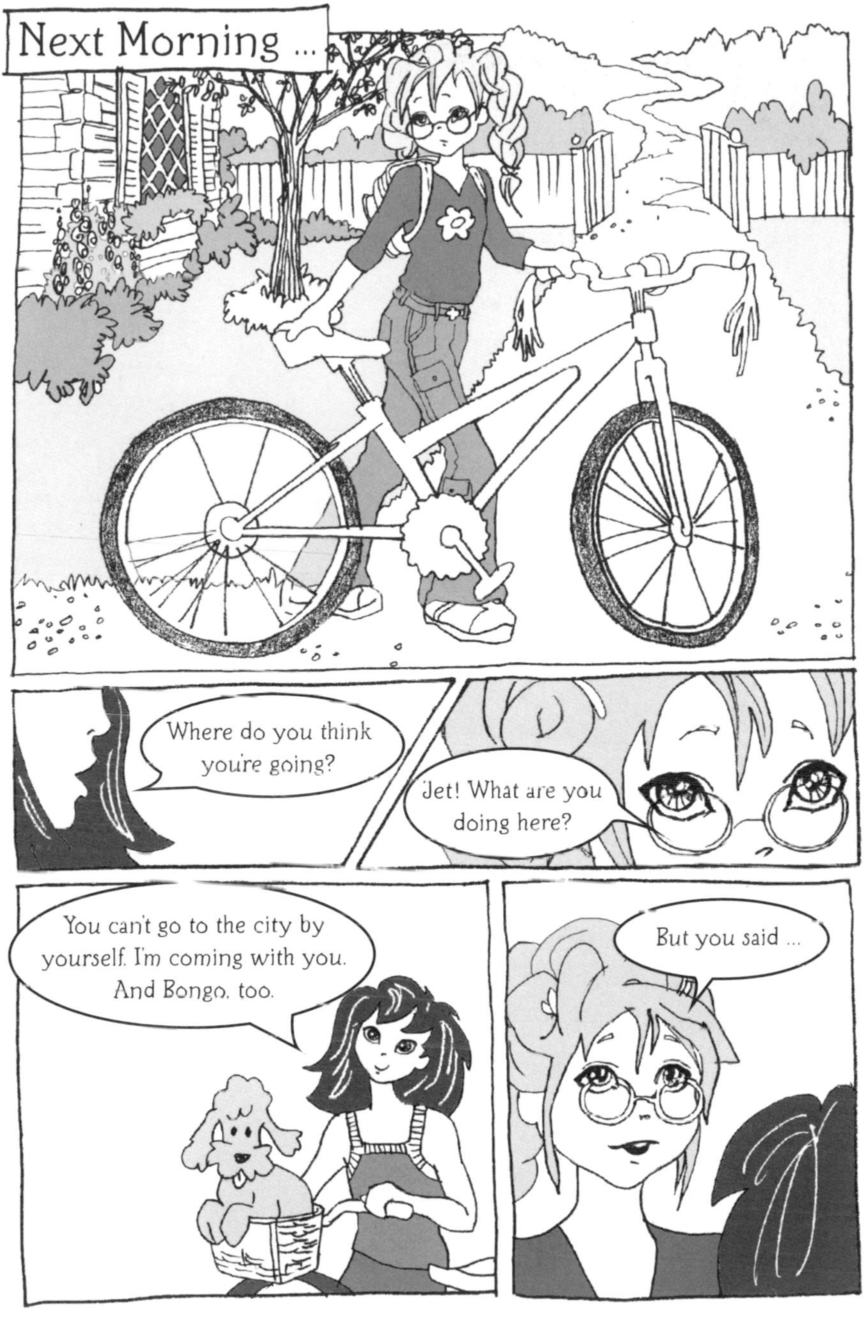
Next Morning ...
Where do you think you're going?
Jet! What are you doing here?
You can't go to the city by yourself. I'm coming with you. And Bongo, too.
But you said ...

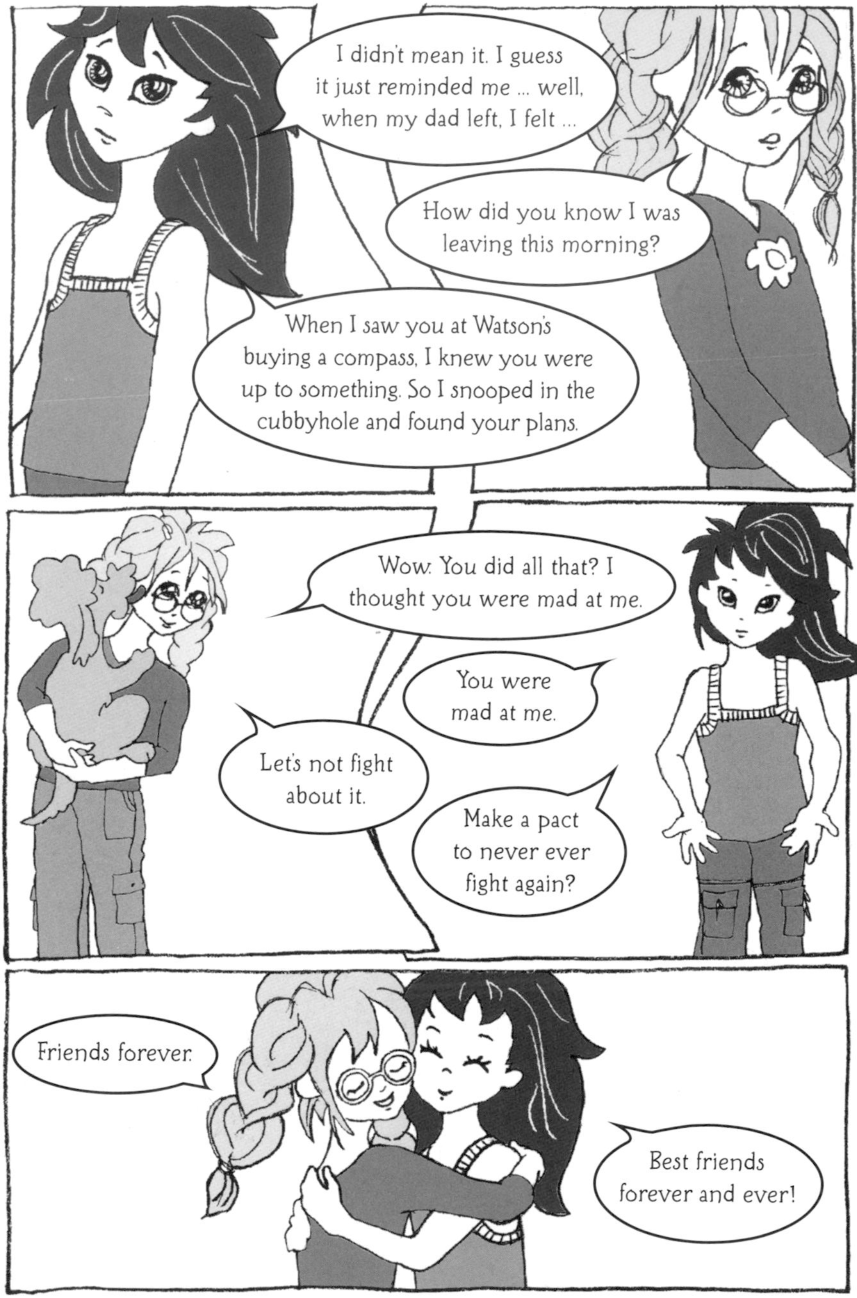
I didn't mean it. I guess it just reminded me ... well, when my dad left, I felt ...
How did you know I was leaving this morning?
When I saw you at Watson's buying a compass, I knew you were up to something. So I snooped in the cubbyhole and found your plans.
Wow. You did all that? I thought you were mad at me.
You were mad at me.
Let's not fight about it.
Make a pact to never ever fight again?
Friends forever.
Best friends forever and ever!

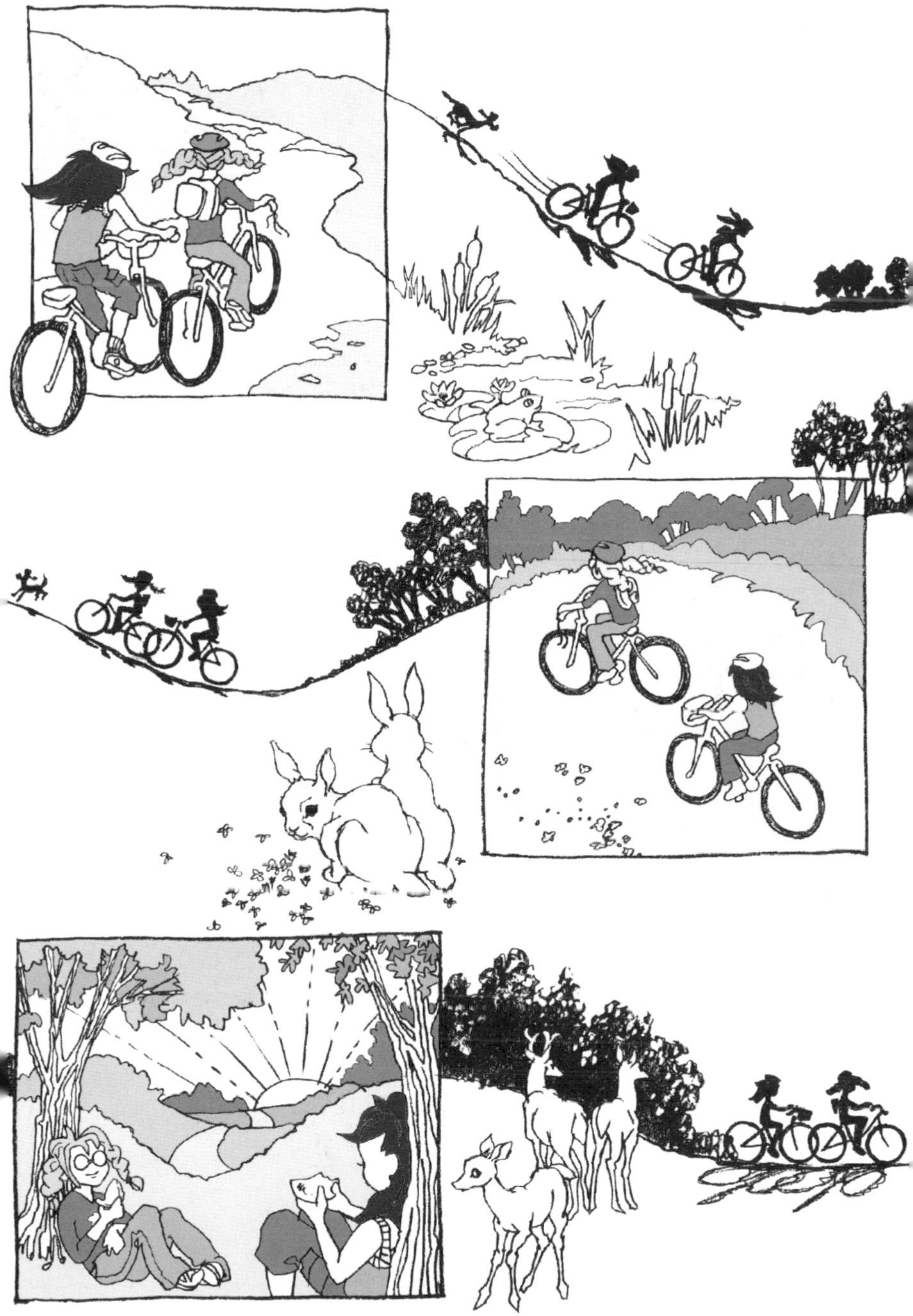

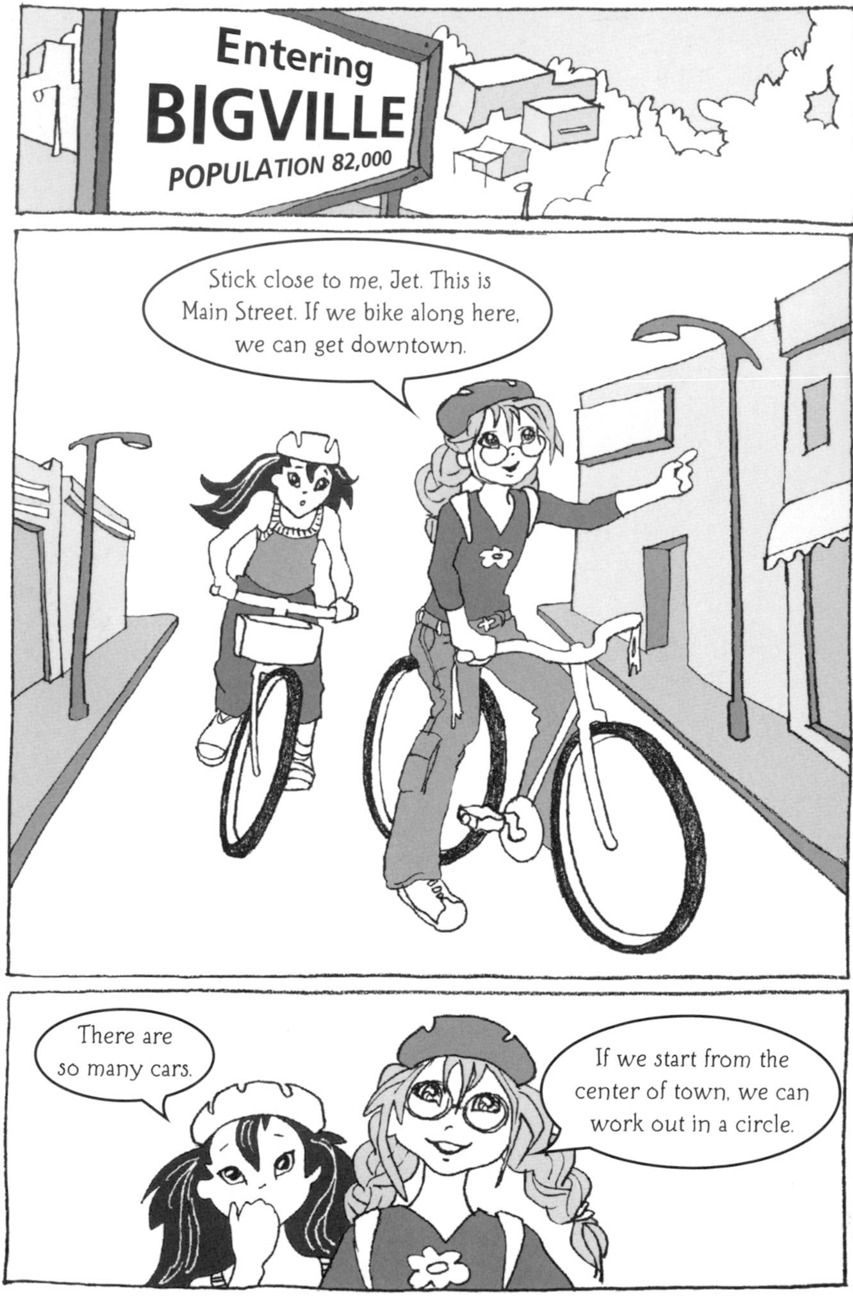
Entering
BIGVILLE
POPULATION 82,000
Stick close to me, Jet. This is Main Street. If we bike along here, we can get downtown.
There are so many cars.
If we start from the center of town, we can work out in a circle.

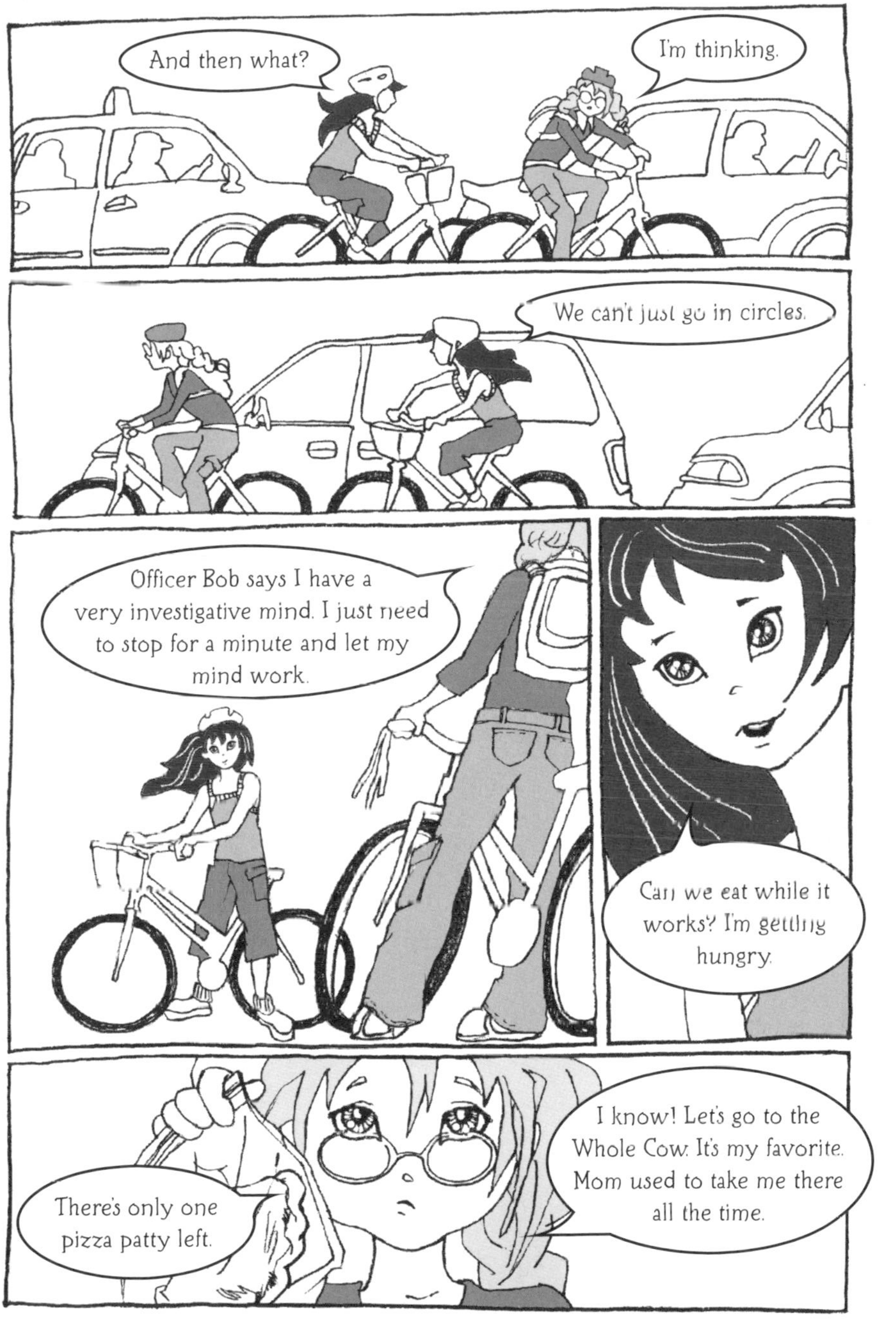
And then what?
I'm thinking.
We can't just go in circles.
Officer Bob says I have a very investigative mind. I just need to stop for a minute and let my mind work.
Can we eat while it works? I'm getting hungry.
There's only one pizza patty left.
I know! Let's go to the Whole Cow. It's my favorite. Mom used to take me there all the time.

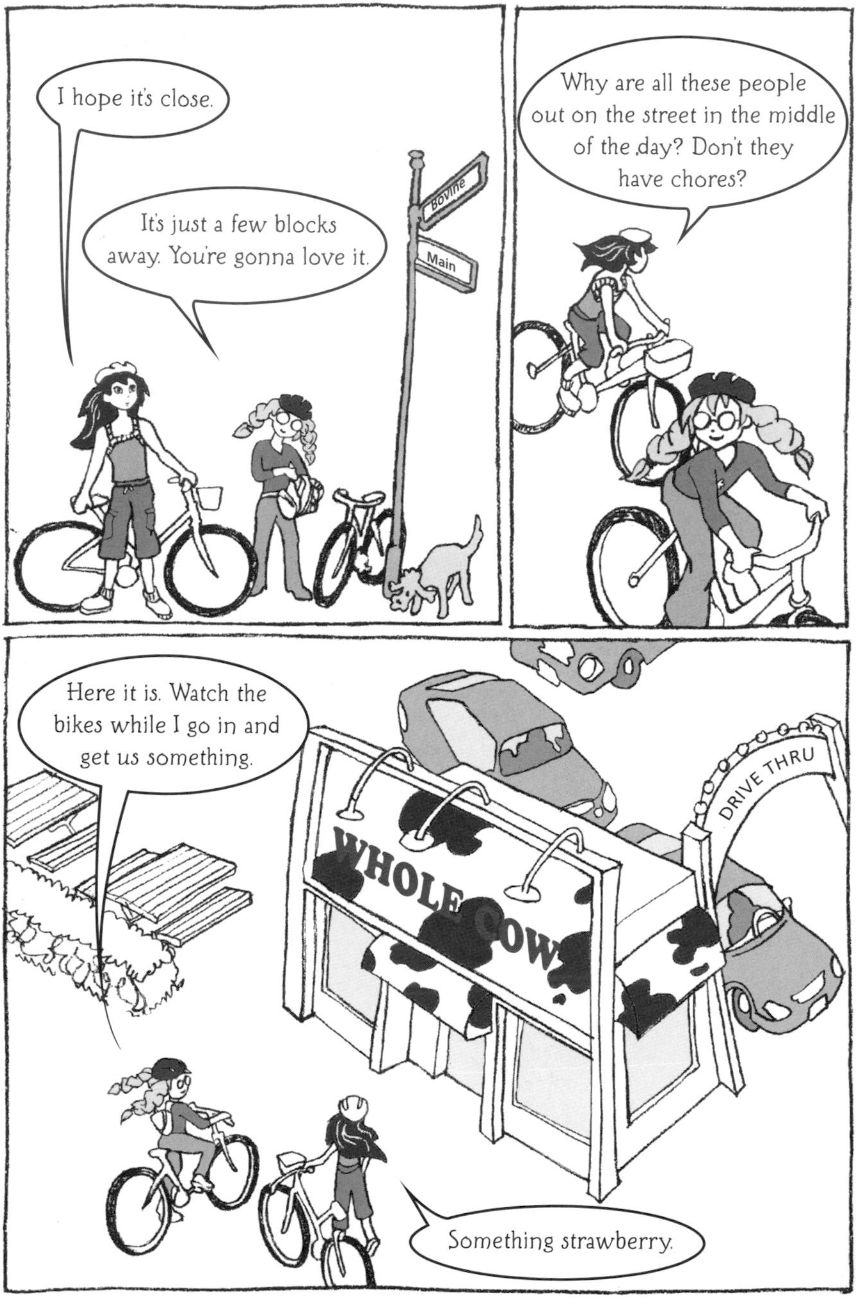
I hope it's close.
It's just a few blocks away. You're gonna love it.
Bovine
Main
Why are all these people out on the street in the middle of the day? Don't they have chores?
Here it is. Watch the bikes while I go in and get us something.
DRIVE THRU
WHOLE COW
Something strawberry.

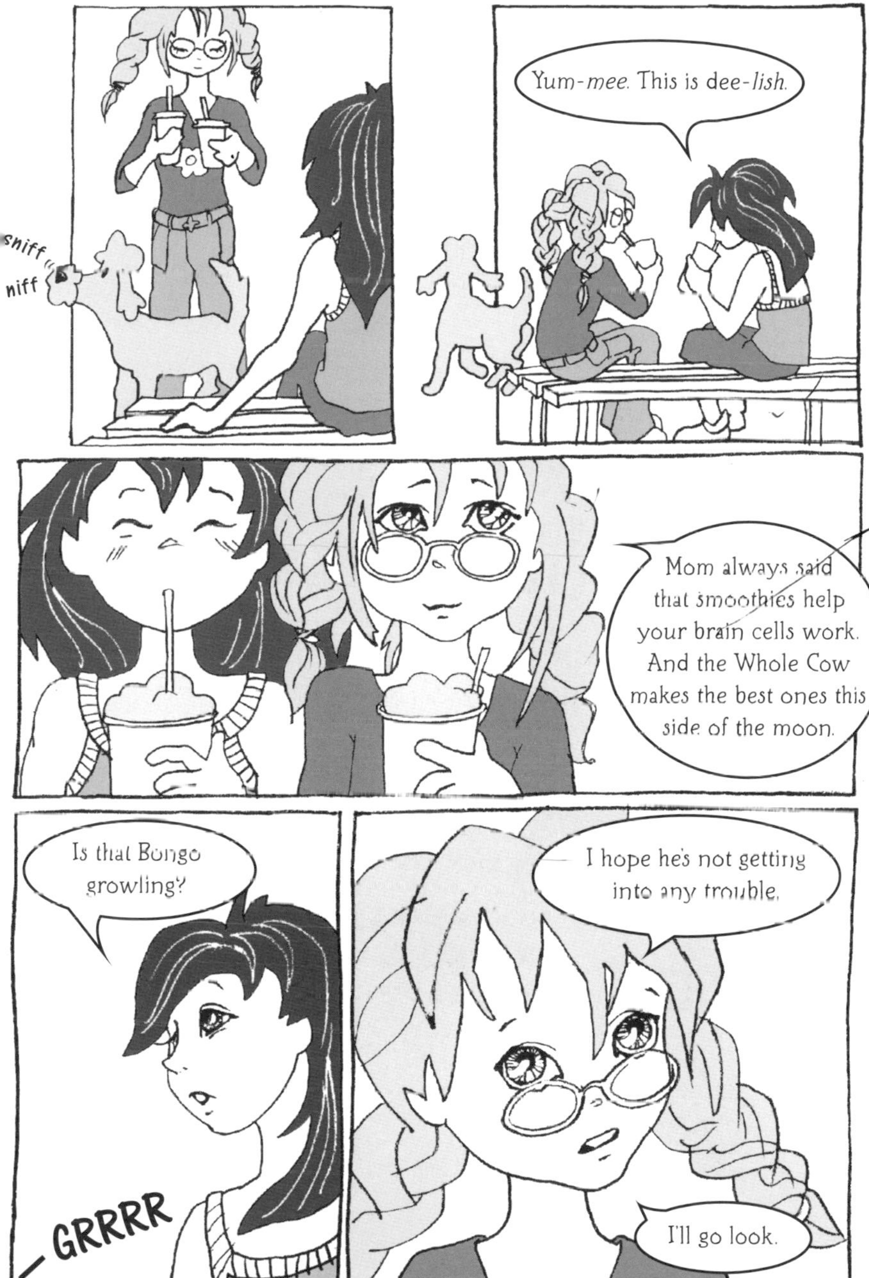
sniff
niff
Yum-*mee*. This is dee-*lish*.
Mom always said that smoothies help your brain cells work. And the Whole Cow makes the best ones this side of the moon.
Is that Bongo growling?
GRRRR
I hope he's not getting into any trouble.
I'll go look.

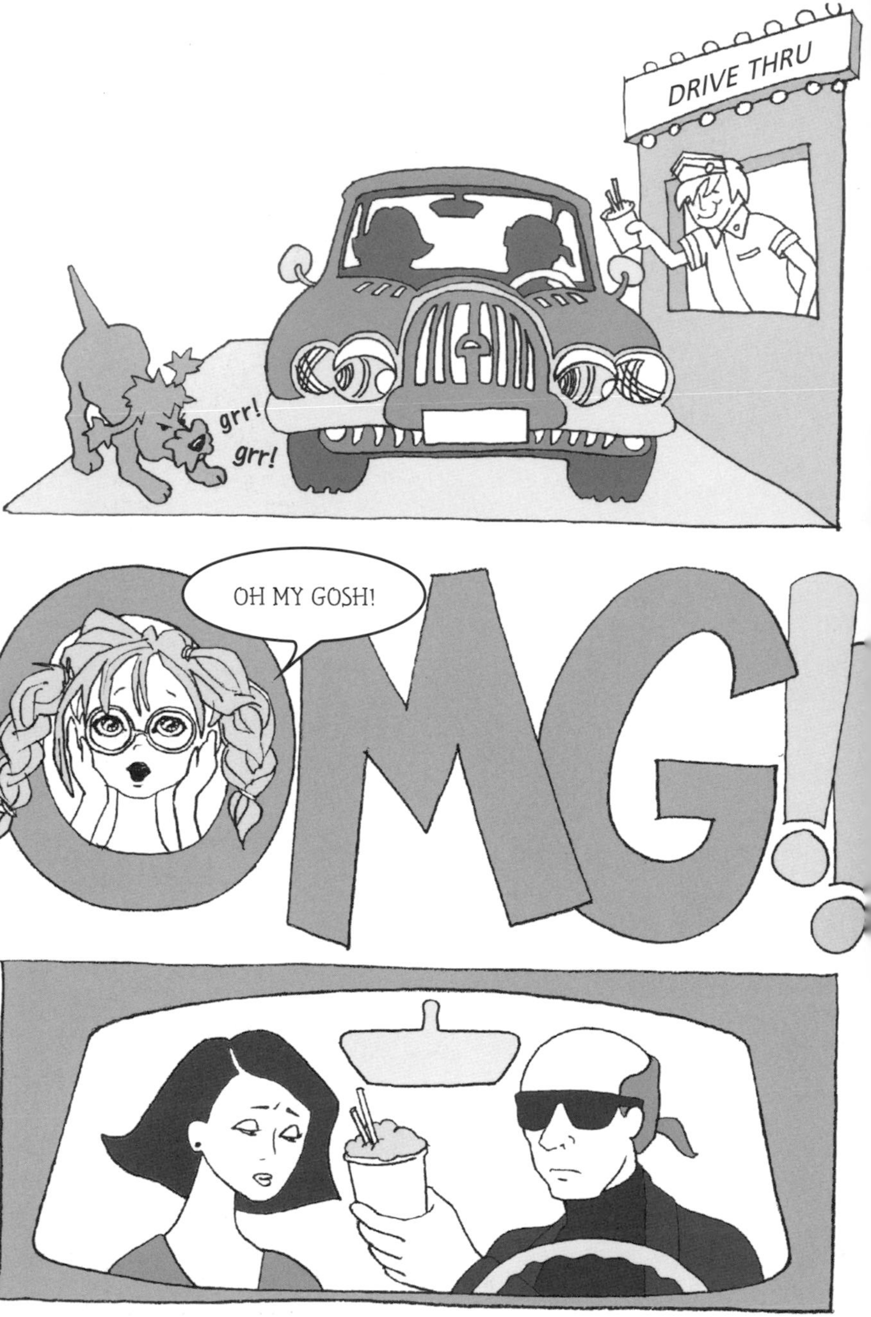
DRIVE THRU
grr!
grr!
OH MY GOSH!
OMG!

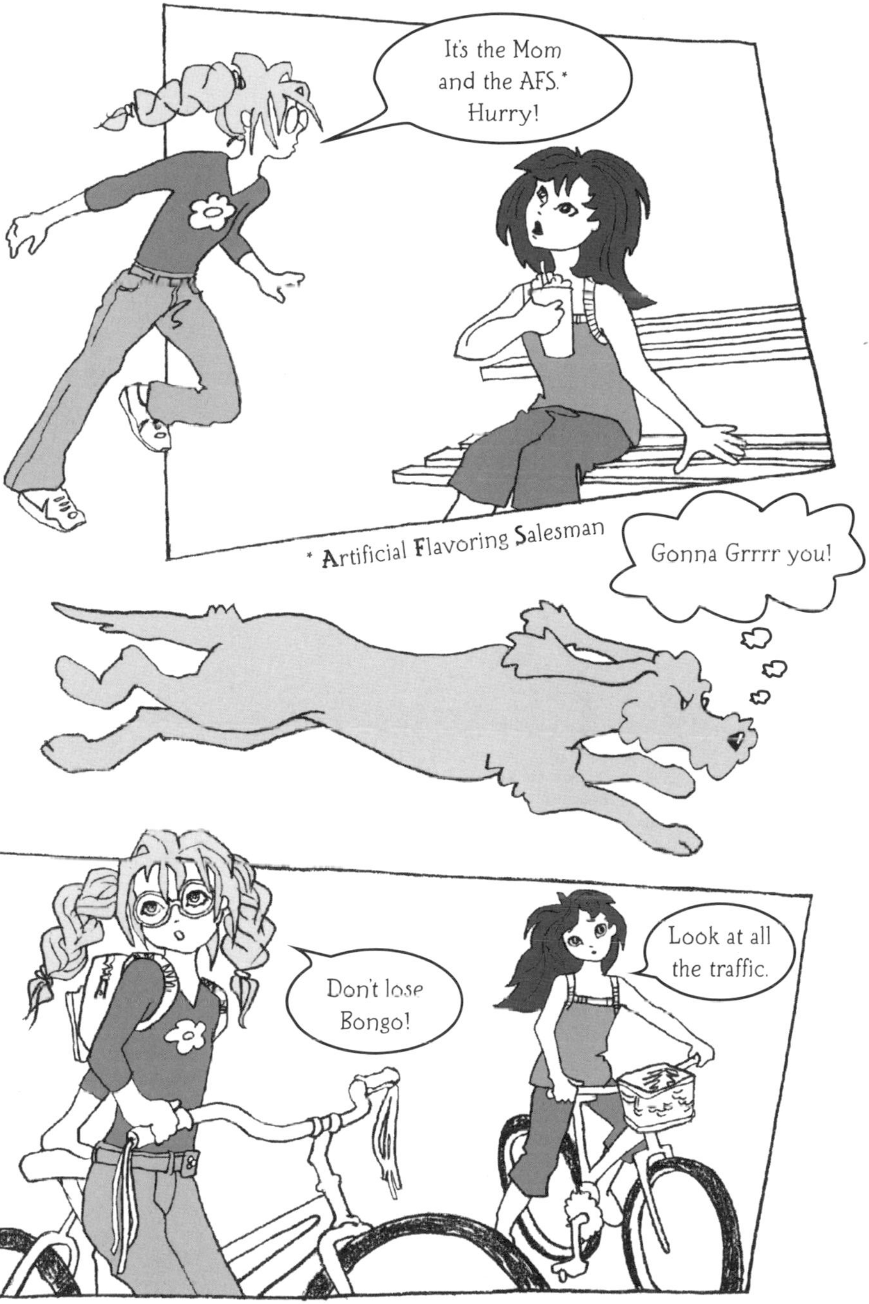
It's the Mom and the AFS.* Hurry!
* Artificial Flavoring Salesman
Gonna Grrrr you!
Don't lose Bongo!
Look at all the traffic.

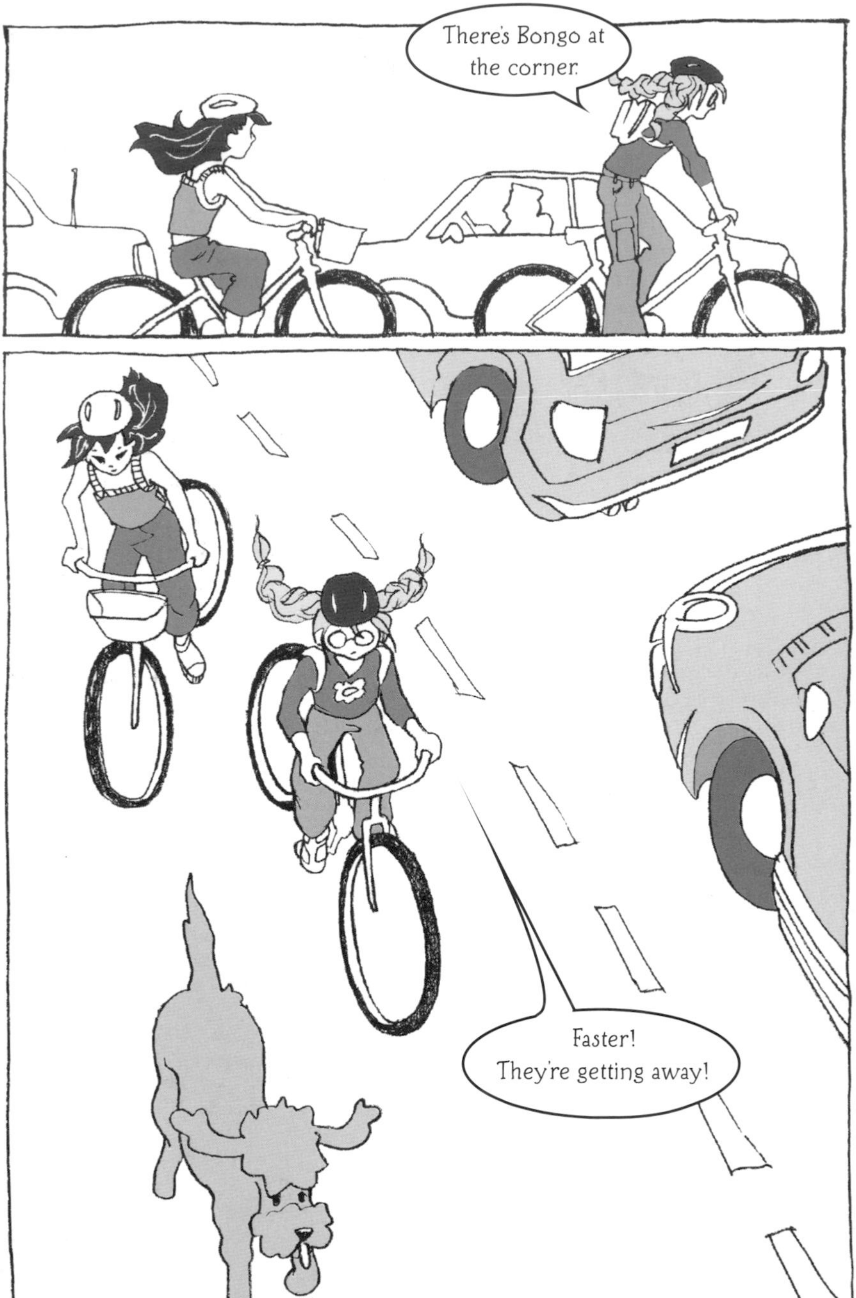
There's Bongo at the corner.
Faster! They're getting away!

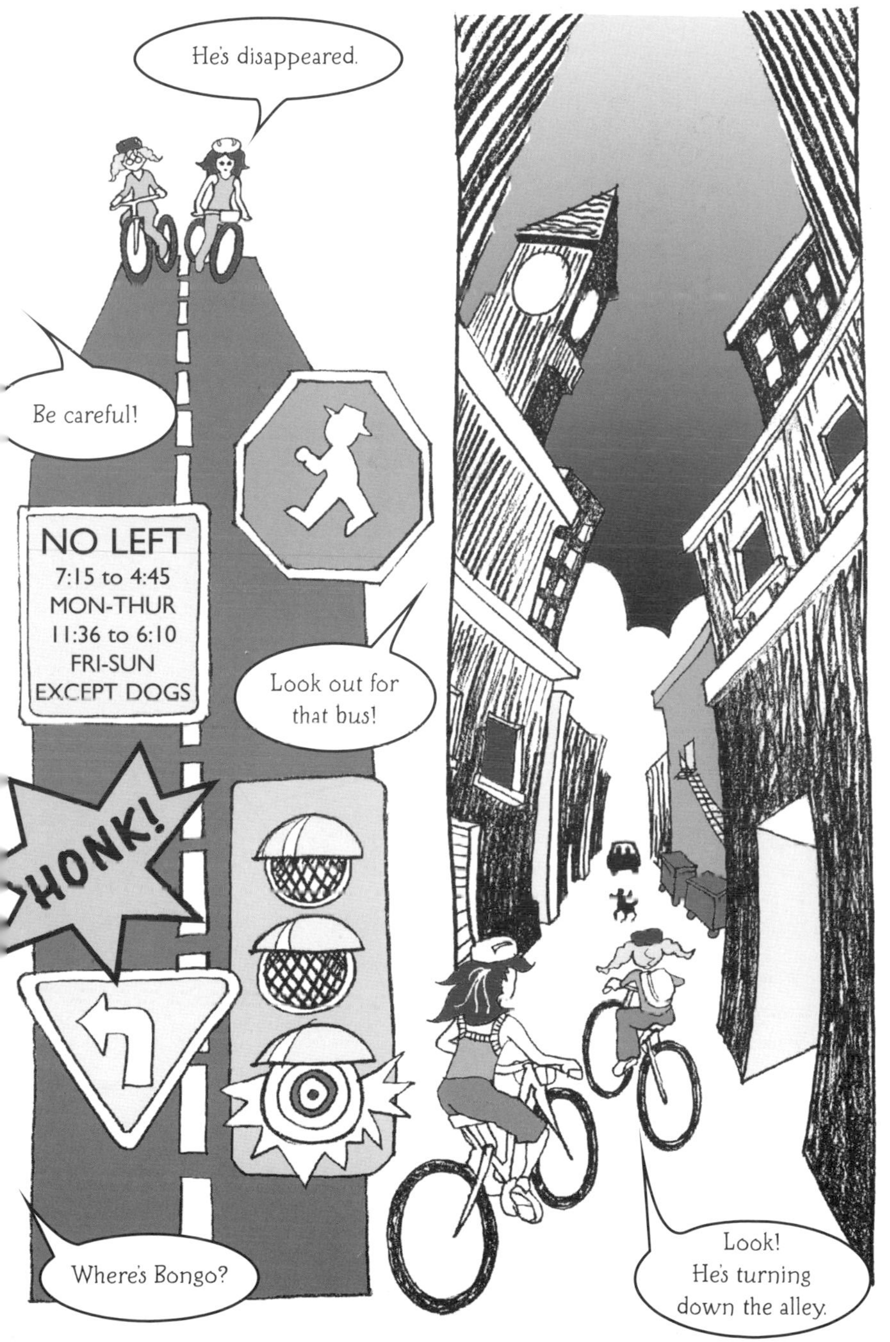
He's disappeared.
Be careful!
NO LEFT
7:15 to 4:45
MON-THUR
11:36 to 6:10
FRI-SUN
EXCEPT DOGS
Look out for that bus!
HONK!
Where's Bongo?
Look! He's turning down the alley.

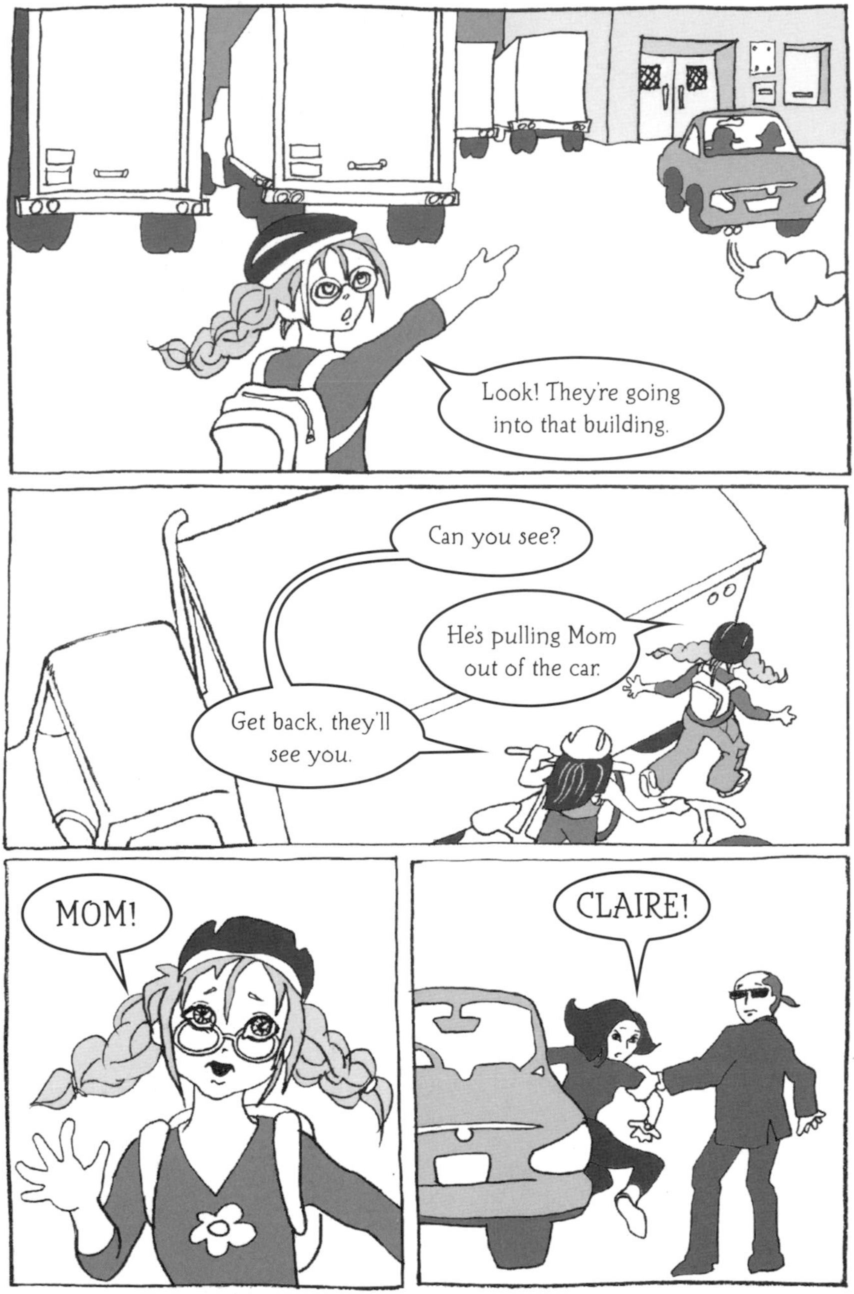

Look! They're going into that building.
Can you see?
He's pulling Mom out of the car.
Get back, they'll see you.
MOM!
CLAIRE!

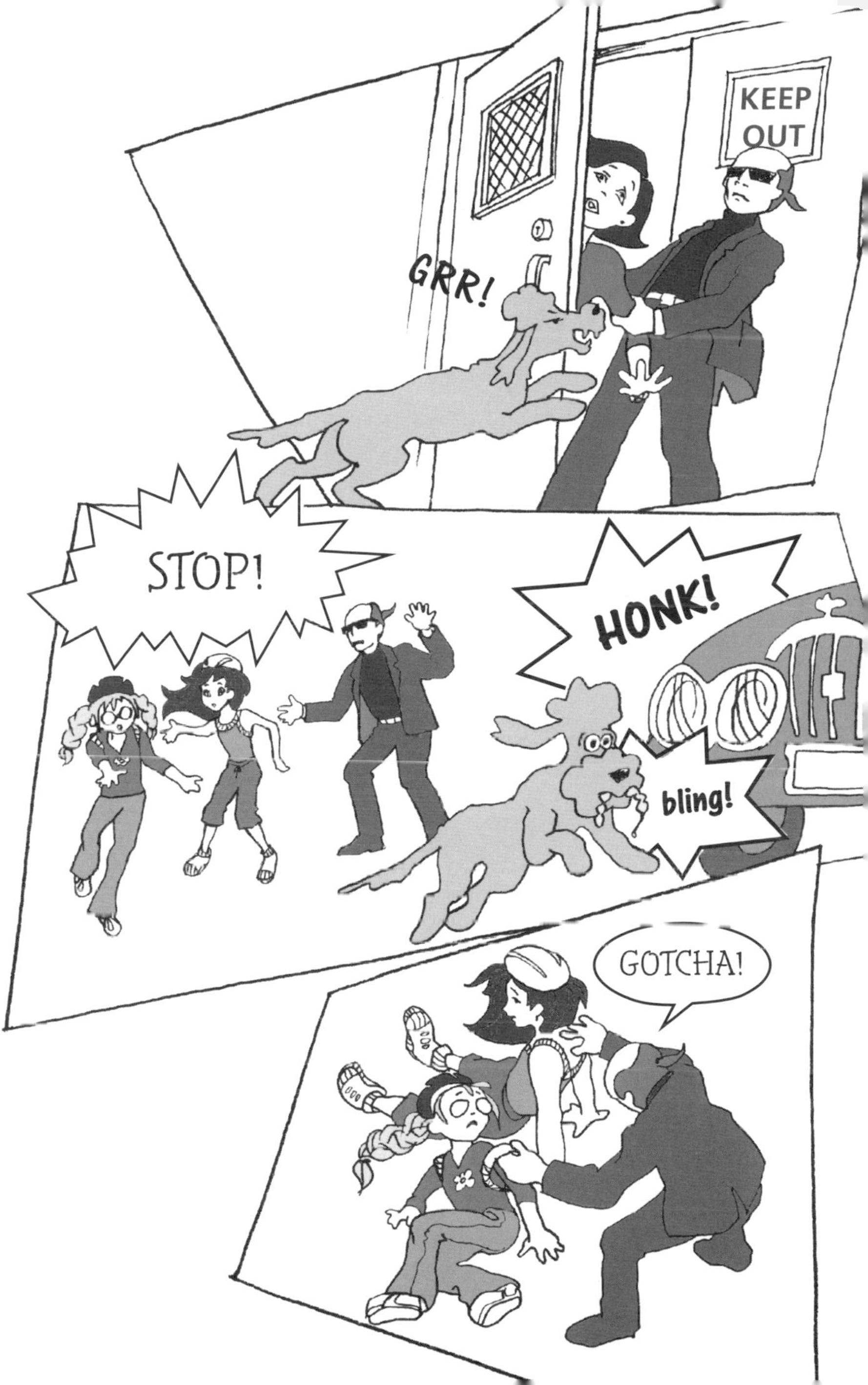

KEEP OUT
GRR!
STOP!
HONK!
bling!
GOTCHA!

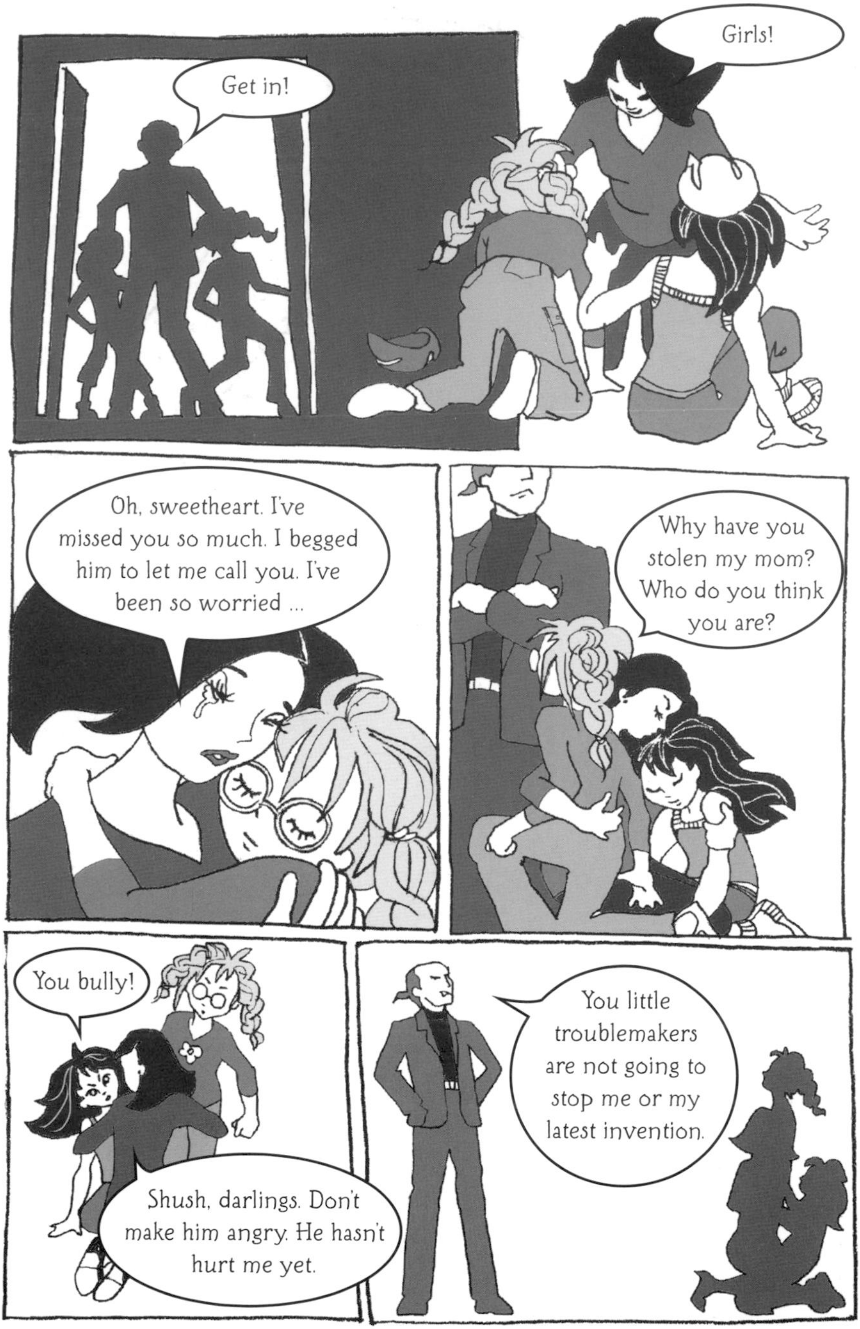
Get in!
Girls!
Oh, sweetheart. I've missed you so much. I begged him to let me call you. I've been so worried ...
Why have you stolen my mom? Who do you think you are?
You bully!
Shush, darlings. Don't make him angry. He hasn't hurt me yet.
You little troublemakers are not going to stop me or my latest invention.

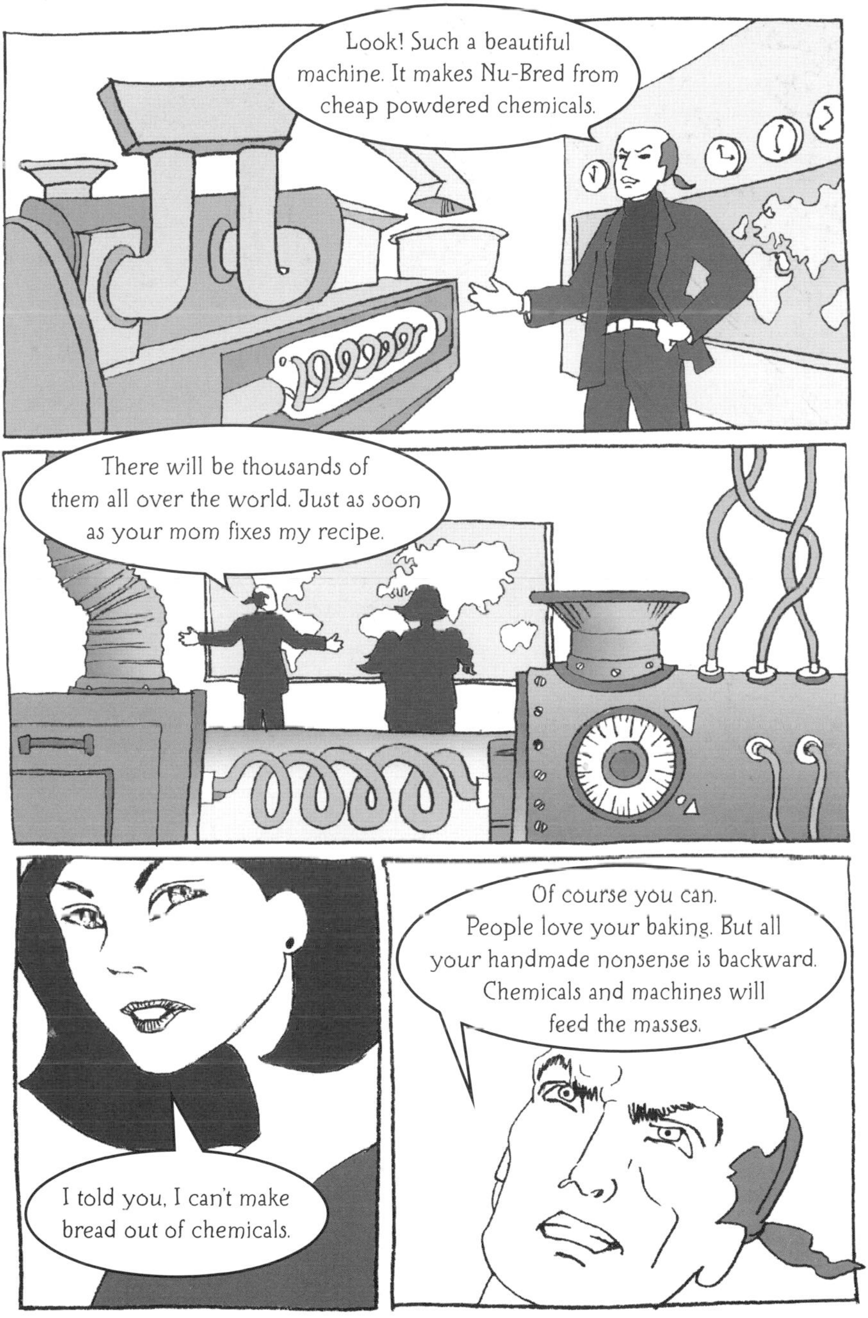

Look! Such a beautiful machine. It makes Nu-Bred from cheap powdered chemicals.
There will be thousands of them all over the world. Just as soon as your mom fixes my recipe.
I told you, I can't make bread out of chemicals.
Of course you can. People love your baking. But all your handmade nonsense is backward. Chemicals and machines will feed the masses.

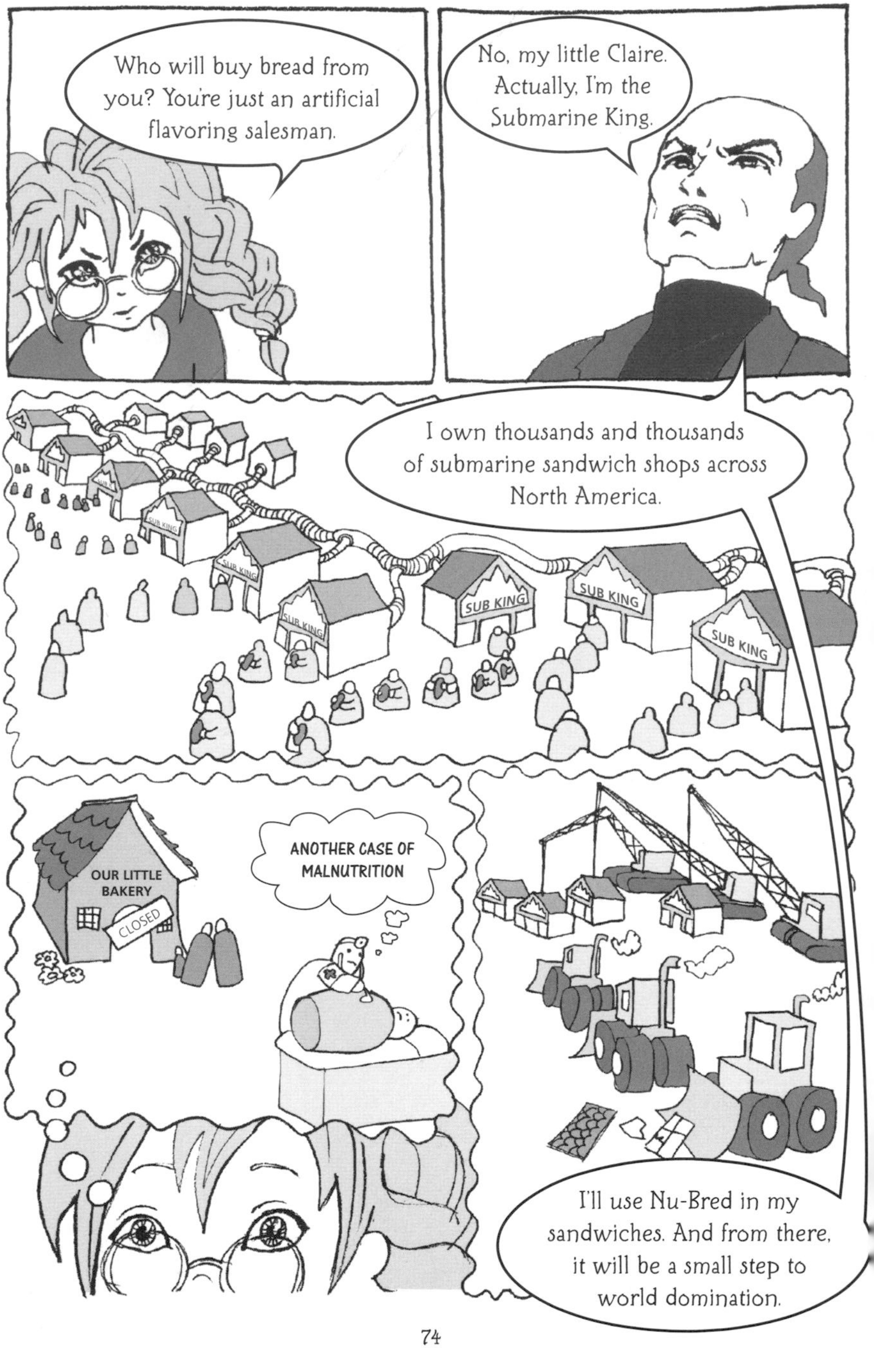
Who will buy bread from you? You're just an artificial flavoring salesman.
No, my little Claire. Actually, I'm the Submarine King.
I own thousands and thousands of submarine sandwich shops across North America.
SUB KING
SUB KING
SUB KING
SUB KING
SUB KING
SUB KING
OUR LITTLE BAKERY
CLOSED
ANOTHER CASE OF MALNUTRITION
I'll use Nu-Bred in my sandwiches. And from there, it will be a small step to world domination.

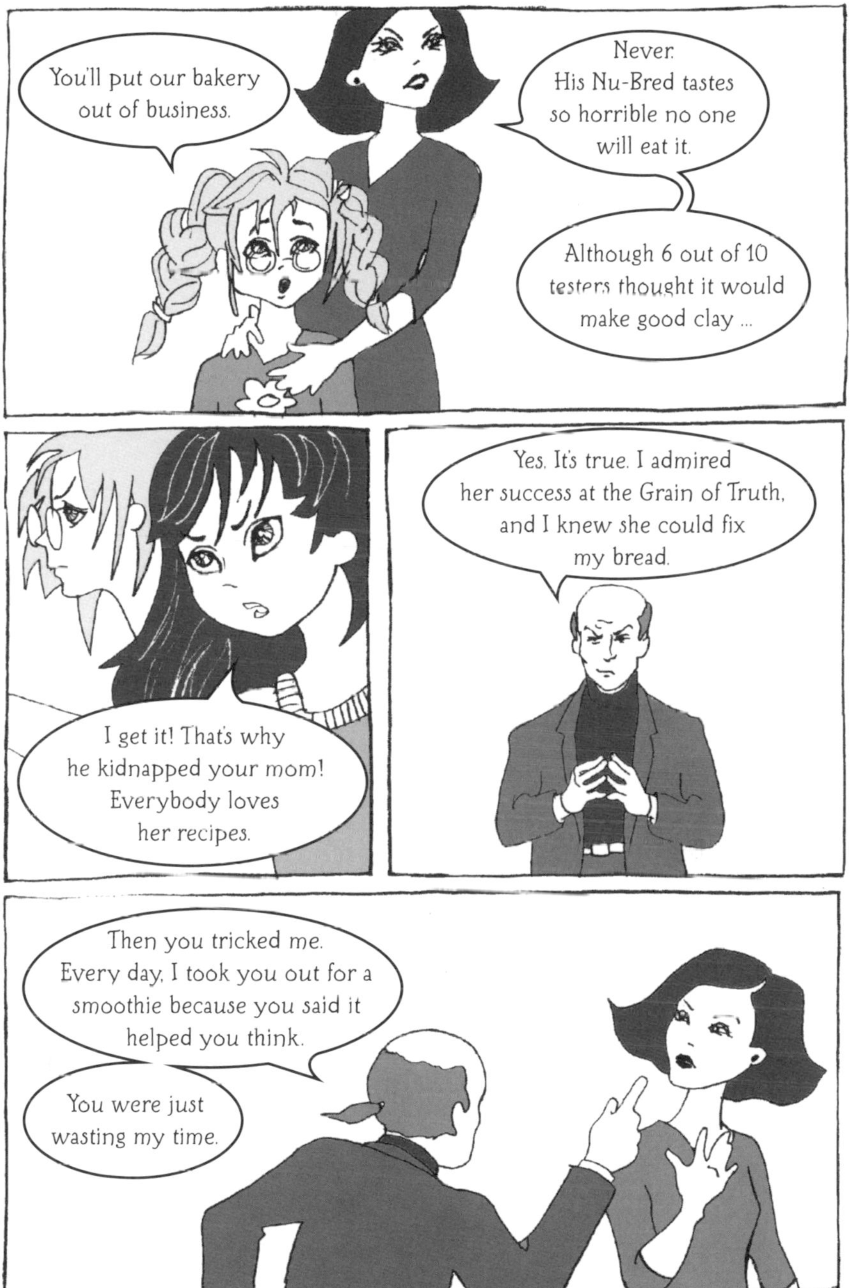
You'll put our bakery out of business.
Never. His Nu-Bred tastes so horrible no one will eat it.
Although 6 out of 10 testers thought it would make good clay ...
I get it! That's why he kidnapped your mom! Everybody loves her recipes.
Yes. It's true. I admired her success at the Grain of Truth, and I knew she could fix my bread.
Then you tricked me. Every day, I took you out for a smoothie because you said it helped you think.
You were just wasting my time.

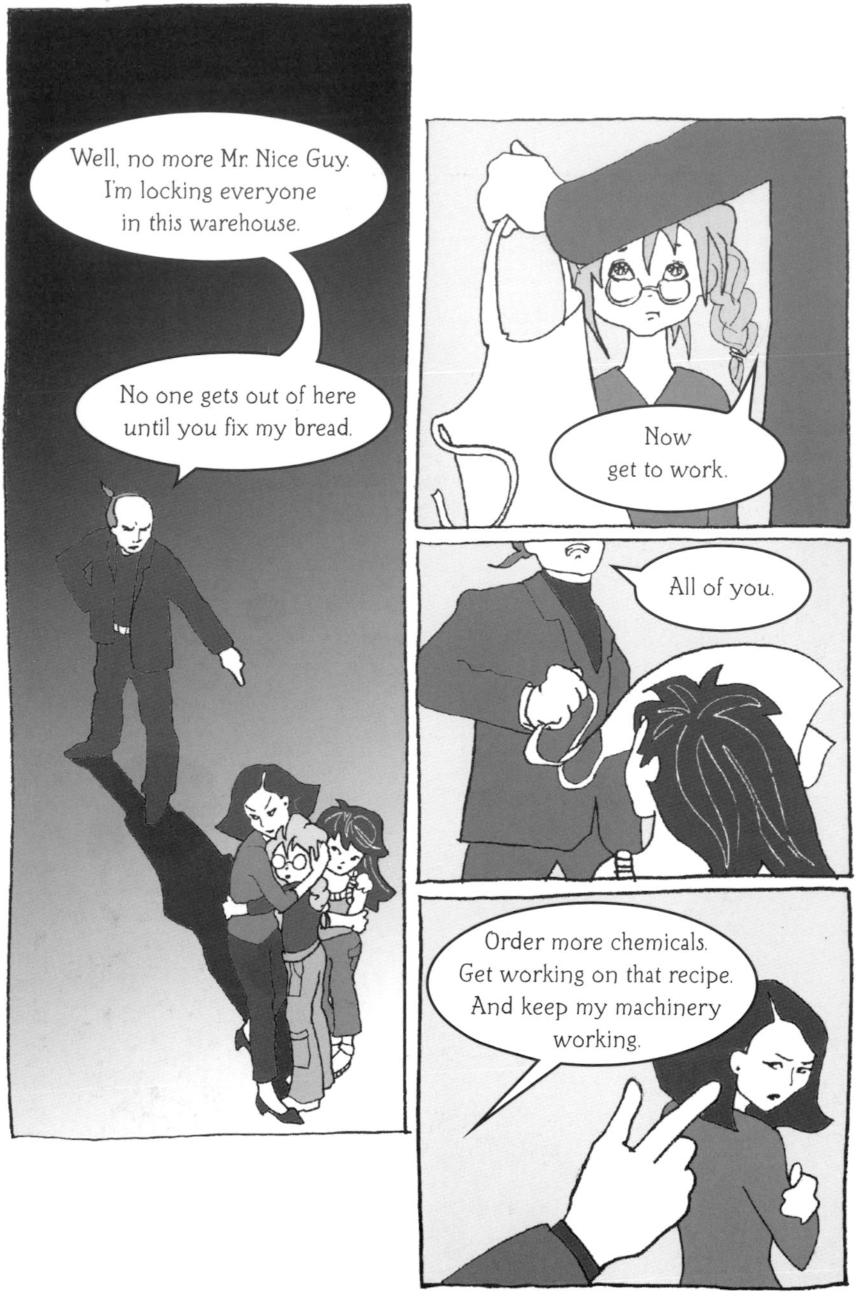
Well, no more Mr. Nice Guy. I'm locking everyone in this warehouse.
No one gets out of here until you fix my bread.
Now get to work.
All of you.
Order more chemicals. Get working on that recipe. And keep my machinery working.

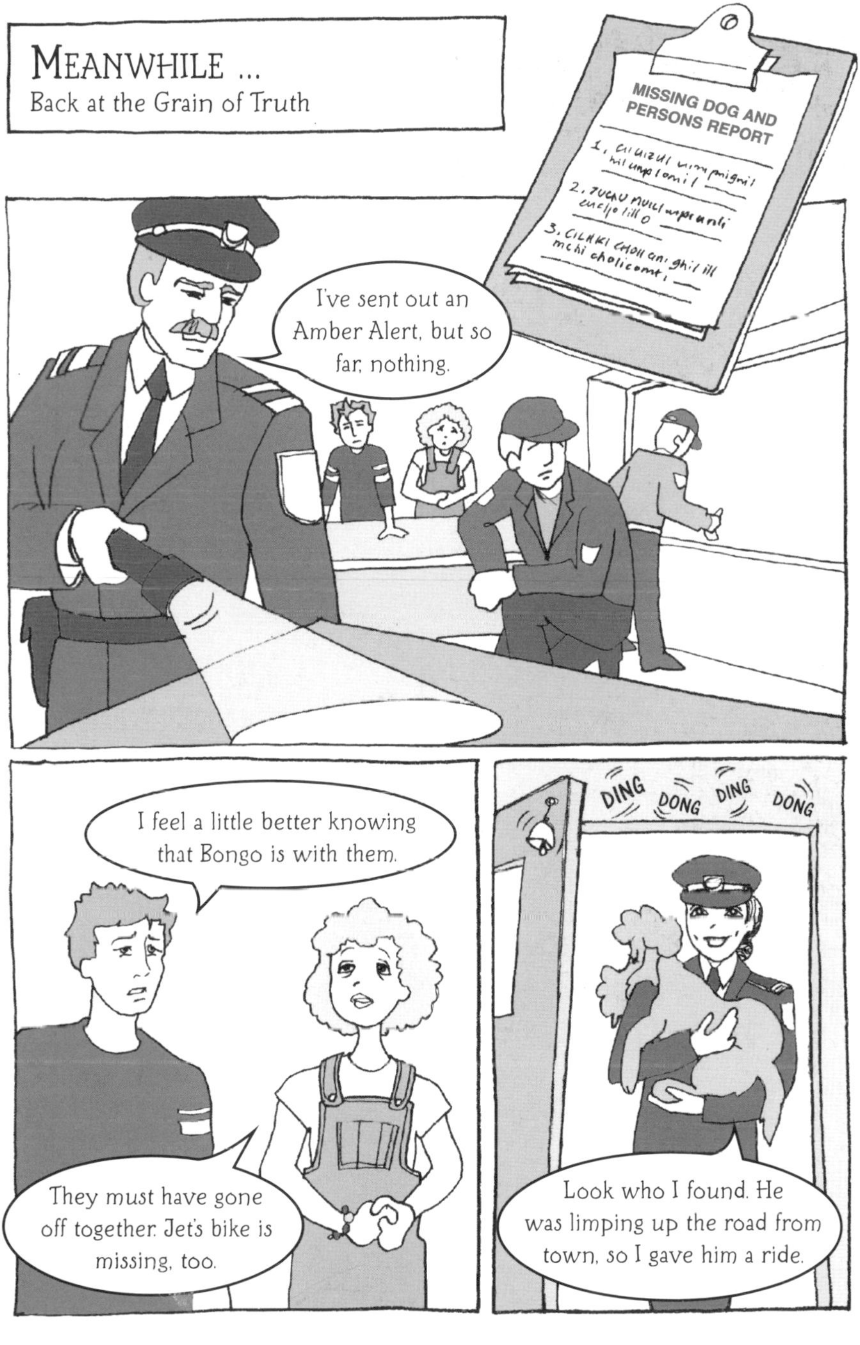
MEANWHILE ...
Back at the Grain of Truth
MISSING DOG AND PERSONS REPORT
I've sent out an Amber Alert, but so far, nothing.
I feel a little better knowing that Bongo is with them.
They must have gone off together. Jet's bike is missing, too.
DING DONG DING DONG
Look who I found. He was limping up the road from town, so I gave him a ride.

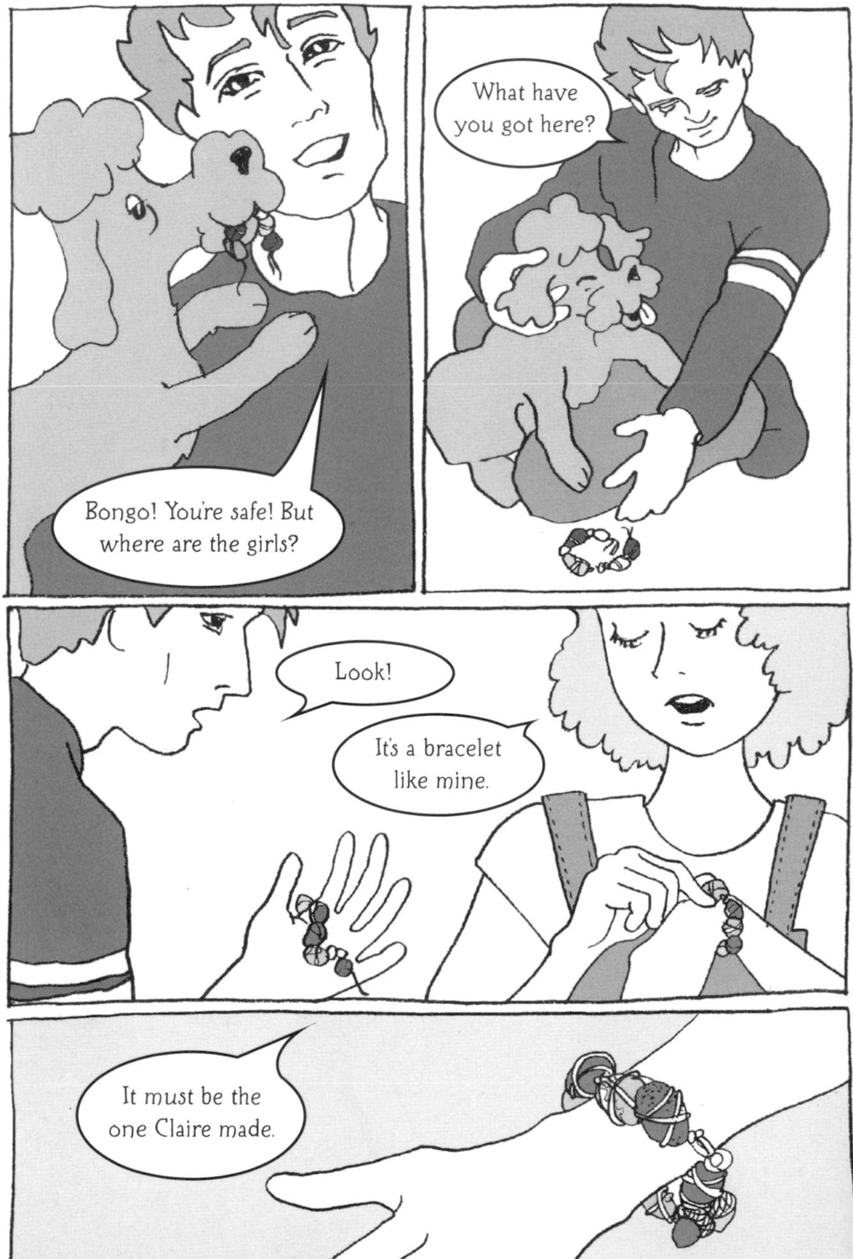
Bongo! You're safe! But where are the girls?
What have you got here?
Look!
It's a bracelet like mine.
It must be the one Claire made.

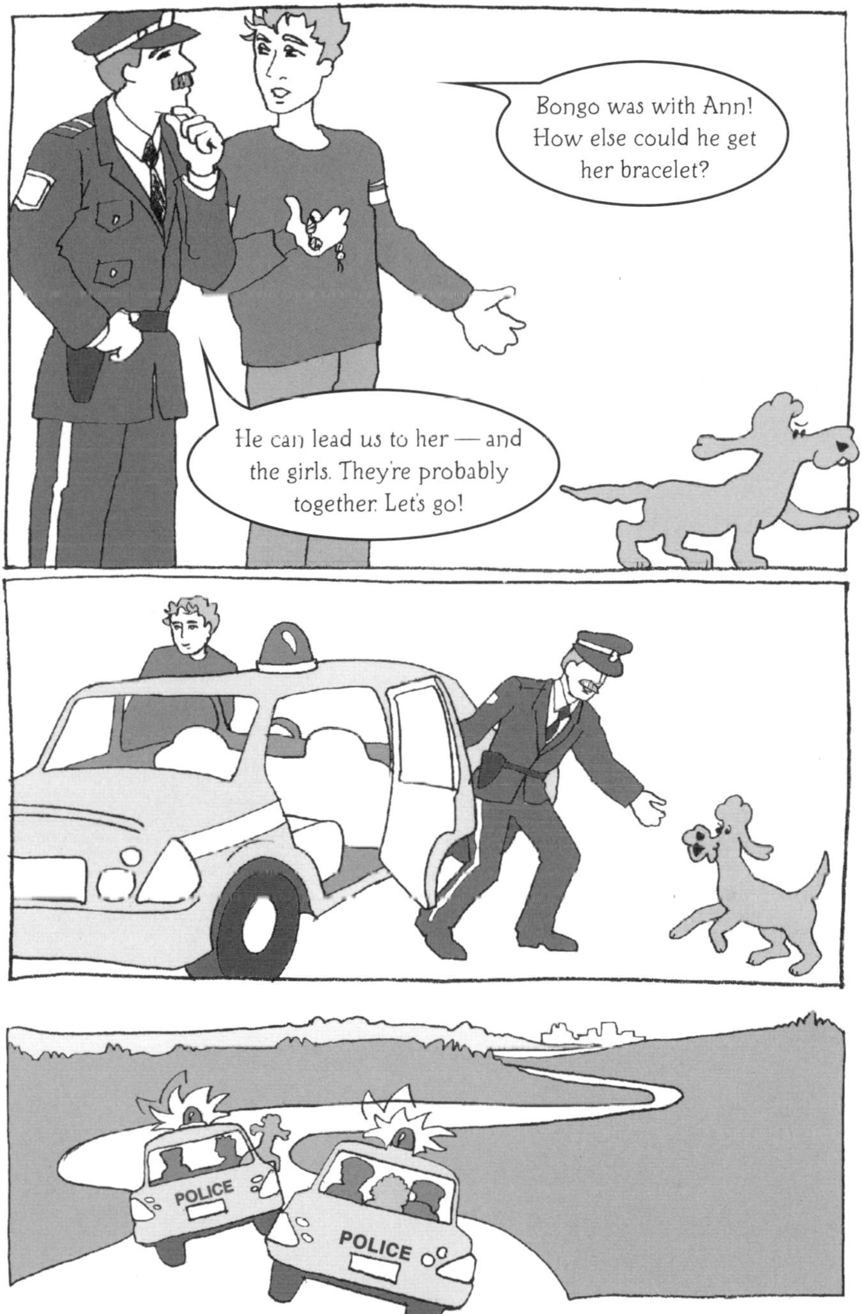
Bongo was with Ann! How else could he get her bracelet?
He can lead us to her — and the girls. They're probably together. Let's go!
POLICE
POLICE

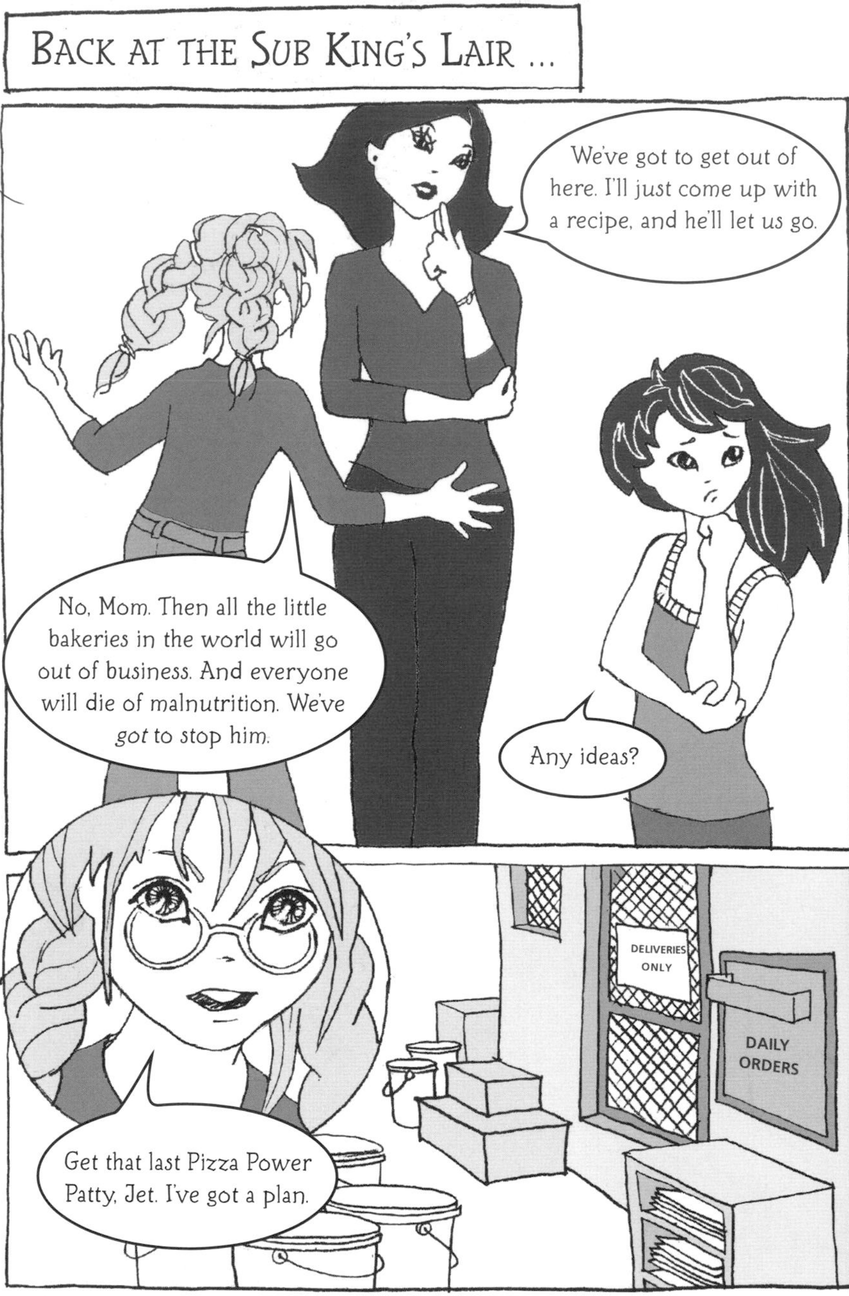
Back at the Sub King's Lair ...
We've got to get out of here. I'll just come up with a recipe, and he'll let us go.
No, Mom. Then all the little bakeries in the world will go out of business. And everyone will die of malnutrition. We've *got* to stop him.
Any ideas?
DELIVERIES ONLY
DAILY ORDERS
Get that last Pizza Power Patty, Jet. I've got a plan.

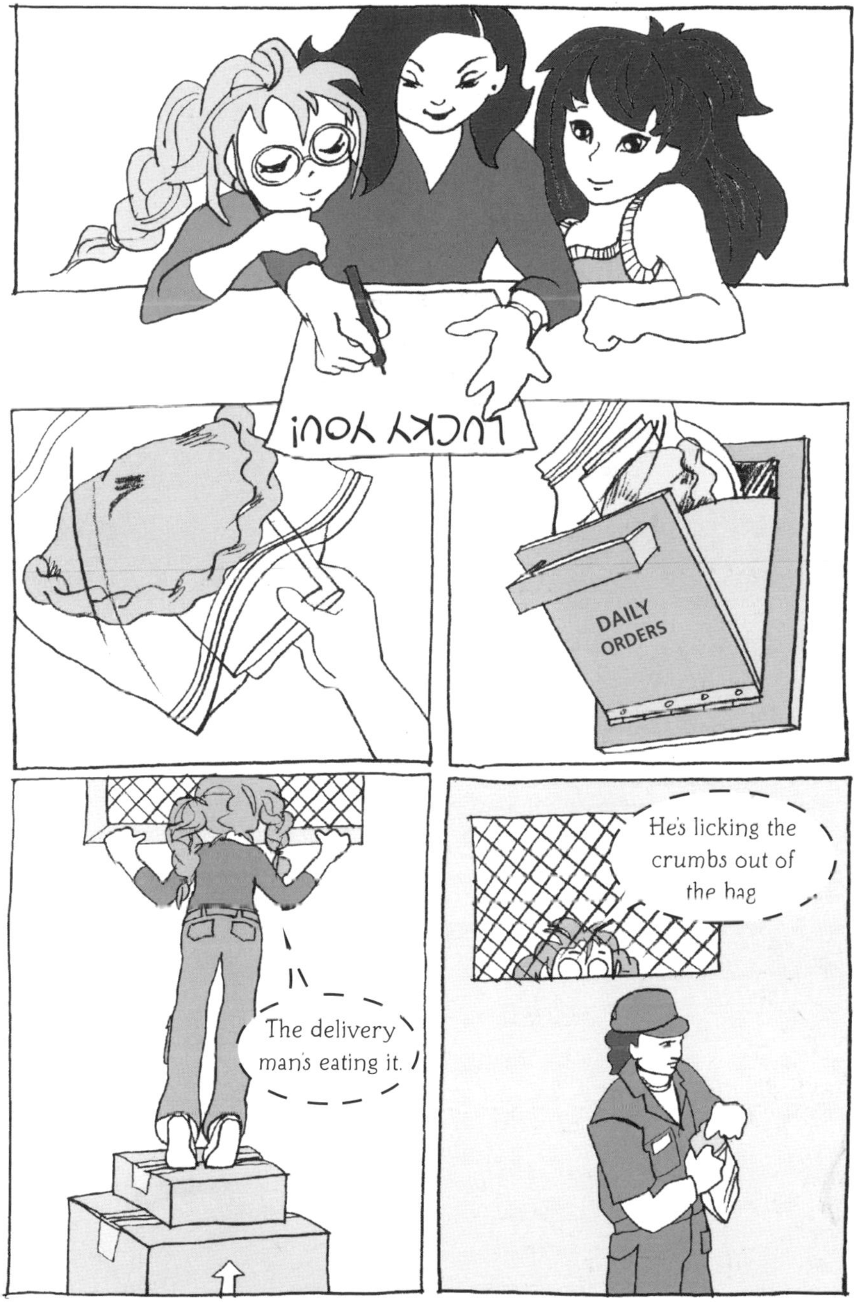
LUCKY YOU!
DAILY ORDERS
The delivery man's eating it.
He's licking the crumbs out of the bag

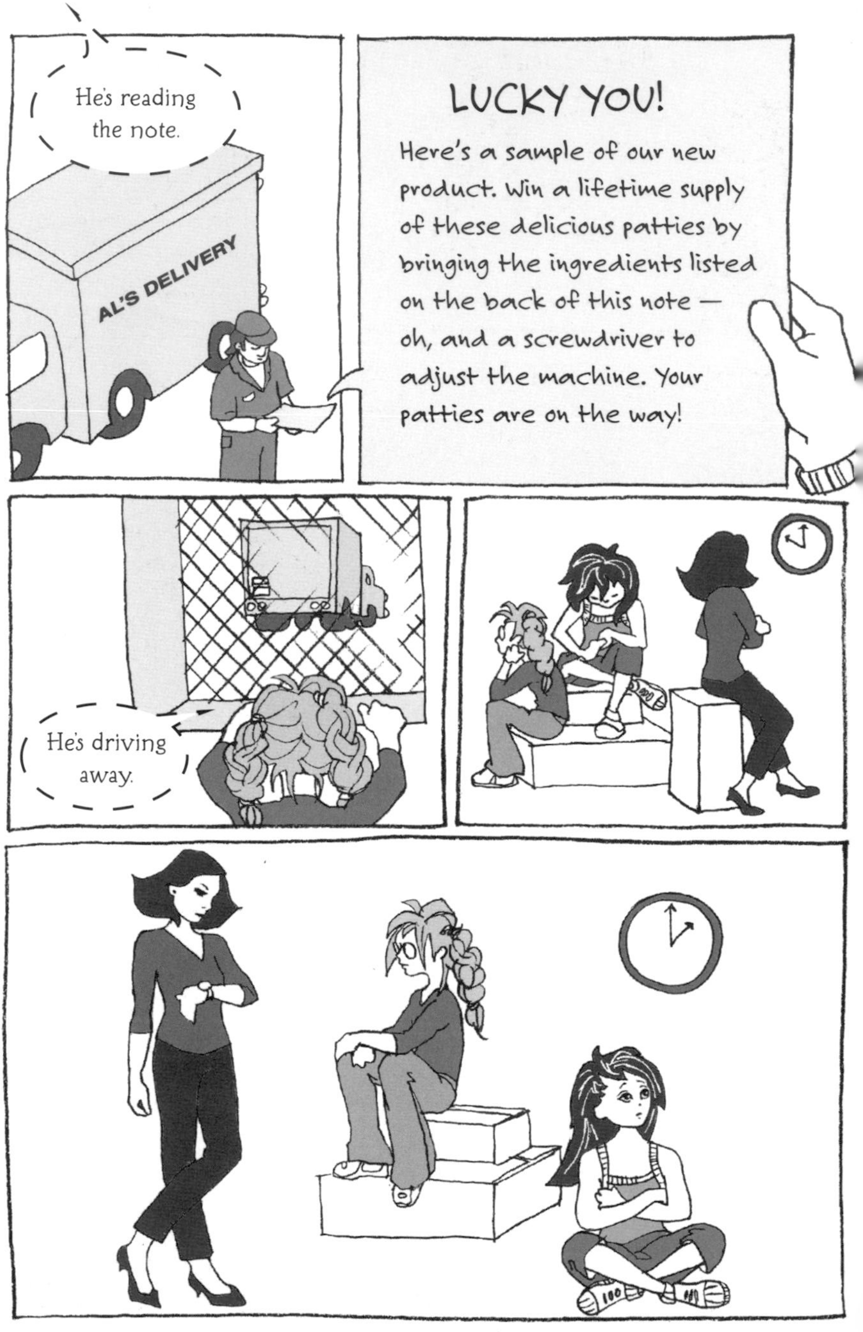
He's reading the note.
AL'S DELIVERY
LUCKY YOU!
Here's a sample of our new product. Win a lifetime supply of these delicious patties by bringing the ingredients listed on the back of this note — oh, and a screwdriver to adjust the machine. Your patties are on the way!
He's driving away.

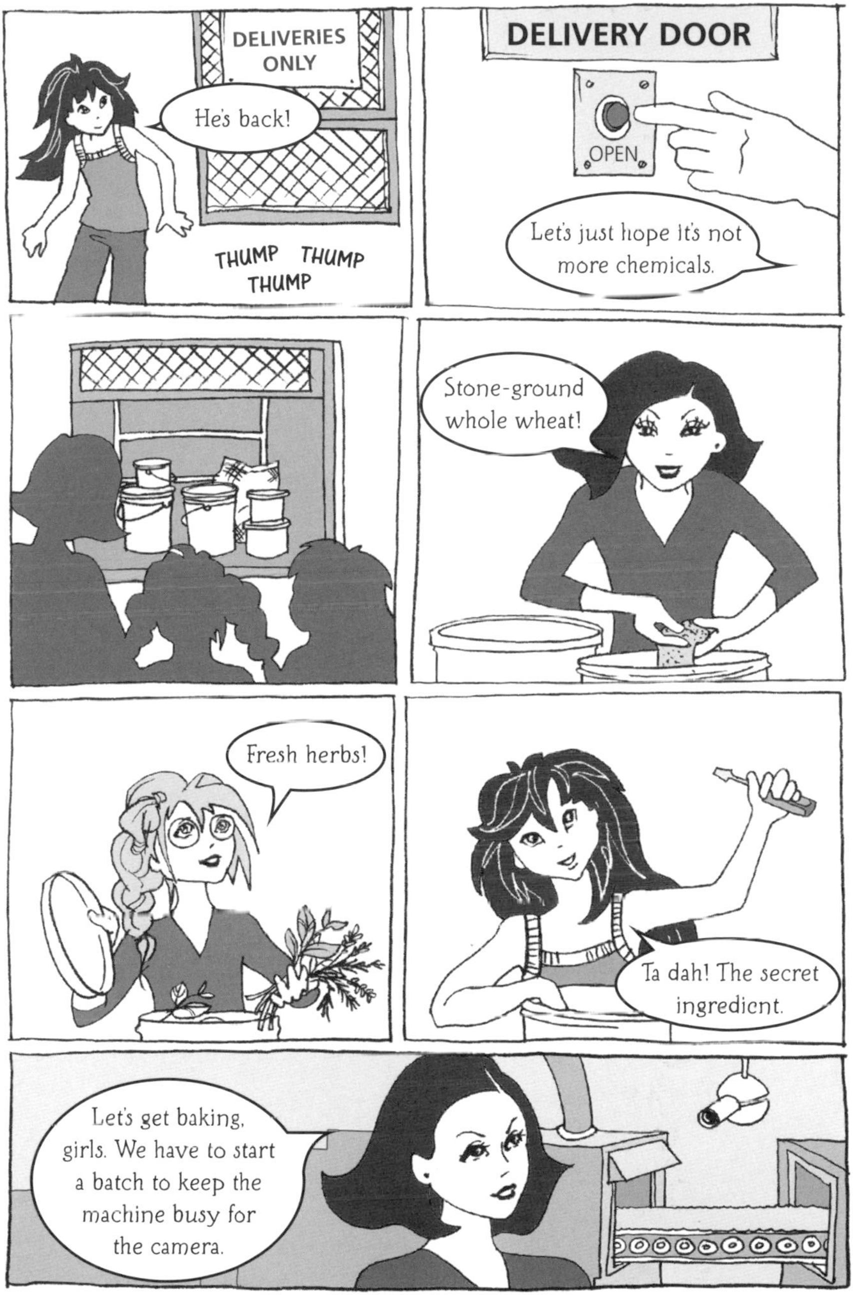
DELIVERIES ONLY
He's back!
THUMP THUMP THUMP
DELIVERY DOOR
OPEN
Let's just hope it's not more chemicals.
Stone-ground whole wheat!
Fresh herbs!
Ta dah! The secret ingredient.
Let's get baking, girls. We have to start a batch to keep the machine busy for the camera.

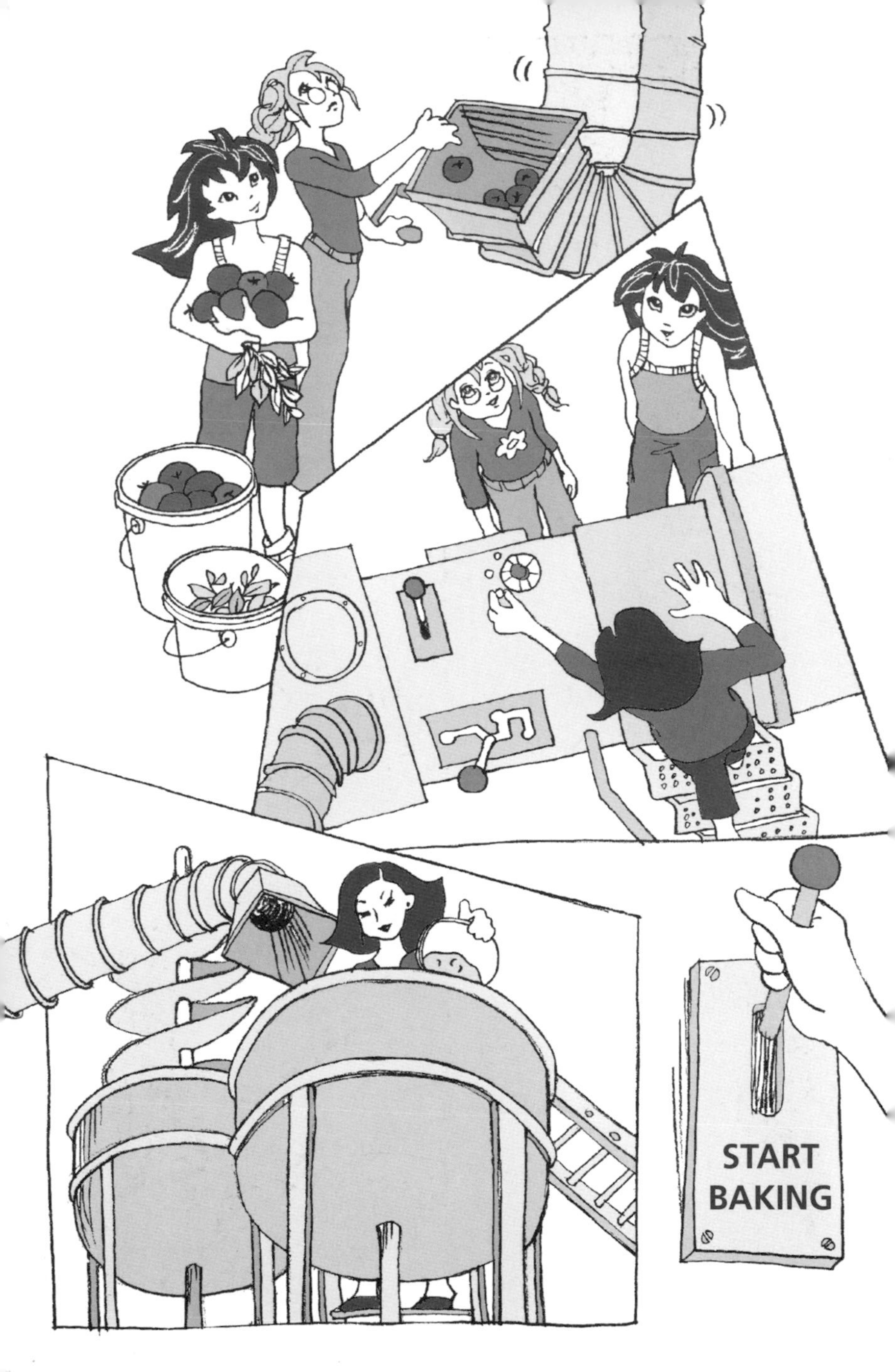
START
BAKING

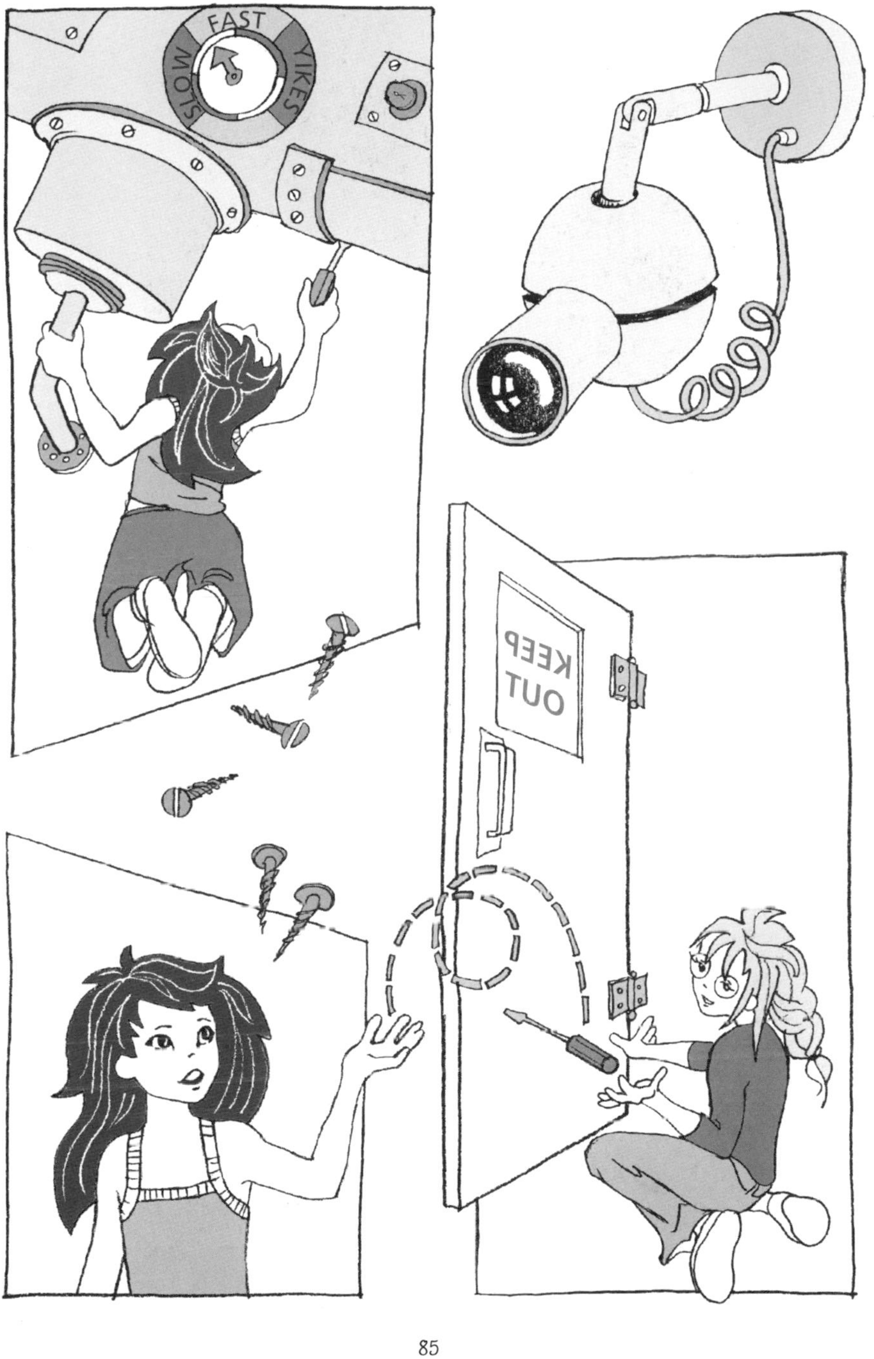
SLOW
FAST
YIKES
KEEP OUT

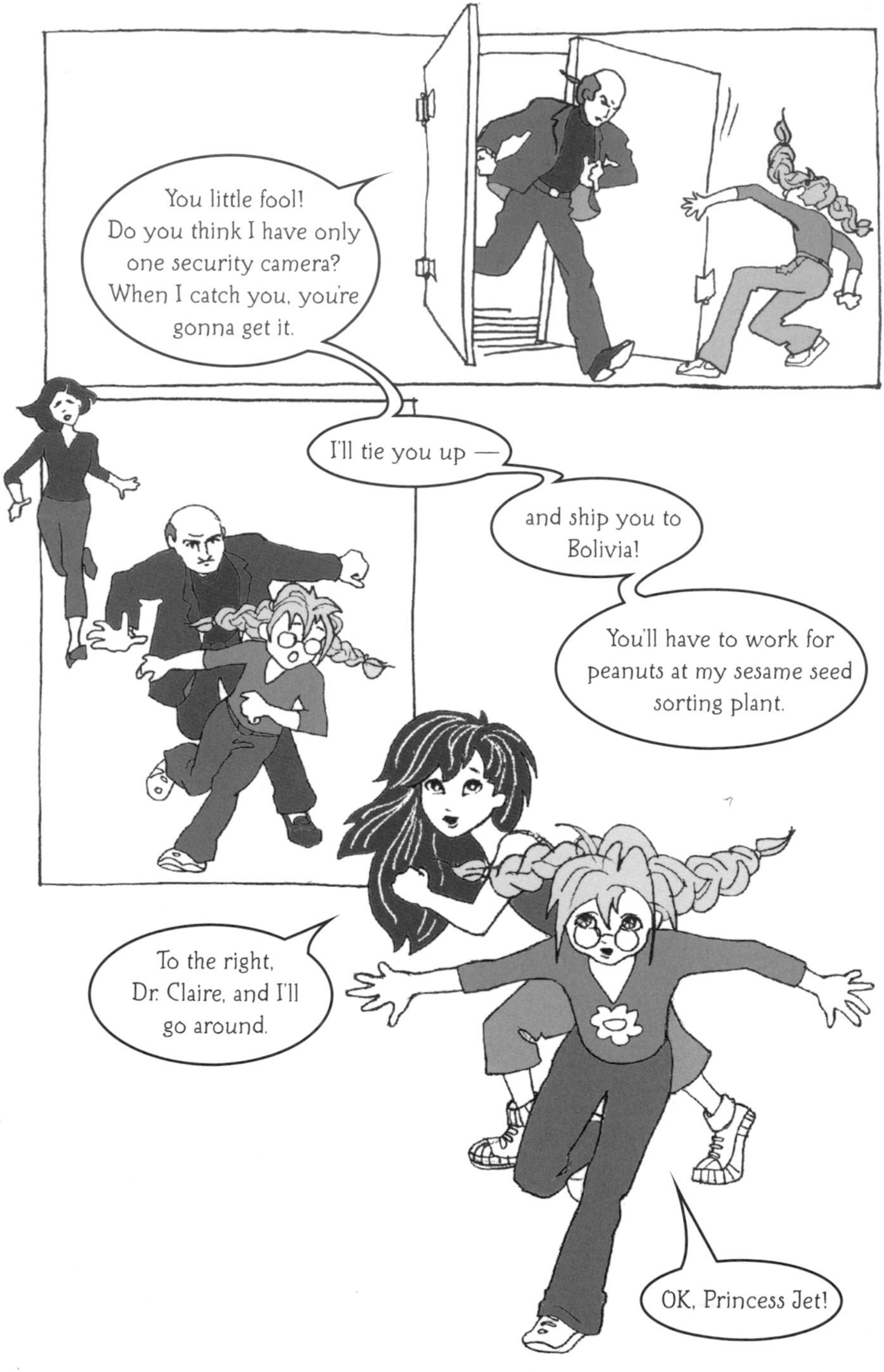
You little fool! Do you think I have only one security camera? When I catch you, you're gonna get it.
I'll tie you up —
and ship you to Bolivia!
You'll have to work for peanuts at my sesame seed sorting plant.
To the right, Dr. Claire, and I'll go around.
OK, Princess Jet!

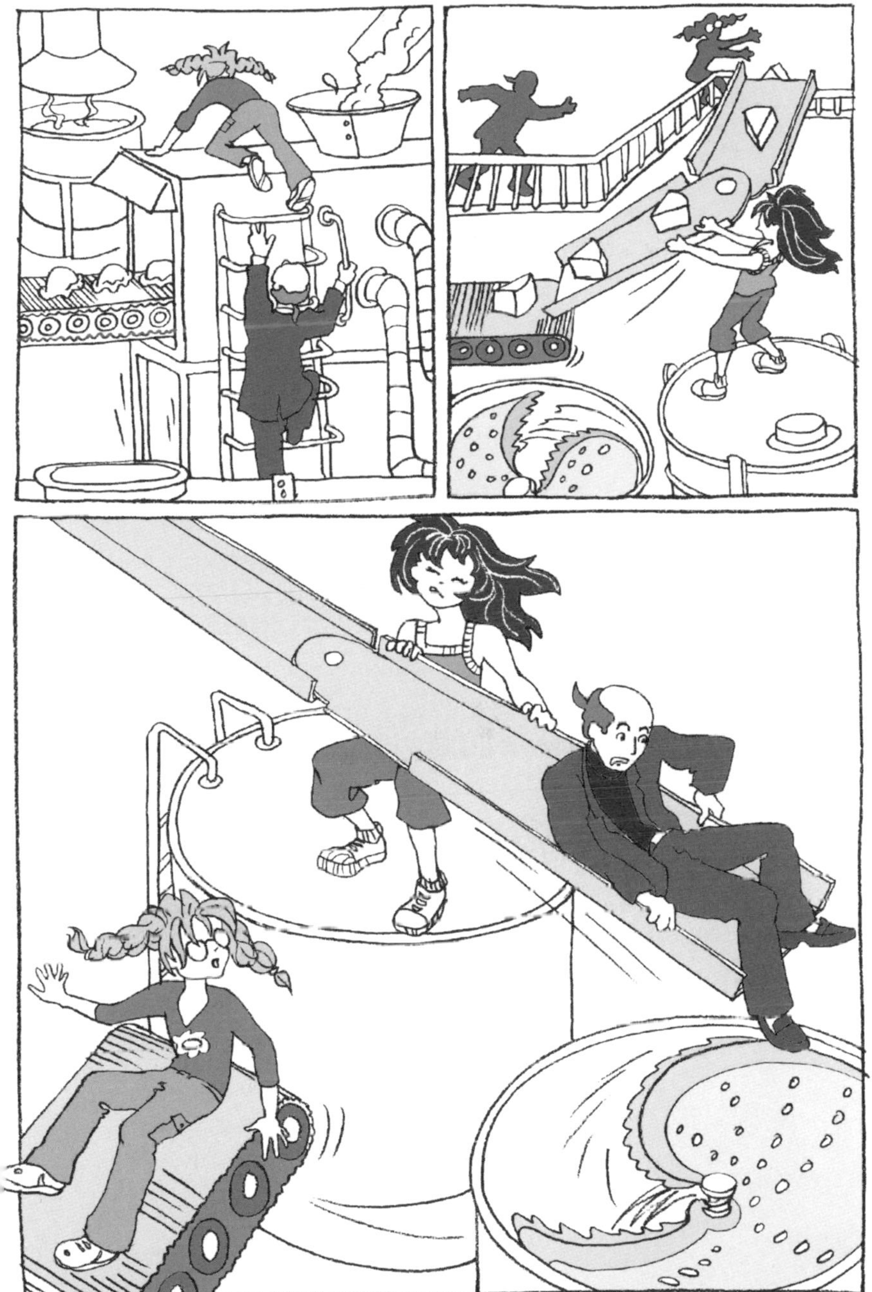

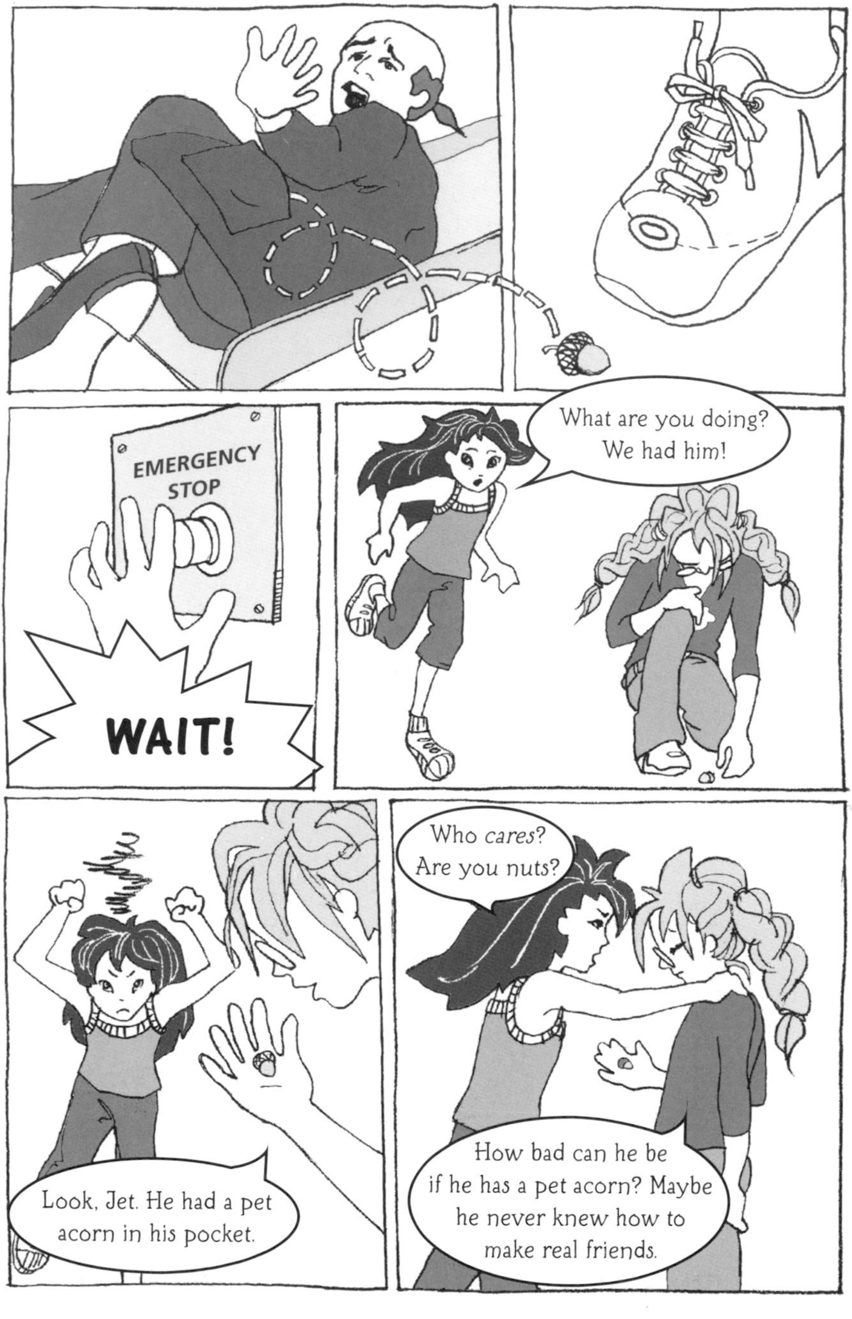
EMERGENCY STOP
WAIT!
What are you doing? We had him!
Look, Jet. He had a pet acorn in his pocket.
Who *cares*? Are you nuts?
How bad can he be if he has a pet acorn? Maybe he never knew how to make real friends.

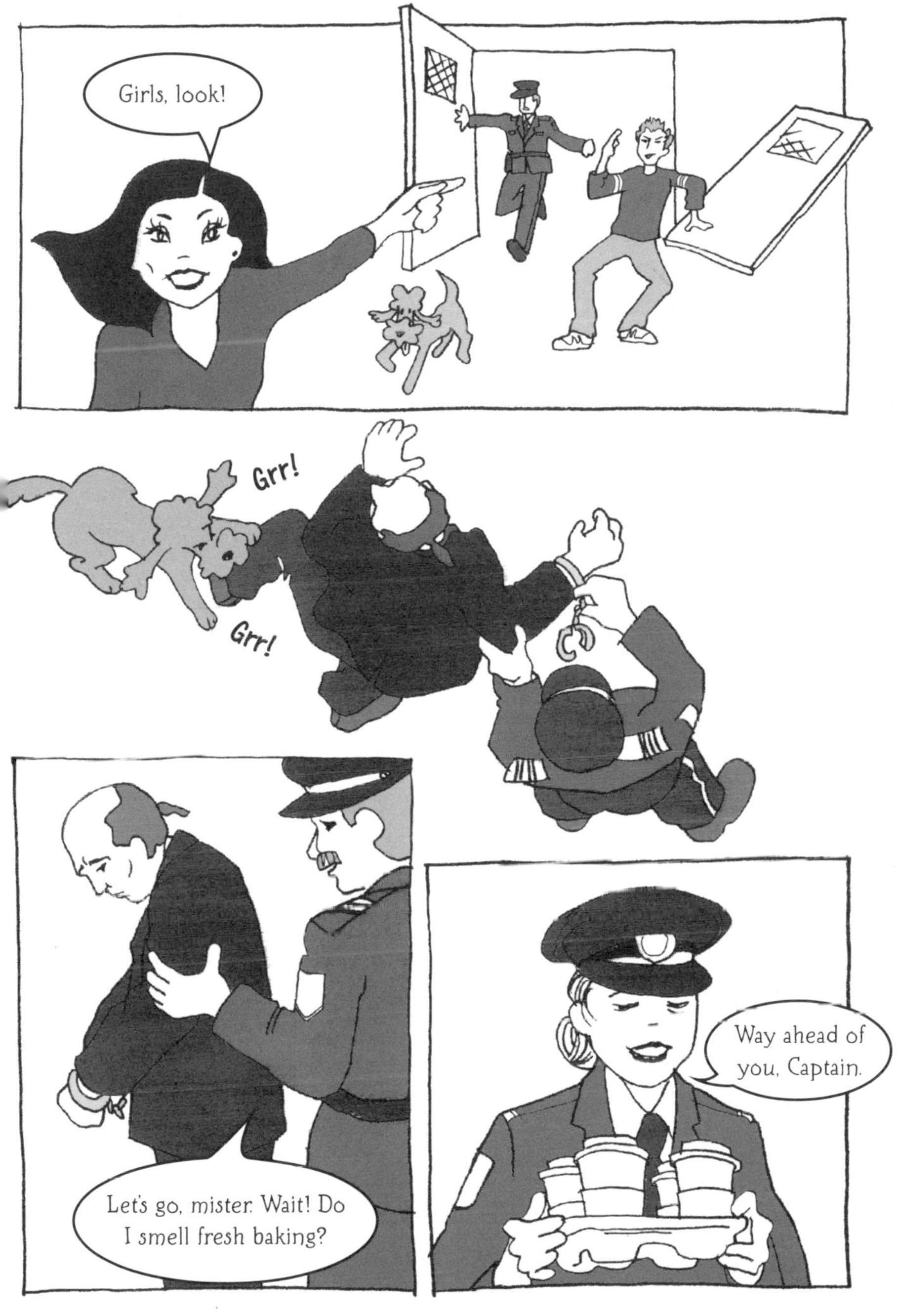
Girls, look!
Grr!
Grr!
Let's go, mister. Wait! Do I smell fresh baking?
Way ahead of you, Captain.

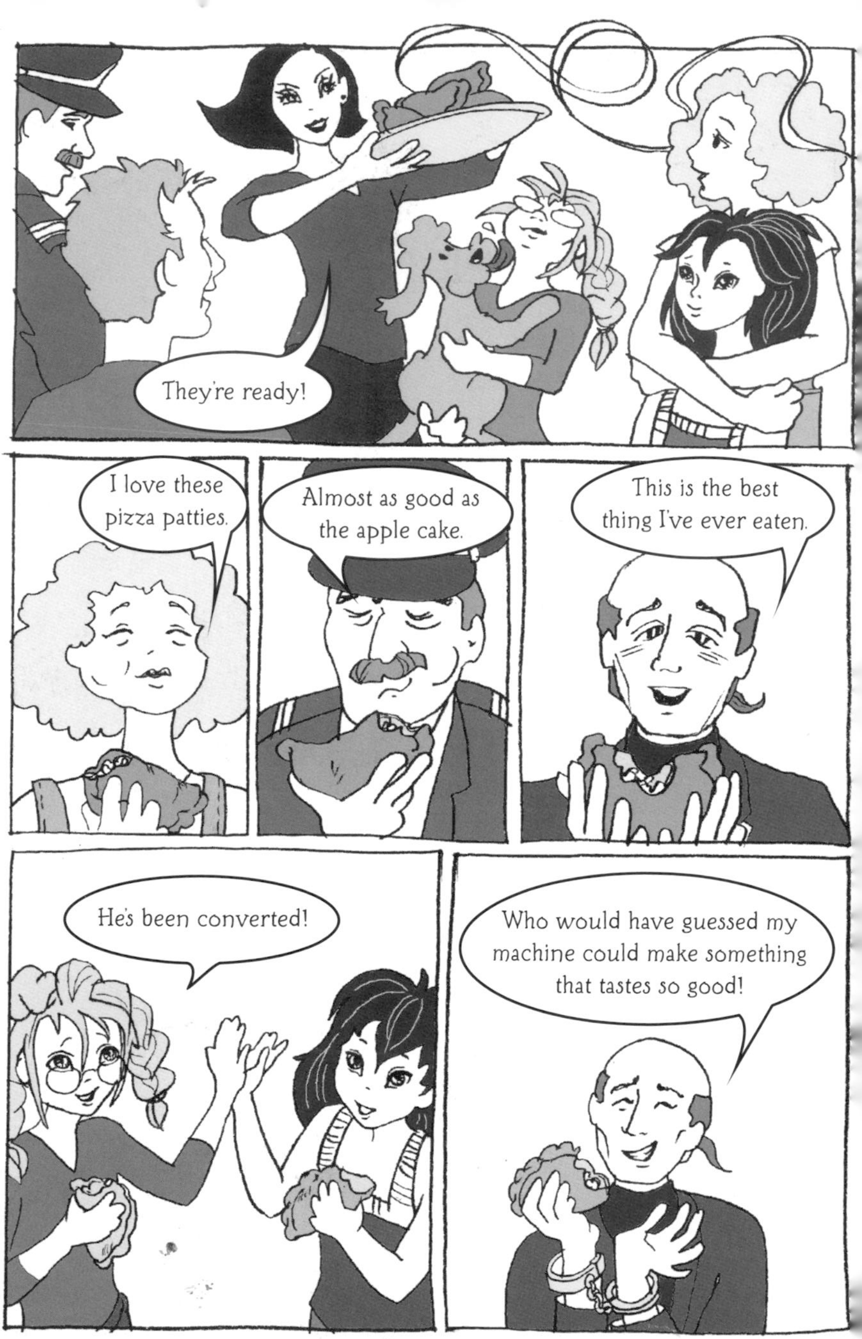
They're ready!
I love these pizza patties.
Almost as good as the apple cake.
This is the best thing I've ever eaten.
He's been converted!
Who would have guessed my machine could make something that tastes so good!

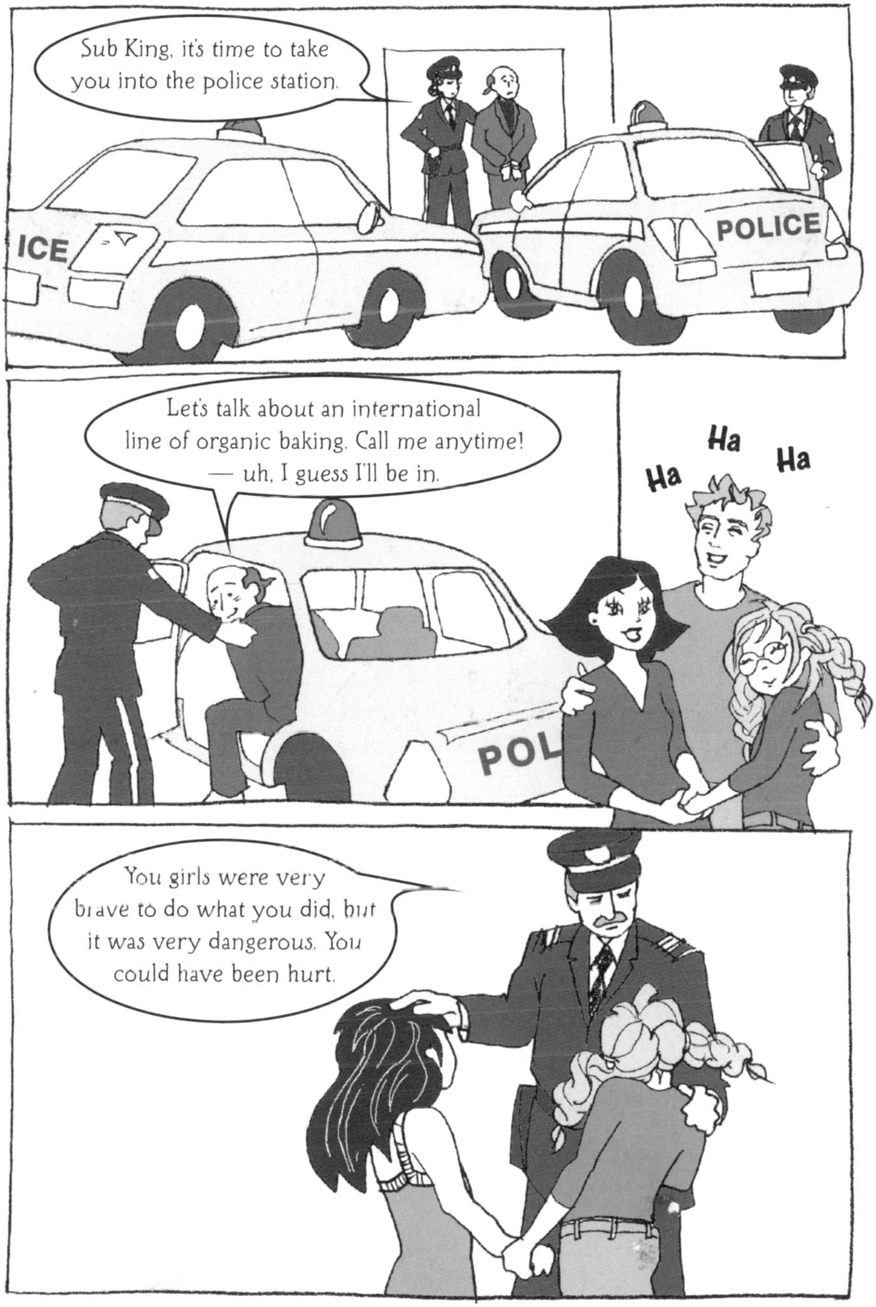
Sub King, it's time to take you into the police station.
ICE
POLICE
Let's talk about an international line of organic baking. Call me anytime! — uh, I guess I'll be in.
Ha
Ha
Ha
POL
You girls were very brave to do what you did, but it was very dangerous. You could have been hurt.

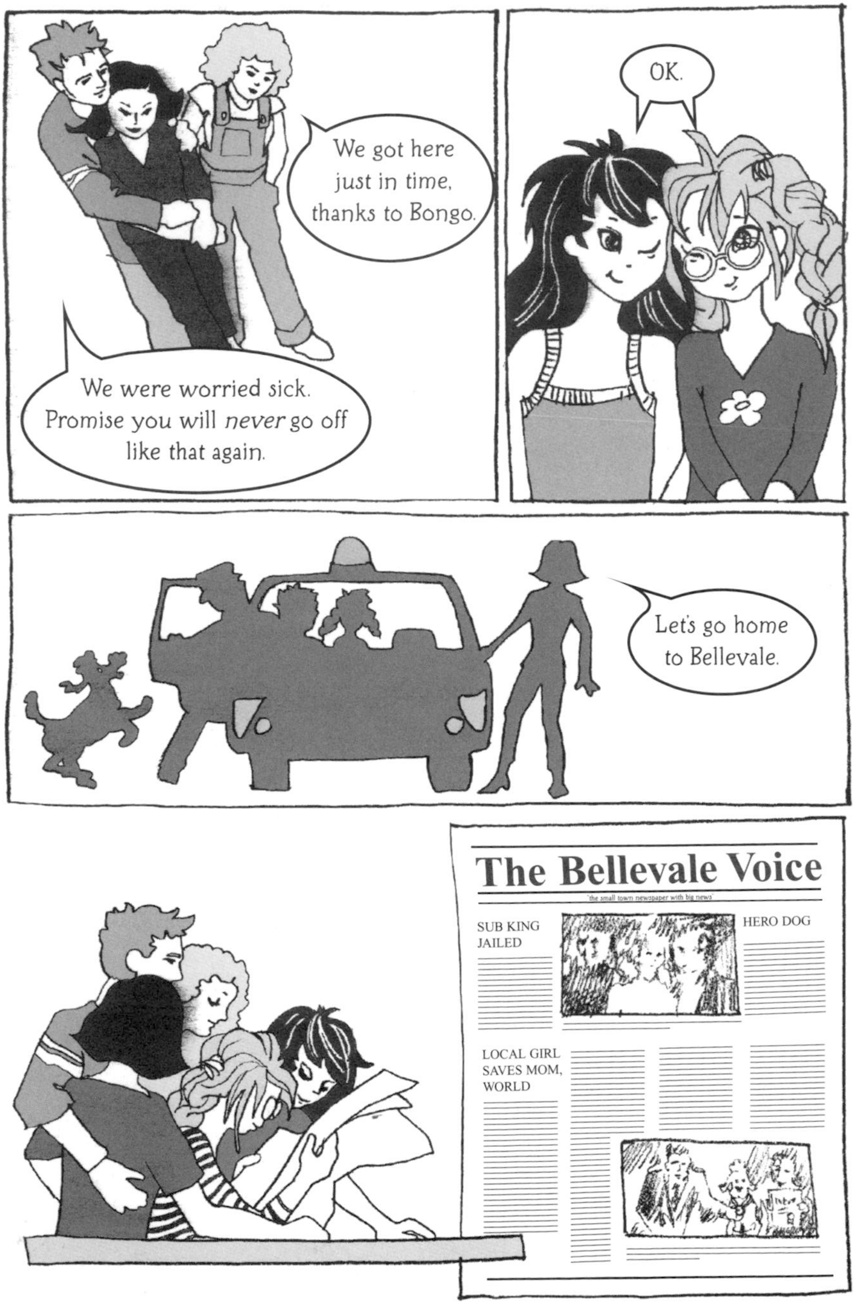
We got here just in time, thanks to Bongo.
We were worried sick. Promise you will *never* go off like that again.
OK.
Let's go home to Bellevale.
The Bellevale Voice
"the small town newspaper with big news"
SUB KING JAILED
HERO DOG
LOCAL GIRL SAVES MOM, WORLD

Dear Diary:

It's so much fun to be back. Officer Bob made Bongo an honorary police dog and gave him a really cool dog tag.

Everybody in the whole village wants to talk to Jet and me about what happened. Lauren said she and I should sit together on the school bus. As if! Now I can't wait until school starts.

Claire

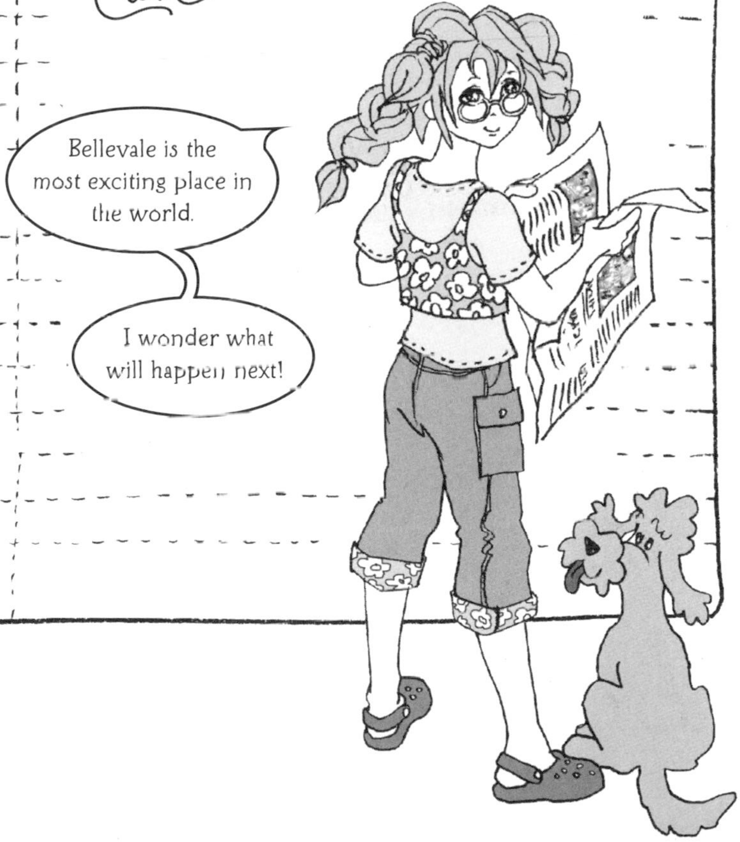

Bellevale is the most exciting place in the world.
I wonder what will happen next!

Claire's Special Recipes from the Grain of Truth Bakery

Try making these favorites from the Grain of Truth. Baking can be lots of fun as long as you follow these safety rules!

- Use oven mitts to handle hot baking sheets and cookie pans.
- Ask an adult to help you use the oven or blender.
- Don't forget to turn off a blender before reaching inside.
- When mixing a bowl of ingredients with an electric beater, turn it off before you put spoons, spatulas or fingers in the bowl.
- When using an appliance, never leave it unattended.

Let the baking begin!

Incredibly Crunchy Cookies

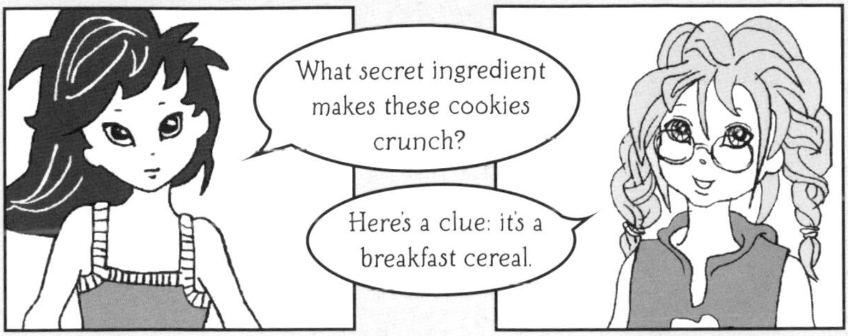
What secret ingredient makes these cookies crunch?
Here's a clue: it's a breakfast cereal.

YOU WILL NEED

125 mL	butter (room temperature)	1/2 c.
175 mL	brown sugar	3/4 c.
2 mL	vanilla	1/2 tsp.
1	egg	1
175 mL	flour	3/4 c.
5 mL	baking soda	1 tsp.
250 mL	rolled oats	1 c.
250 mL	crispy rice breakfast cereal	1 c.
250 mL	chocolate chips	1 c.

small and medium-sized mixing bowls, fork, spoon, baking sheet, spatula, cooling rack

1. Preheat oven to 180°C (350°F).

2. Combine butter and sugar in the larger mixing bowl and stir with a fork until creamy. Add vanilla and egg and blend well.

3. In a smaller mixing bowl, combine flour and baking soda and mix thoroughly. Add to bowl with butter-sugar mixture and mix gently until just combined.

4. Add the rolled oats, crispy rice cereal and chocolate chips and stir to combine.

5. Using a spoon, drop dough in 4 cm (1 $\frac{1}{2}$ in.) balls onto baking sheet about 8 cm (3 in.) apart. Flatten balls slightly.

6. Bake for 10 minutes or until cookies have browned and smell dee-vine! Let baking sheet cool for about a minute, then lift cookies from baking sheet with a spatula and slide onto cooling rack to cool completely.

Makes 30 cookies.

Crazy Apple Cake

Everyone is crazy about this apple cake.

Especially when Claire bakes it.

YOU WILL NEED

2	large apples	2
	or	
3	medium-sized apples	3
375 mL	flour	1 ½ c.
175 mL	brown sugar	¾ c.
5 mL	ground cinnamon	1 tsp.
15 mL	baking powder	1 tbsp.
175 mL	vegetable oil	¾ c.
50 mL	orange juice	¼ c.
5 mL	vanilla	1 tsp.
2	eggs	2

20 cm (8 in.) square baking pan, fork

1. Preheat oven to 180°C (350°F).

2. Peel and cut apples into 2.5 cm (1 in.) chunks, discarding the peel and core. Set apple chunks aside.

3. Combine the rest of the ingredients into the cake pan and stir with a fork for about 3 minutes until all the flour disappears and batter is smooth, thick and all the same color.

4. Add the apple chunks and stir until they are evenly distributed in the batter.

5. Bake for 35 to 45 minutes, until a toothpick inserted into the middle of the cake comes out clean. Place on rack to cool.

Makes 9 pieces.

Super Pizza Power Patties

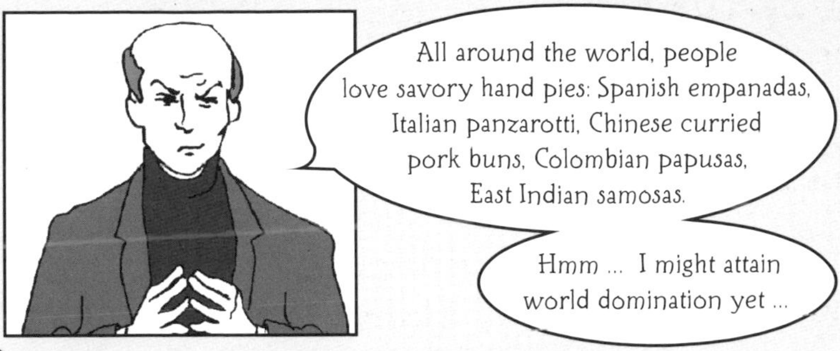
All around the world, people love savory hand pies: Spanish empanadas, Italian panzarotti, Chinese curried pork buns, Colombian papusas, East Indian samosas.
Hmm ... I might attain world domination yet ...

Patty Dough

YOU WILL NEED

750 mL	flour	3 c.
15 mL	instant dry active yeast	1 tbsp.
2 mL	salt	1/2 tsp.
5 mL	sugar	1 tsp.
300 mL	very warm water	1 1/4 c.
50 mL	vegetable oil	1/4 c.
	oil for brushing	
	flour for sprinkling	
	water for moistening	

large mixing bowl, large fork, pastry brush, plastic wrap

1. Combine flour, yeast, salt and sugar in large bowl and mix well with fork. Add warm water and vegetable oil and stir gently until all the flour is worked in and the dough forms a wad that comes away from the sides of the bowl as you stir. The dough should be very soft and a little bit sticky. If all the flour does not mix in readily, stir in a tablespoon at a time of warm

water until dough is soft. If it is too gooey to hold into a ball, sprinkle on a tablespoon more of flour over the dough and mix it in.

2. Sprinkle flour over a clean countertop. Turn dough out of bowl onto the flour. Knead the dough gently for about 5 minutes until it is smooth and elastic. It will stick to your fingers just a little bit. Divide into 6 equally sized balls.

3. Brush dough balls all over with oil, place on a plate and cover with plastic wrap. Allow dough to rise for 20 to 30 minutes in a warm place while you prepare the filling.

Pizza Filling
YOU WILL NEED

175 mL	tomato sauce	$^3/_4$ c.
10 mL	dried oregano	2 tsp.
30 slices	pepperoni	30 slices
500 mL	mozzarella in 1 cm ($^1/_2$ in.) cubes	2 c.

Make and Bake!
YOU WILL NEED

patty dough
pizza filling
flour for sprinkling
vegetable oil for brushing
water for moistening

rolling pin, baking sheets, pastry brush, cooling rack

1. Preheat oven to 180°C (350°F). Brush baking sheets with oil.

2. To form the patty, first sprinkle a few tablespoons of flour on a clean countertop and, using a rolling pin, gently and evenly flatten out a ball of patty dough into an 18 cm (7 in.) round about 0.25 cm ($^1/_8$ in.) thick. Sprinkle on more flour if the dough sticks to the countertop or rolling pin. Be careful not to rip any holes in the dough as you work with it.

3. To fill the patty, spread 30 mL (2 tbsp.) of tomato sauce on the lower half of the circle, 2.5 cm (1 in.) from the edge. Fan out 5 slices of pepperoni on top of the tomato sauce. Place 75 mL ($^1/_3$ c.) mozzarella cheese on top of that, and then sprinkle on a bit of the herbs, keeping the filling 2.5 cm (1 in.) away from the edge of the circle.

4. To close the patty, use your fingertips or a pastry brush to moisten the edge of the dough with a little water. Fold the dough in half over the filling to make a semi-circle. Press the edge closed. To seal tightly, fold dough 0.5 cm ($^1/_4$ in.) over along the outside edge and pinch shut. Transfer to baking sheet and brush the top of patty with oil using a pastry brush.

5. Repeat to fill the remaining 5 patties.

6. Bake patties for 25 minutes or until lightly browned. Place on rack to cool.

Makes 6 Super Pizza Power Patties.

Fruit Yogurt Smoothie

You can make this smoothie in a blender — or just press the fruit through a food mill, and then use a fork to whip everything together into a frothy drink.

YOU WILL NEED

250 mL	strawberries (6 to 10)	1 c.
1	banana	1
125 mL	yogurt	1/2 c.
125 mL	orange juice	1/2 c.
50 mL	water	1/4 c.

blender (or fork and food mill), mixing bowl

1. Wash the strawberries and remove their green tops. Cut each strawberry in half. Peel the banana and cut in four.

2. Put banana slices, strawberry halves, yogurt, orange juice and water into the blender. Place lid on firmly and blend until the ingredients become a smooth, thick liquid.

To make without a blender, combine the strawberry halves and banana slices in a food mill and grind into a mixing bowl. Add yogurt, orange juice and water and beat together with fork.

3. Pour into two glasses and enjoy!

Makes 2 drinks.

Nu-Bred Play Clay

Nu-Bred tastes horrible, but 8 out of 10 researchers agree that it makes great modeling clay.

YOU WILL NEED

1 L	flour	4 c.
250 mL	salt	1 c
300 mL	water	1 $\frac{1}{4}$ c.

large mixing bowl, measuring cup, fork, baking sheet

1. In a large mixing bowl, combine flour and salt and mix well. Add water and mix to blend. Turn dough out onto a clean countertop and knead by hand to make a smooth soft clay.

2. Make into fun shapes and bake at 100°C (200°F) for several hours or until completely dry. Baked shapes can be painted after they cool.

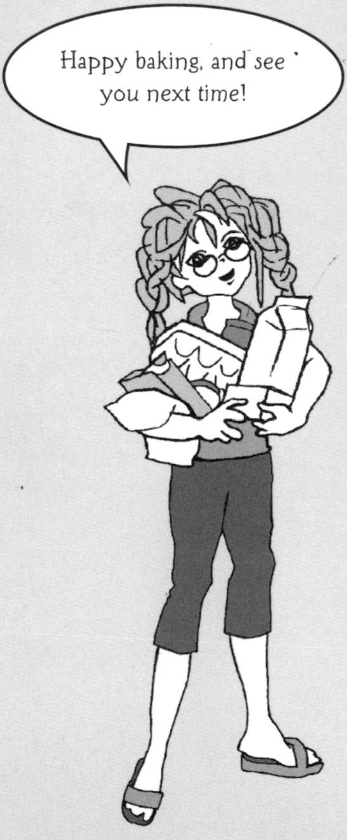
Happy baking, and see you next time!

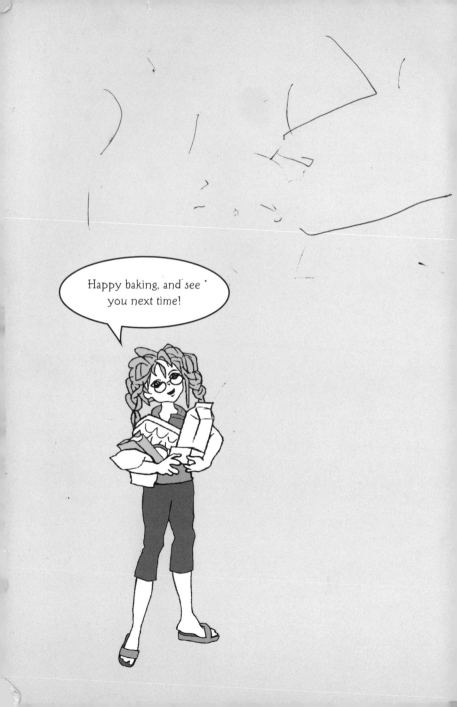